PRAISE FOR *SCREAM QUEEN*

"Great creepy fun! A postmodern edge-of-your-seat thriller, with enough smarts to know when to scare you and when to make you laugh. Having survived a decade in television, I thought I'd seen it all, but th__ _____ SCARIER than meeting a Hollywood N__ _____
—Ron Oliver,

"Edo van Belkom has found a ____ _____ where it makes its home . . . Hol_____ ers of supernatural terror will en___ _____ crew caught up in a life and death _____ _____ used to imitating. Producers and d_____ _____
—Andrew N_____ _____ of *The Devil's Advocate*

PRAISE FOR EDO VAN BELKOM

"Edo van Belkom can write horror and he can write, period."
—The *Sunday Telegram*, St. John's, Newfoundland

"Van Belkom tells a chilling story with a master's sure hand. He knows the dark scary places of the soul . . . and he takes us there with pleasure."
—Matthew J. Costello, author of *See How She Runs*

"One can only hope that he follows the solid and widely appealing course set by *Martyrs*, and takes his rightful place among the mainstream horror writers who are clearing the literary forests of the new century."
—Michael Rowe, *Fangoria*

"Van Belkom is a storyteller, first and foremost. He has all the talent and verve of a young Robert Bloch."
—Garrett Peck, *Masters of Terror*

"Edo van Belkom is a true original."
—Ed Gorman, author of *Black River Falls*

"Worthy of the young Stephen King."
—Elizabeth Hand, *The Magazine of Fantasy and Science Fiction*

"Edo van Belkom is a one-man factory of fear."
—Stanley Wiater, host of *Dark Dreamers*

"Van Belkom writes with verve and no small amount of ambition. Indeed he has a great deal to be proud of . . . The comparisons to Stephen King are apt. . . ."
—James Schellenberg, *Crystalline Sphere*

"Edo van Belkom is a superb craftsman when it comes to weaving stories that will both chill your blood and turn you on."
—*B.C. BookWorld*

"Van Belkom proves to be a master of the 'Twilight Zone' story: a story that truly surprises you at the end. . . ."
—Denise Dumars, *Fandom.com*

"Edo van Belkom is well on his way to becoming the north country's top practitioner of nightmare tales."
—Robert J. Sawyer, author of *The Terminal Experiment*

SCREAM QUEEN

Edo van Belkom

PINNACLE BOOKS
Kensington Publishing Corp.
http://www.kensingtonbooks.com

PINNACLE BOOKS are published by

Kensington Publishing Corp.
850 Third Avenue
New York, NY 10022

Copyright © 2003 by Edo van Belkom

All rights reserved. No part of this book may be reproduced
in any form or by any means without the prior written con-
sent of the Publisher, excepting brief quotes used in reviews.

If you purchased this book without a cover, you should be aware
that this book is stolen property. It was reported as "unsold and
destroyed" to the Publisher and neither the Author nor the Publisher has received any payment for this "stripped book."

This novel is a work of fiction. Names, characters, places, and
incidents are either the product of the author's imagination, or
are used fictiously. Any resemblance to actual persons, living
or dead, or events is entirely coincidental.

All Kensington Titles, Imprints, and Distributed Lines are available at special quantity discounts for bulk purchases for sales
promotions, premiums, fund-raising, and educational or insti-
tutional use. Special book excerpts or customized printings can
also be created to fit specific needs. For details, write or phone
the office of the Kensington special sales manager: Kensington
Publishing Corp., 850 Third Avenue, New York, NY 10022,
attn: Special Sales Department, Phone: 1-800-221-2647.

Pinnacle and the P logo Reg. U.S. Pat. & TM Off.

First Pinnacle Books Printing: April 2003

10 9 8 7 6 5 4 3 2 1

Printed in the United States of America

For Dick Laymon
1947–2001

ACKNOWLEDGMENTS

I'm indebted to several people for their help with this novel. I am especially grateful for the insights into the world of show business and horror moviemaking provided by director Ron Oliver (*Prom Night 3*), and regular *Fangoria* contributor Michael Rowe. I'd also like to thank fellow writers Robert J. Sawyer and David Nickle for their feedback on the manuscript. And of course, thanks to my wife, Roberta, whose love and support over the years have made this and all my books possible.

PREPRODUCTION

One

She knew a bit about scary movies, but she wasn't a rabid fan or anything like that.

Most horror films were pretty lame, and after seeing her cousin's arm torn from his shoulder in a combine accident, it was hard to think of anything to do with blood and gore as a form of entertainment.

And she had no real aspirations of becoming a movie star.

She'd thought about it, of course—what young woman in southern California didn't?—but she was only pretty in a small-town sort of way, not really Hollywood beautiful. Her body was hard from years of helping out on the farm, not thin and curvy like so many of the female leads were today. And while she'd acted in a few high school plays, no one had ever taken her aside and told her she had *talent*.

But she did have some experience with ghosts.

The family farm had been haunted by the spirit of her great-grandfather, who could sometimes be seen walking the cornfields around harvest time, checking the stalks—same as he'd been doing on the day that he died.

And so, when she saw the ad in *Variety* calling for women between the ages of twenty and thirty who loved horror movies and had some experience and/or belief in the occult, she thought, *Why the hell not?*

The next day she went to the casting call with few expectations, figuring she had nothing to lose but a few hours of her time. Well, that had been over a month ago and now she'd been called back for her third, and she hoped, final interview. Or maybe this time it would be an actual screen test. That's what was supposed to happen when you auditioned for a part; you read some lines, or acted out a scene with somebody who was already in the movie, and the casting directors and producers decided if you were right for the role. But the producers of this show hadn't asked her to act, or to read any lines, or do anything like that. All they'd done was ask her a lot of questions, and then told her to tell them a little bit about herself. That had been easy enough, but she wasn't sure how that was going to get her a part on a television show. What was so interesting about a farm girl named Jody Watts who came from a part of the country where cows outnumbered people four to one?

She stopped for a moment at the corner and read the street name on the lamppost. Then she checked that with the directions she'd been given over the phone.

One more block to go.

Her first meeting with the Gowan brothers had been in a ground-floor room in the Hollywood Roosevelt Hotel on Hollywood Boulevard across from Mann's Chinese. There had been a line of young girls that had gone out the door and around the block, and dozens of newspaper and television reporters taking pictures and asking dumb questions like "Are you afraid of the dark?" and "What's your number?" The second meeting had also been at the Roosevelt, but there had been fewer girls and no reporters. The producers had taken pictures of her, and asked her more questions about herself, but she'd done no acting. This time out, they'd asked her to come to an address near Little Tokyo, more specifically to the studio and warehouse the brothers had on Traction Street.

Looking around, it seemed like an odd place to meet a pair of television producers for a network show, but then again the Gowan brothers weren't exactly television producers. Since her first interview, Jody had done a bit of research at the local library, and had read all about "the Boo Brothers" as they were sometimes referred to in the trades. The Gowan brothers were basically B-grade horror filmmakers whose makeup and special effects were just a few steps above homemade. They made one or two features in their downtown studios each year, going direct-to-video in the United States and sometimes releasing theatrically in other parts of the world, mostly Asia and eastern Europe.

So maybe this would be a screen test after all, she thought. Or at the very least, on the level. Maybe they'd do her up in some ghoulie makeup and ask her to scream for them. That would be fun. And even if she didn't get the part, she'd at least have a Polaroid or two of herself as a zombie to send to the folks back home.

They'd sure get a kick out of that. . . .

She stopped at the next corner and read the street sign over her head—TRACTION STREET.

Nice name, Jody thought. *Wonder where it leads to. Coma Avenue, maybe. Or, knowing the Gowan brothers, it probably just comes to a Dead End.*

Jody smiled at that, then turned down Traction Street looking for the Gowan Brothers studio.

She didn't have to look far. Halfway down the block she noticed a hand-painted sign over an old steel door that read GOWAN BROTHERS ENTERTAINMENT. Jody put her hands on her hips and took a long look at the building that stretched down the block away from the door. It was an old, old warehouse, with reddish brown bricks that had long ago turned black and dirty with age. There were blacked-out windows lining the wall on the second floor, many of them broken and patched on both sides with plastic and glue. The building looked like crap and reminded her of a few of the barns back home.

Maybe they put all their money up on the screen, she thought hopefully, then recalled the one Gowan Brothers movie she'd rented, *Night of the Sorority Vampires*, and knew that that couldn't possibly be true.

"Oh, this is just great," she muttered under her breath. No wonder they first met the girls at the Roosevelt. One look at this studio and people would think they were auditioning for a porno.

Well, Jody had no interest in that.

She thought about turning around and heading back home, but it had already taken her over an hour just to get down here . . . she might as well check it out now that she was here. She could always say, "No, thanks," if she didn't like what they had in mind. And then of course, there was always a chance that these guys were for real.

Jody laughed and shook her head.

She knew she was just nervous and looking for any excuse to back out of this thing and go home. Judging the Gowan brothers by the look of their studio was like judging a book by its cover. And that was just wrong. As much as she hated to admit it, she'd enjoyed *Night of the Sorority Vampires*, and had watched it a second time before returning it to the video store.

So, stop stalling and let's get this over with.

After taking a moment to smooth out her dress, she took a deep breath, let out a long sigh, and tried the door.

It opened.

"Hello?"

"Hello?" came the response, sounding more like a question than an answer.

She'd expected to find some sort of office, but it was little more than a dimly lit room full of shadows. Jody moved cautiously forward, unable to see the floor and what might lie at her feet.

"I'm looking for the Gowan brothers," she said, still not knowing to whom she was speaking.

"You're in the right place." It was a female voice. Perhaps that of a secretary.

The lights in the room suddenly came on, and she was indeed inside an office, although a rather shabbily decorated one. The desks and chairs were old and worn and the only things on the walls were movie posters from Gowan Brothers productions

TEENAGE BRAIN-EATING ZOMBIES

ATTACK OF THE BLOOD FREAKS

TERROR DOLLS OF CASTLE PAIN

THE DEVIL IN HIS BONES

DEATH RITES OF THE SHE-DEMON

REVENGE OF THE MANIAC 2

A woman stepped into the light, but rather than being a sharply dressed secretary, she wore a form-fitting Raiders T-shirt and a pair of tight, faded jeans. Somehow, Jody wasn't surprised.

"I'm Jody Watts."

The woman nodded, sipped her Evian, and gestured with her thumb at the door behind her.

"They're waiting for you in back."

"What's in back?"

"The studio, prop storage, and the brothers' office." She paused, perhaps reading Jody's face. "They don't like having an office up front. Every once in a while someone comes in looking for them . . . and they'd rather not be around when that happens, if you know what I mean."

Jody nodded politely.

"Follow the hallway on the left." She took another sip from the bottle. "It'll take you all the way around the studio to their office."

"Thank you."

The woman smiled politely, then sat down at her desk, immediately looking as if she'd been working hard all morning.

Jody went through the doorway and found a long hallway that ran the length of the building, with doors on the right every twenty feet or so. The hallway was dimly lit, but she could just see well enough not to lose her way or trip over anything on the floor. The hallway turned right at the far end, following the outside of the building all the way to the back. At the end of that hallway, Jody came upon a door with a sign on it that read BOO!

This must be it, she thought.

She knocked on the door and it slowly swung open, creaking loudly on its hinges for what seemed like an eternity.

The space on the other side of the door was also dimly lit, but unlike everywhere else, this room seemed more spooky and foreboding. She could see things on the floor and hanging from the walls: severed heads and broken limbs, things that looked like wolves and monsters . . . and the bodies of children, strung up by their legs.

"C'mon in," said a voice. *"We* won't bite."

A small laugh came from somewhere deep inside the room.

She stepped through the doorway and immediately felt a presence about her. She looked around, but couldn't see anyone in the darkness.

And then she felt a hand on her shoulder.

Jody gasped.

A match flared and in the faint orange glow a long, thin face smiled at her. She recognized the face of Ike Gowan, the older, and she thought, better looking, of the two brothers. He was dressed in black tails with a high collar and scarf of the type Edgar Allan Poe might wear.

"Did you find the place all right?" he asked, his face still lit by the match.

She nodded.

He used the dying flame of the match to light a candle, then took her by the hand. In the dim orange glow of candlelight, Jody saw that he was leading her through a maze of giant bugs, hanging entrails, eviscerated animals, and cases of beer.

"Don't mind the mess," Ike said, stepping over a giant black spider that had only seven legs. "But be careful where you step, because I can never remember which are the real spiders and which are the puppets."

Jody felt herself flinch at the mention of spiders, and hoped Ike hadn't noticed.

But of course, he had.

"Hah!" he said, leading her safely over the giant bug. "You're afraid. . . . I like that."

Jody managed a nervous smile.

If the brothers were trying to freak her out, they were doing a good job of it. She felt chilled, even though she knew it was warmer inside the warehouse than it had been out on the street.

They came upon another door, this one opening up to a room that looked a little like the inside of a Victorian mansion.

Ike lit a few more candles and slowly the room became filled with a flickering yellow light that sent shadows dancing across the walls.

Jody hadn't rented the film, but she recognized the room and the iron maiden off in one corner from the box cover of *The Horror of Nightmare House,* the Gowan brothers' most recent release.

"Have a seat," Ike said, gesturing toward a plush chair at one end of a small wooden coffee table.

She sat down, feeling her heart thumping in her chest like a drum. What was going on here? she wondered. It was supposed to be an audition, but it was as if they were already making a movie.

"This is our interview room," Ike said, smiling. "It's where we've chosen to conduct our, uh . . . *final* auditions."

"To see what the actors are made of," said a second voice, slightly higher in pitch than Ike's.

Another match flared, giving way first to a candle flame and then a small bank of lights that illuminated the face of Erwin Gowan, the younger, and weirder, of the two brothers.

Looking at the two men, even in the odd light, it wasn't too hard to figure out which brother looked after which facet of their operation. Ike was the older, more handsome businessman who usually wore designer golf shirts, slacks, and loafers. He cut the deals and the checks, and was the one who was given the job of saying no. Erwin, on the other hand, often looked as if he were still in high school, preferring to wear flowered Hawaiian shirts, checked shorts, and leather sandals. His hair was long and unruly, and he had a beard that was equally a mess. In a word, he was *strange,* but was probably the one who came up with most of the creative mayhem that characterized their movies.

"You remember my brother, Erwin," Ike said, gesturing to where Erwin sat on an overstuffed, upholstered couch. Erwin was dressed in tattered and dirty clothes, as if he were some grave digger in a Lugosi black-and-white film from the 1930s.

Jody extended her hand, but Erwin didn't get up from the couch, forcing Jody to get up and move closer to him. She shook his hand with enthusiasm and did her best to keep her smile bright.

Whatever they want, she thought, *as long as it doesn't involve me getting on my back and spreading my wings. . . .*

"Thanks for coming," Erwin said, smiling devilishly.

She straightened her sundress, feeling uncomfortable and out of place dressed in the brightly colored outfit, and sat back down.

Ike took the chair across the table from Jody and picked up a clipboard from the table next to him. Then he clicked his pen twice and said, "How much have we told you about our new show?"

Jody shook her head. "Not much, actually."

"Right, well, we didn't want people to know what we were up to until it was absolutely necessary—" Ike said.

"But now that we're less than a month away from production," Erwin interjected, cutting off his brother in midsentence, "we can finally let people in on the premise."

There was a long moment of silence in which Ike shot Erwin a look of contempt. Erwin sank back into the couch; then Ike cleared his throat and continued.

"We're producing a reality-based television show called *Scream Queen*. The show will put a number of young actors into a real-life haunted house where they will all spend the night. In addition to being haunted, the house will be rigged with a few choice special effects designed to scare the hell out of the contestants."

Ike paused after he said those words. A slight breeze suddenly wafted through the room, flickering all the candles and causing the shadows on the walls to jump and dance like flies around a dead horse. When the flames settled, the smile on Ike's face gave Jody the creeps.

"There will be cameras all over the house to record everyone's reactions to things that happen inside, and contestants will be given cameras of their own to record themselves or what they see during the night. And, if you make it through the night you'll earn ten thousand dollars, whether you win or not."

"It sounds a little like a movie I've seen before—"

"*The House on Haunted Hill.* Nineteen fifty-eight, starring Vincent Price." Erwin turned to his brother. "I told you people would make that comparison."

Ike seemed annoyed. "It's not like that film at all."

Erwin sneered. "Sure. Right."

"We're taking the concept a lot further. And if anything, it's an . . . *homage.*"

"Sounds pretty classy when you say it in French, doesn't it?" Erwin's voice was dripping in sarcasm.

"Like it or not, Erwin . . ." Ike raised his voice to a shout. "I got you the budget you've always wanted." Ike stared at Erwin, visibly annoyed by his brother's sniping.

"Right," Erwin said at last. "Sorry."

In the silence that followed, Jody could hear the sound of a door opening somewhere beyond the shadows. It was followed by a moan, then silence again.

"In addition to all the scary stuff, each contestant will be sent into a room and be required to perform a classic scene from a horror movie."

Erwin cracked another devilish smile at this.

"What kind of scene?" Jody asked.

"You know, the final victim, the discovery of the body, a demonic possession . . . that sort of thing."

Jody nodded. "That sounds great."

Ike continued. "Now, the show will air on three consecutive weeks leading up to Halloween. On that night, studio audiences at selected horror theme parks and conventions around the country will watch the final episode and vote on their favorite 'Scream Queen.' The winning Scream Queen will not only receive fifty thousand dollars in cash, but will also get the starring role in the next Gowan Brothers horror film."

"Wow!" said Jody.

"Uh, excuse me, Ike," Erwin said, "but I thought the top prize was going to be a hundred thousand dollars."

Ike just looked at his brother, teeth clenched and one eyebrow twitching. "No, we're now going to use that fifty thousand for promotional purposes, namely for things like buttons, postcards, and fridge magnets to be handed out at conventions."

Erwin shook his head. "Uh-uh, we decided a hundred

thousand would go to the winner because fifty thousand doesn't sound like much of a prize."

Jody was about to say that if she were lucky enough to win, fifty thousand would be a great prize, but she never got the chance.

"That was yesterday," Ike said, the volume of his voice rising once again. "Today we decided we needed to spend a little extra on promotion."

"Who's we?"

"Myself and Bartolo from the network."

"Why wasn't I informed of this?" asked Erwin.

Jody had seen her own brothers argue enough times back home to know that this could go on for a while. She leaned back in her chair and tried to make herself comfortable.

"Because it didn't concern you," Ike said, clicking his pen in frustration. "We agreed at the beginning that you would look after the creative end of things, and I would take care of the finances."

"I want to be informed, though."

"On money matters you're strictly on a need-to-know basis. If I let you in on everything you'd just get in the way and slow things down."

Erwin's lips turned out in a pout, and were made to look even larger by the shadows cast upon his face. He was breathing in short, choppy breaths, almost as if he were about to cry. "My name is Erwin Gowan. I'm a Gowan brother just like you, and that means I have a fifty percent stake in everything to do with this production. How could you make a decision like that without asking me?"

Jody couldn't believe what she was seeing. It was as if she were back in kindergarten all over again.

"It didn't affect you. Your budget hasn't changed."

"Really? And what other things did you do that don't affect me? I bet the trailer you ordered for me is smaller than yours, isn't it?"

"I'll need to take meetings during the production."

"And all the letterhead I've seen reads 'Ike and Erwin Gowan' even though E comes before I in the alphabet."

How on earth did they ever get a movie made? Jody wondered.

"I'm the older one," Ike said.

"And the smarter one, too, right? I know that's what you're thinking."

Ike said nothing.

"Well, how smart will you be when I pull my fifty percent out of this production? How are you going to make a movie without any new ideas or creative talent? Why don't you just film your big deals, your transactions . . . Oh, wouldn't that make for a great reality TV show?"

Ike smiled nervously at Jody, then turned back to face his brother. "C'mon, Erwin, there's no need to get into all this now."

Jody was becoming uncomfortable watching the brothers argue. It had started out as just a little playful ribbing between siblings, but now they were getting nasty with each other.

"Watch!" Erwin said, gesturing wildly with his hands as if he were putting each word up on the big screen, "as Ike Gowan loses half a million dollars on the stock exchange. . . . *Watch!* as Ike Gowan gets bilked out of ten thousand dollars from a con man he trusts, just because the guy says he knows Mel Gibson. . . ."

"Shut up!" Ike said. Dark shadows were beginning to appear in high relief on his forehead as the veins there became more prominent. Ike held his pen tightly in his white-knuckled fist, clicking it as if it were a timer on some bomb.

"C'mon, guys," Jody interjected. "Take it easy. Fifty thousand is—"

But Erwin just kept on taunting his brother.

"Read! the reviews of the latest Gowan Brothers movie: 'The budget must have all gone up his nose because it

sure isn't up there on the screen,' says Roger Egbert of the *Picayune Daily Terror.* "

Ike rose from his chair and stood over Erwin. "I'm warning you, shut up! Just shut the fuck up!"

But Erwin wasn't about to shut up, he was on too much of a roll. *"Watch!* as Ike Gowan spends three million-dollar to make a one-million-dollar movie."

"That's enough, you asshole!"

Suddenly there was a large kitchen knife in Ike's hand.

"Hey!" Jody said.

Erwin saw the knife in his brother's hand, but didn't seem to take the threat seriously. "You don't have the balls to use it, Ike, so why don't you just put it away?"

Ike stood there, the knife inching closer to his brother's face. "This time I'll do it, I swear."

Erwin shook his head confidently. "No, you won't. Now put it away."

Jody wasn't sure what she was seeing. Obviously the brothers had been down this road before, but had probably never come to blows. Well, there would always be a first time, and she wasn't going to just sit back and watch it happen.

"Listen to your brother," she said. "Hurting him isn't going to solve anything."

She moved forward, but Ike turned to face her, stopping her in her tracks.

"He needs to be taught a lesson," Ike said.

Erwin laughed. "Don't worry, he hasn't got the guts to do it. He's even afraid to cut scenes from our movies because he doesn't want to hurt anyone's feelings."

"Shut up!" Ike firmed his grip on the knife.

"Come on." Erwin sighed. "You look pathetic standing there with that thing in your hand. . . . Either use the damn knife or put it away!"

Ike paused, and for a moment it looked as if it were all over, but then he lunged over the table at his brother.

Jody screamed.

Ike landed on top of Erwin and, in a single motion, stabbed the knife deep into his brother's neck.

Blood spurted from around the wound in Erwin's throat in long thin jets, one of them catching Jody across the face.

She screamed again.

Ike continued stabbing at the ruined neck of his younger brother, tearing it open, shredding the flesh.

Jody's brothers had fought plenty of times while they were growing up and the worst that had ever happened was a bloody nose. But this . . . this was *murder.* Or it would be if she didn't do something about it.

She dove forward, her shoulder hitting Ike in the upper body, knocking him off the couch.

They both fell to the floor.

She scrambled to her feet and backed away, wary of the knife.

Ike got up from the floor slowly, his chest heaving, the knife still in his hand, dripping blood. "You'll pay for that."

Jody shook her head in disbelief. All she'd wanted was a part in a stupid television show. "I didn't want you to kill him."

Ike looked over at his brother. Erwin's head was slumped over onto his right shoulder. Blood continued to leak out of the open rent in his neck.

"He's already dead," Ike said, his eyes alight with evil and his face looking ghoulish in the candlelight. "And now it's your turn, bitch!"

Jody backed away from Ike to stall for time. If she did nothing she'd end up dead like Erwin. But if she fought back, winding up dead would be the worst that could happen to her. If she did something right now, there was a good chance she might escape . . . that she might survive this nightmare.

"Ready or not, here I come." Ike laughed like a madman.

Jody took a quick step forward and kicked at Ike's hand, sending the knife flying through the air. Then she pushed him out of the way and raced for the side of the room that had a door.

She found the door in the darkness, but it was locked. The doorknob wouldn't turn.

Ike had gotten up off the floor and was coming toward her, his bloody hands looking to wrap themselves around her neck.

She kicked at the door and beat it with her fists, but to no avail.

Ike was almost upon her.

She screamed in terror.

It was a high-pitched, keening wail that came from somewhere deep down in the pit of her stomach.

"Cut!" Ike said.

Suddenly, the lights came on and Jody found herself in the middle of a soundstage.

There was applause coming from crew all around her.

Ike was standing in front of her, smiling.

Over on the couch, Erwin opened one of his blood-spattered eyes . . . and smiled as well.

Jody just stared at the two men, trying to look dignified while struggling to catch her breath.

"Fantastic!" said Erwin, pulling the empty blood bag from his neck and rising up from his chair.

"The best yet," Ike added with a nod of his head.

Jody was dumbfounded. "You mean . . ."

"Psyche!" Erwin said with a burst of childlike laughter.

"Congratulations!" Ike said, putting a hand on Jody's shoulder. "You got the part."

Two

"Are we there yet?" said Erwin, the sarcasm in his voice unmistakable.

"That was funny the first time you said it," Ike said. "But the joke starts to wear thin after the fifth or sixth time."

"Well, when I asked it the first time I thought we were almost there. How was I supposed to know we still had another *hour* to go?"

Ike said nothing in response to his brother. If he had known that the house his location manager had found for the shoot was so far from L.A., he might not have agreed to use it. Sure it had looked good in the photos he'd been e-mailed, and it was big enough to handle the entire production, and the price had certainly been right . . . but it was a two-hour drive out of L.A., and on the outskirts of a small town no one had ever heard of. If something went wrong during production, or someone got hurt on-site, they might not have the means or the budget to make things right. They *could* have had the budget if they spent everything the network gave them to produce the series, but they'd decided to do the show on a shoestring and save the bulk of the money for the movie they'd be making afterward.

The thought of the network deal still brought a smile to Ike's face. He'd basically gotten the network to fund a television series that would be a four-hour advertisement for the next Gowan Brothers horror film. In addition to the money they'd given them for the television show, the network had also paid up front for the television broadcast rights to the new movie, giving the Gowan brothers more money to produce this one than they'd had on their previous four films. It was a sweet deal, no doubt about it, and it was the thing that was going to put the Gowan brothers on the map. After this one they'd be doing studio films with enough money for top-shelf animatronics and CGI effects, name stars, and most important of all, they'd be rich. . . .

Their driver turned the Navigator off the two-lane highway they'd been traveling for the past two hours and onto a gravel road that led straight into a forested area that was made up of tall pines and dark shadows, even in the middle of the day.

"Are we there yet?" Erwin said again. "I've got to pee."

This time Ike turned toward the driver. "Well?"

"Five minutes down this road."

"Can you wait that long?" Ike asked.

"No, I can't," said Erwin.

Suddenly, a line of water splashed against the dashboard.

"What the—" exclaimed the driver, jerking the wheel left in surprise and almost putting them into a tree before managing to get the big SUV back onto the dirt road.

Ike slowly turned around to face his brother. "Damn it, Erwin, that wasn't funny."

Erwin sat there with a big grin on his face and a tiny green squirt gun in his hand. "What do you mean? It was hilarious."

Ike had to smile. "Yeah, a real pisser."

The driver let out a sigh and shook his head ever so slightly.

"Just no more surprises until we get to the house, okay? I want to get there in one piece."

"All right," said Erwin, "but are we there yet?"

"Yes," said the driver. There was relief in his voice. "Here it is."

They rounded a curve in the road and the trees slowly began to part. There in front of them stood the old house they'd seen in the pictures.

The driver brought the car to a stop and the brothers just sat there, looking at the house.

"It looked scarier on the computer screen," said Erwin.

At first glance, Ike had to admit that his brother was right. The old Victorian mansion didn't appear to be all that menacing in the middle of the day. The sun shining down on it only exposed its missing shingles, broken windows, and sagging rooflines. And the trees around it were overgrown, crowding the building as if they were working on reclaiming the structure and returning it to the land. But the more Ike studied the house, the more he began to appreciate its design and construction.

At the north end of the building was a two-story turret that housed large, round, glassed-in rooms on both the first and second floors. The turret was capped by a shingled spire that towered over the rest of the house, giving it a focal point, and an ominous, fortresslike quality. There was also evidence of Gothic influences in the pointed arches that supported the roof over the porch, which went all the way around the ground floor. The longer Ike looked, the more the house gave him the creeps. "It'll do," he said at last.

"Hi, guys," said a voice that was tinged with a bit of an Australian accent.

Ike looked up and saw William Olsen, their location manager, approaching them from the direction of the trailers that were set up in the empty field on the eastern side of the house. Olsen was in his late forties, with a thick brown beard and long, unruly blond hair. He had a real knack for finding places that looked great on film, and that could stand in for multiple locations.

"Well, what do you think?" he asked.

"It's fine," Ike said, not wanting to let Olsen know what he really thought, just in case it might encourage the guy to ask for more money on their next project.

"It looked scarier in the pictures we saw," said Erwin.

"Not to worry, boys," Olsen said. "I know it doesn't look like much now, but the network sent us this crackerjack lighting guy. He's got all sorts of special lights set up around the house, and at night . . . I swear, you'll think the whole fucking thing's come to life."

"That good, eh?" said Erwin, already sounding pleased.

"And the lights even shine through the windows into the house so we can save a bit on interior lighting."

Ike liked the sound of that. "Sounds good," he said.

"Aw, it's great, wait till you see it."

Ike took a look around the property. There were people moving between the trailers, and there were others going in and out of the building, probably carpenters and electricians making the house safe for the effects guys who would be arriving over the next few weeks.

One of the people hanging around was obviously not a carpenter or a plumber. The man was walking an average-sized dog on a leash and if it weren't for the rat sitting up on his shoulder he might have been mistaken for someone from town who had just wandered onto the set.

Ike looked at Olsen and gestured in the man's direction.

"Oh, right, let me introduce you to Ryan Mayhew, he's our animal wrangler. I asked him to come by because I knew you two would be here today. I hope you don't mind."

Erwin shrugged.

"Not at all," Ike said.

Olsen turned toward Mayhew. "Ryan, would you come here a minute? I want you to meet the Gowan brothers."

The animal wrangler walked toward them, his hand extended in greeting. "I'm pleased to meet you, Mr. and Mr. Gowan."

"Mr. Gowan was our dad," said Erwin.

"I'm Ike, and this is my brother, Erwin."

"Oh, you don't have to introduce yourselves to me, I know who you two are. I've enjoyed all your movies, even if there weren't many animals in them."

"We could never afford them before," Ike said.

"Besides that," said Erwin, "it's easier to make puppets that we can chop into small bits than work with *live* animals. You know, I've never met a dog that could emote well after its head had been hacked off with an ax."

Mayhew's face looked pained, as if he was having trouble appreciating Erwin's attempt at humor.

"Does the rat do any tricks?" Ike asked, changing the subject.

Without a word, Mayhew bent down and placed a cube of cheese on the toe of his shoe. Then he snapped his fingers and the rat climbed down Mayhew's chest and pant leg to get to the cheese. After putting the food in its mouth, the rat climbed back up the wrangler's body to its perch on his shoulder.

Mayhew smiled, proud of his animal's accomplishment.

Ike was skeptical, not sure how they could work that trick—if you could call it that—into the show. He glanced at the dog. It was little more than a mutt, looking as if it had been dragged out of the pound earlier in the day. "What about him? He do anything special?"

"He doesn't look all that scary to me," said Erwin.

"Just watch," said Mayhew. He took three steps away from the dog, caught the dog's attention, and then gave it a silent signal by tapping his cheek three times in succession.

All at once the dog's appearance changed. Its lips pulled back to expose two long rows of pointed fangs. It snarled and spat like a hellhound, lunging forward and moving backward as if it were in a pit and fighting for its life.

"Jesus," said Erwin, taking a couple of steps back to get out of the dog's way, then moving behind Olsen where he could look at the dog more safely over the man's shoulder.

Even Ike moved aside, afraid that the dog might take a chunk out of one of his loafers.

Mayhew let the dog snap and snarl for a little while longer before tapping his other cheek. The dog suddenly fell silent and looked to the wrangler for a treat.

"Wow!" said Erwin.

"Yeah," Ike said. "Wow!"

Olsen slapped a hand on Mayhew's shoulder. "Thanks, Ryan, that was great," he said.

The animal wrangler nodded, then turned and led the dog away. The rat remained perched on the man's shoulder, hardly moving as he walked.

"That was cool!" said Erwin.

"But do we really need animals?" Ike asked.

Olsen nodded. "The house has got them. At one point in the house's history the basement was overrun by rats, thousands of them. . . ."

"And the dog?"

"Well, the guy who owned this house, who did the killing, had a dog, and they figure the dog proved very helpful in, uh . . . disposing of a few of the man's victims."

"Ah," Ike said with a slight nod.

"What did the dog do," said Erwin, "bury them?"

"Uh, no," Olsen said. "He ate them, actually."

Erwin clapped his hands and rubbed his palms together. "This is going to be great."

"Let's get to the production trailer," Olsen said, smiling. "There are a bunch of people there waiting for you."

"Lead the way," Ike said.

Romano Ramirez hooked the end of the crowbar under the aged plank and pulled. Nails screamed, dust flew, and the wood slowly came away from the riser.

Another step was laid bare.

Romano and his brother, Eduardo, had been building theatrical sets in southern California for the past fifteen years. Most of their work had been on low-budget, nonunion productions, but they'd never been on a job like this one before.

First of all, why would anyone want to fix such an old run-down house? It would be a lot easier to build a brand-new one, especially when they had to use second-hand wood for all their repairs. And even though they were making repairs, they'd been instructed only to fix the house so that no one would break their neck walking around inside. Romano could only shake his head at that. He and his brother had worked for some tightfisted producers over the years, guys like Roger Corman and those two cheapskates, Golan and Globus, but they'd never seen a project that cut as many corners as this one.

Romano swung the crowbar under another step. This time the hook punched a hole in the rotten plank, leaving behind a mess of tiny wooden shards that would have to be removed by hand.

At this rate, he'd be working on the stairs leading to the second floor all afternoon. The head carpenter had told him that six steps needed to be replaced, but there were twice that many in need of repair. Sure, the others would hold as long as the people using them stepped lightly . . .

Like ghosts.

Which was the other thing that bothered Romano about the house. Even though the sun was shining and it was hot outside, the inside of the house felt cold. Not cool like a house that hasn't been opened in years, but *cold* like the inside a cooler full of ice.

It was almost like the place was really haunted, or maybe even cursed.

Romano glanced at his watch. There were fifteen minutes to go till break time, but he needed to get out of the house now. He felt uneasy, like there was somebody looking over his shoulder all the time, watching what he was doing to the house and not being too pleased about it.

He began to gather up the broken bits of wood, careful not to catch his bare hands on any of the exposed nails. His hands had become hardened by fifteen years of work, but calluses were no match for a rusty four-inch nail.

Just then, something moved at the top of the stairs.

Romano dropped a sliver of wood and looked up in time to see a shadow moving across the wall inside one of the upstairs rooms.

But there was no one upstairs . . . wouldn't be anyone up there until he repaired the steps leading up to the second floor.

Romano continued to peer into the room, wondering if what he'd seen might have been just a shadow from a tree outside the upstairs window.

Yeah . . . that would explain it.

He took a deep breath and let out a sigh, then began backing down the stairs with the load of broken wood in his arms. *The sooner this job is done, the better,* he thought. *There's something wrong with this place, and it's not just rotten wood on the stairs.*

At the bottom of the stairs Romano turned for the door, but as he did, he noticed something standing in the doorway leading into the kitchen. It was a dark, deformed figure that looked vaguely human. Much of the head was missing and its arms seemed to bend at strange and impossible angles.

Romano's heart began to race and his breath quickened. He wanted to move, to run, but all he could do was look at the horrible vision.

As he watched, the thing's misshapen arms reached out to him, as if he were a long-lost love.

And then . . . it moved toward him.

Romano screamed, turned for the open doorway, and ran.

He was through the door in seconds, but out on the porch his right foot broke through a rotten plank.

As he fell . . .

Broken wood spilled from his arms.

Jagged planking shredded his right leg, tearing it open from ankle to thigh.

His shinbone snapped in two with a loud *crack!*

And then he hit the porch hard, his outstretched hands and left cheek pierced by upturned nails in the scattered wood.

And then he was still.

For a moment, there was only silence, then the shouts and pounding footsteps of workers running toward the house.

His brother, Eduardo, was first on the scene. "Romano!"

Romano opened his right eye and saw there was a nail poking through his right hand. He tried to speak, but cut his tongue on the point of the nail that had pierced his cheek.

"What happened?" his brother wanted to know.

"La casa . . ." he whispered, too low for anyone to hear.

Instead of asking again, Eduardo got busy tying off Romano's thigh to try and stop his brother from bleeding to death.

"Bring the truck!" Eduardo shouted. "We've got to get him to the hospital."

The rest of the workers moved quickly.

Romano closed his eyes, hoping that if he lived, the job would be finished before he was well enough to return to work.

Three

"Geez, Mom, I thought you would have been happier for me."

Jody Watts sat by the open window in the living room of her apartment, her feet on the sill so the bloodred nail polish she'd just applied to her toenails could dry in the breeze.

She didn't like talking on the phone all that much, and especially didn't like answering the phone—it brought back too many painful memories—but one of the conditions of her moving out to Los Angeles was that she call her folks each week whether she wanted to or not. So far she'd never missed a call, although the calls were getting shorter and shorter.

"I am happy for you, dear, it's just that . . . I don't know, it sounds a little dangerous to me."

"It *sounds* dangerous," Jody said, dabbing some color onto a spot on her big toe she'd missed earlier. "But it's a television show, Mom. There's going to be all sorts of special effects to scare us and make us scream, but it's all just a bit of harmless fun."

"You're going to be spending a night in a haunted house, right?"

"Yes."

"A real haunted house, one that's full of ghosts and spirits . . ." Jody's mom's voice trailed off, but her words were obviously intended as a question.

"That's what the producers said, but I don't know where the house is yet, or why it's haunted."

The phone line was silent, but Jody could almost feel her mother shaking her head thousands of miles away. "Oh, I don't like the sound of that *at all.*"

"I've seen ghosts before," Jody said, knowing she was starting to grasp at straws.

"My grandfather was a kind and gentle man," her mother said. "He died quietly and naturally while doing something he loved. . . . And because of that his ghost became a spirit guide, a guardian, a loving entity that would never harm anyone."

"So, maybe this house will have the same kinds of ghosts."

"Oh, Jody . . ."

The tone was unmistakable. It was the voice her mother had always used to show disappointment in her daughter. Hearing it now made Jody feel all of five years old again.

". . . I've seen the kinds of movies those two boys make. They're sick and depraved and I can only imagine that this television show of theirs will be just as obscene. If the house they've found is truly haunted, then you can be sure it'll be haunted by all manner of wraiths and poltergeists, demons and ghouls."

"C'mon, Mom, do you really believe that?"

"Jody, honey . . . you can't believe in the ghost of your great-grandfather and not believe in other kinds of ghosts. If one kind exists, then the other kinds exist as well."

Jody was silent. Her mother was making too much sense—if such a thing could actually be said about ghosts and the supernatural—to argue the point. It was easier simply to ignore her concerns and keep on dreaming the American dream. "It's a TV show, Mom. The producers aren't going to let anything bad happen to the contestants, especially not when everything will wind up on videotape and there will be a record if anything goes wrong."

"Did they make you sign a waiver?"

Jody felt as if she'd just been busted. "Yes."

"So if something happens to you, you'll have no recourse. You won't be able to sue them, or anything."

"What's the worst thing that could happen?"

"Well, you could get killed for one. . . ."

Jody felt a chill run down her spine.

"Or you could hurt yourself running through a dark house and wind up falling down a flight of stairs, paralyzed for life. . . . Or you could be so traumatized by what happens to you inside the house that you might not be able to do any kind of meaningful work for the rest of your life. . . . Or you could pee in your pants on national television, and no one would ever take you seriously again. . . . Or you could—"

"All right, Mom! I get the picture."

Now it was Jody's mother's turn to be silent.

"I'm sorry, honey," she said at last. "I'm just worried about you is all. You're still my baby, you know, and it's my *job* to worry about you."

Jody smiled at that. The chill down her spine was gone, replaced by a warm and fuzzy feeling all over her body. Still, the phone felt uncomfortable cradled between her ear and shoulder. "I've got to go, Mom."

"Where are you off to?"

Jody let out a sigh. Thousands of miles between them and her mother was still treating her as if she lived at home. "They gave us all a bit of money as a sort of advance so I joined the health club down the street for thirty days. I'm working out every day so I'll be ready for the show."

"But you don't need to lose any weight, dear."

"Thanks, Mom," Jody said, knowing her mother would say the same thing no matter how much she weighed.

"But it's not so much for that . . . I'm just thinking that since there will probably be other girls on the show who are prettier and sexier than me, I might as well be the strongest one in the group."

"That's my girl!" said a third voice.

"Dad?"

"He must have been listening in on the other phone," said her mother.

"Damn right I was," said Jody's dad. "Now you listen, Jo . . . you be ready for whatever those Hollywood boys dish out."

"I will, Dad."

"And when you meet up with one of them ghosts, you kick it in the ass for me, you hear!"

"I hear, Dad."

"Bye, hon," said her mother.

"Bye, Mom."

"And good luck," her mother added as she hung up.

"Thanks, Mom," Jody whispered under her breath as she put down the receiver, glad to be off the phone. "I just might need it."

Four

Ike, Erwin, and the rest of the production team ran around to the front of the house. By the time they arrived a construction van was speeding down the drive, kicking up a cloud of dust and dirt in its wake.

"What the fuck happened here?" Ike demanded, climbing up onto the porch.

He was met there by the head carpenter, a short, dark-haired man named Luis who had worked for the brothers on their last six features and had done most of the renovations on Ike's home in Palm Springs.

"One of the men had an accident," Luis answered, pointing to the hole in the floorboards of the porch. There was blood spattered nearby, and plenty of broken pieces of wood splayed about, some of the nails jutting out from them tipped with blood.

Erwin picked up a few jagged boards and began playing with them, first acting as if they were knives, and then closely examining the way they'd broken, as if he were working out some new effect in his mind.

"Where is he now?" Ike wanted to know.

"A few of my men took him to the hospital."

Ike wondered what this was going to do to the insurance policy he'd taken out on the production. "How many went with him?"

Luis shook his head and shrugged his shoulders. "Two or three, I'm not sure. They left in a hurry."

Ike looked down the drive and saw that the van was gone from view. He knew that this was where he was supposed to ask if the guy was hurt badly, if he was going to be all right, but that wasn't the foremost thing on his mind. "With one man in the hospital and two gone with him to hold his hand, who's going to finish the work on this damn house?"

Luis's head bowed ever so slightly. "Don't worry, Mr. Gowan, it'll get done, even if we have to work straight through the night."

Ike nodded. "I've got a twelve-man special effects team coming in three days and I can't afford to have them waiting for the paint to dry, you understand me?"

"Yes, sir, Mr. Gowan. Everything will be ready."

Ike stood there in front of Luis wanting to bully the man further, but realizing there was nothing to be gained from it. Luis was a good carpenter, and was able to get a lot out of his men for what they were being paid. He was also good at bending to Ike's will, and letting Ike have the last word. Ike liked that, but every once in a while he wished Luis would give him some lip, talk back, or complain about the money and materials or whatever, just so Ike could throw his weight around and act the way a big Hollywood producer was supposed to act.

"All right, then," Ike said at last. "You all get back to work now."

"Yes, sir," Luis said.

Ike turned for the production trailer and saw that several of the men had been watching him talk to Luis.

"What are you standing around for?" he bellowed. "Get back to work!" He clapped his hands. "Let's go!"

In moments, everyone had made themselves busy.

And the air was filled with the sound of power tools and pounding hammers.

A smile crept across Ike's face.

It was good to be the guy in charge.

* * *

The production trailer was ten years old and twenty feet long. It was just large enough inside to fit twelve chairs around an eight-foot table, and still have enough room for a second four-foot table to hold a couple of coffee machines and a few trays of cookies and donuts.

"Is this the best you could do?" Ike asked as he stepped into the trailer and took a seat at the head of the table.

"Best I could do with the money you budgeted for trailers," answered location manager William Olsen.

Ike nodded knowingly.

Since they were holding back a good portion of their budget for the feature film, they had to cut costs somewhere and the network wouldn't be pleased if most of the money they'd invested didn't end up on the screen. So, they'd had to cut costs elsewhere and fancy trailers had been high up on the list of things they could do without.

Erwin took the chair at the opposite end of the table from his brother, still fiddling with two broken pieces of wood and marveling at the way the bent nails could be dragged over the skin of his forearm without breaking the flesh.

Ike noticed his brother's activity. "Erwin, what are you doing?"

Erwin looked up. "Oh, well . . . if I drag the nail this way with the point trailing away, it doesn't hurt me. But if we film it like that, then play it backward, it would look as if the nail is about to rip open the skin."

"Yeah, so?"

"So the audience would be cringing waiting for the nail to go in and for blood to come out, but of course it never would."

Ike thought it over. "Maybe we could use it for a distraction before a jump."

"You mean like just before a wolf breaking through a window," Erwin said, excitement in his voice.

"Yeah, something like that." Ike nodded.

As the brothers had been talking, the trailer filled up with the key members of the production crew including the lighting and sound directors, director of photography, assistant directors, production manager, and William Olsen's assistant. Most of the people present wouldn't be called upon at this meeting, but it was good to have them around so they could begin to get a feel for what needed to be done, and to get an idea about how the Gowan brothers wanted these things to be done.

When they were all settled in, Ike sat up and said, "Good morning, everyone."

The rest of the table responded.

Ike quickly dispensed with the pleasantries and focused his gaze on Olsen. "Bill," he said, "Erwin and I aren't here for more than half an hour and we've already got a man in the hospital. What kind of death-trap money pit did you stick us with?"

The heads of everyone sitting around the table turned in the direction of the shaggy-haired Australian.

"The price we're paying is a bit higher than we'd usually pay for something in such bad condition, but it's not my fault the owner of this place reads the trades. I didn't tell him who I was, but he was able to piece it together."

"Couldn't you lie to him?"

Olsen smiled. "I did lie to him. . . . But really, no one has shown any interest in the property for twenty years, and then some guy's asking to rent the place for three months. What would you think if you were him?"

"I'd think you were crazy," Erwin said from the other end of the table.

"Exactly, or I'm with some production."

"Did he try and bleed you?" Ike asked.

"Of course he did, but he had no idea what productions normally pay . . . and I convinced him that when we were done, the place would be worth double what it's worth now."

"And he believed you?"

Olsen just smiled, and his smile seemed to be infectious, slowly spreading to everyone else in the room.

Ike couldn't let Olsen think he'd done something great, even if he had. "It's still more than we budgeted."

"Maybe, but two percent over budget for the location is still a bargain. Haunted houses don't come cheap these days, especially one with, uh . . . real ghosts inside them."

Erwin was suddenly interested in what was going on. "Is this place really haunted?"

Olsen shrugged. "I don't believe in any of it myself, but there seems to be a few stories about ghosts wandering around over the years, inside the house and on the grounds."

"Really?"

"Yeah, there's a bit of back story to the house, too. Even a write-up in this old book about haunted houses."

"Okay, let's hear it."

Olsen reached into his pocket and pulled out a pair of reading glasses. After sliding them on, he opened up a thin hardcover book with a faded red cover and worn spine and held the book up to his face. There was some gold lettering on the front and spine, but much of it had been rubbed off over the years. He'd marked the page he needed with a bit of yellow ribbon, which was probably part of the book. He cracked opened the book, pulled aside the ribbon, and began to read the entry.

THE SHIELDS HOUSE, Kettleman City, California.
The two-story five-bedroom Victorian house is situated

some ten miles east of Kettleman City, a small town about 100 miles northwest of Los Angeles, east of Interstate 5.

Deserted now, the house was once the home of Reginald Shields, owner of a turn-of-the-century sawmill located on the southern shores of Tulare Lake. When Reginald died in 1937, his youngest son, Marcus, took over the house, going into debt to buy out the other siblings so he could own the house outright. The sawmill went bankrupt in 1948 and just twelve months later Marcus Shields was penniless. However, he managed to keep up payments on the estate for two more years by farming the land around the house, and by picking up travelers and wanderers roaming Interstate 5 and taking them to his home to kill them. Afterwards, he would sell the personal belongings of his victims on the many regular trips he made to cities like Los Angeles and San Francisco.

State Police became suspicious of Shields when citizens of Kettleman City began to wonder how he'd been able to prosper when so many of his crops had failed. Although not officially suspected of any crime, Shields panicked when sheriffs' deputies asked him to visit their office the next time he was in Kettleman City, and hanged himself the night before he was scheduled to meet with the police.

The Shields house is reported to be haunted by the ghosts of Shields and possibly of his victims. Several families lived in the house throughout the late 1950s and 1960s, but none for longer than two years. The house was vacated when an infestation of rats made it uninhabitable in the spring of 1970.

Olsen closed the book and looked around the table.

Ike was silent for several moments. "That's it? That's all you've got on this house?"

Olsen shrugged. "What do you mean, 'That's all'? It's actually got some history to it, and we're lucky to have it."

"Really?"

"Yeah, really. You didn't exactly give me an easy task, you know. I had to find a place we could have the run of for two months and an owner who didn't care if we knocked out a few walls, or broke a few windows. I had to find it in less than two weeks, within a couple hours' drive from Los Angeles, and I had to get it all for a song." Olsen paused to take a deep breath. "And after all that, oh, wouldn't it be nice if it was actually haunted, too?"

Ike smiled. Olsen could be pushed around, but every once in a while he pushed back, just enough to let you know he'd reached his limit. When he did that Ike could be certain that Olsen had done the best he could under the circumstances and there was no point in badgering the man further.

"Okay, so we're lucky to have this place." Ike sighed. "It's just that the story . . . I mean it's interesting and all, but it just sounds so . . ."

"Boring!" Erwin offered from the other end of the table, throwing the word out like a catcall.

Ike nodded. "Yeah, that's it, boring."

"You'll get no argument from me on that account," Olsen said, raising his hands—one of them holding the book—as if he were being robbed at gunpoint. "This whole thing is written up like an encyclopedia. But it proves that the place *does* have a ghost story attached to it and that's all you need if you've got a decent writer to work it."

"Yes-s," Ike said slowly, then snapped, "Where's Dunbar?"

Everyone's attention moved two people to the left of Olsen where Carl Dunbar, a young, slightly chubby, bespectacled writer from Los Angeles with two horror novels and a few television writing credits to his name, sat idly twirling a pencil through his fingers.

"Who, me?" he said, seemingly uncertain of himself.

"Yeah, you," Ike echoed. "Let me hear the spin you've put on this lame-oh ghost story."

"Yeah, okay." Dunbar sat up in his chair, opened a tan file folder, and leafed through a few typed pages. He cleared his throat once, then began to read.

THE SHIELDS HOUSE, Kettleman City, California.
Unassuming.
Charming.
Grand.
These are the first thoughts that might run through someone's mind after gazing upon the empty house situated just 100 miles northwest of Los Angeles. Set in a rural valley, it looks like the stuff of an American fable, where rock-solid families were born and raised and took their rightful place in the generational strength that has made this country great.

On closer inspection, however, it is obvious that the house is run-down; a broken and shattered shell of a home, holding no warmth, no comfort. Indeed, it looks to be full of dread, a home of untolled terrors.

But while it has taken years for the structure to take on this appearance, the home is actually closer now to its real character than at any time in its history. For no matter how new the house had once been, how freshly painted and scrubbed, it had always been a scarred, broken place . . . where evil lived under the facade waiting for its chance to rise, to break out and take its rightful place in the annals of those houses which hellish monsters call home.

Dunbar paused a moment to take a look around.
No one said a word.
He continued.

In 1937 an unassuming son of a lumber magnate named Marcus Shields took possession of the house after his father, Reginald, died in an industrial accident, which at the time was noted to have occurred under "mysterious circumstances. " *Shields paid off his siblings in order to have the house to himself, then spent several unremarkable years managing the family business. A hardworking, yet unexceptional businessman, Shields eventually ran the sawmill into the ground, declaring bankruptcy in 1948. He managed to live off savings and investments for another twelve months, but once again failed in the business world when his investments went sour and his land proved barren.*

A millionaire all his life, he was penniless by the summer of 1950.

But rather than mark the end of Marcus Shields's life, his business failings and financial losses only served as a transition point upon which he changed careers decades before such midlife shifts became fashionable.

Almost overnight he gave up being a man of business, and became instead a man whose only business was death.

In short, he became a serial killer.

And at last Marcus Shields had found something he was good at.

Someone snickered.

Posing as a kind of bumbling local resident, Shields gave rides to travelers he met on the interstate, then offered them overnight accommodation in his large and empty home.

But at night the inside of the empty home became filled with the anguished cries and screams of his tortured victims.

A teenage boy on the road in search of a job . . .

A woman on her way to the city to work for an uncle . . .

A young father searching for work and money to send to his starving wife and children . . .

All of them begging Shields for death.

And he granted their wishes, but only after he was done with them, exercising every manner of sexual deviancy upon their bodies. And when he was done with them, he'd dispose of the bodies in countless heinous ways, from burning them in bonfires to feeding them to his dog. But while Marcus Shields kidnapped, tortured, and killed secretly and existed in anonymity, there were always eyes upon him, watching.

And the suspicions grew about the man who lived alone, and the terror sounds that could sometimes be heard on the cool night air. And the questions began to be asked.

How was it that a man could survive, indeed prosper, with no crops to harvest, and no job to speak of?

And what of the screams?

The sheriff wanted to know, and it was only a matter of time before what was left of the cracked facade of Shields's insane world came crashing down around him. But he could not allow that, could not face his shame, and so he took the coward's way out, taking his own life on the eve of his capture, damning himself to remain in the house—a soul tortured for all eternity by his very victims' insatiable need for vengeance.

And today, the evil continues to unravel, day after night, night after day, as the ghosts of Shields and his victims walk the halls in search of . . .

Fresh blood.

Revenge.

And a queen whose scream will be music to their ears.

Dunbar put down the papers he'd been reading from.

The trailer was absolutely silent. A few people seemed to be holding their breath.

Ike smiled.

At the other end of the table, Erwin was grinning ear to ear.

Then, after a few more moments of silence, Ike began to laugh.

"I—I can change it if you like," stammered Dunbar. "There's a few spots I'm not really happy with and I can rework it if you think it needs something, I don't know . . . different—"

"No!" Ike cried.

Dunbar looked startled.

"Olsen, where'd you get this guy?"

"Stephen King was busy," Olsen deadpanned.

Nervous laughter percolated around the table.

Dunbar looked crushed. Defeated. If he had circulated among any type of Hollywood crowd he would probably have heard a dozen different stories about working for the Gowan brothers, few of them pleasant, and all of them seasoned with bitterness. Working for Ike Gowan was like sticking your head into a meat grinder. And if the production succeeded, it would be the Gowans who'd take the credit, but if it failed, the blame would all be firmly placed on the shoulders of the cast and crew.

"I'll rework it," Dunbar said, pushing his chair away from the table as if he wanted to leave the meeting early.

"Don't change a thing," Ike shouted. "The network censors might not like it, but we'll worry about that later. Right now it's perfect, I love it!"

"Really?" Dunbar's face was a mix of relief and disbelief. The sag had gone from his shoulders and he looked a half foot taller.

"Yeah, really." Ike looked up at the trailer's ceiling as if there were some film being projected there that only Ike could see. "We'll print the copy up big and use a few words and phrases in the montage that opens the show. Yeah, maybe with someone like Lance Henrickson doing the voice-over. . . . What do you think, Erwin?"

"It's got sex, it's got violence, and a dog who eats human flesh," Erwin said with a shrug. "What's not to like?"

Five

Jody wasn't sure what media consultants did exactly, but one of the production assistants for the show had called a couple of days ago and told her to be at the Lester and Loew offices at ten A.M. on Thursday.

The place was located in an office on top of a camera store on Wilshire Boulevard. The L&L logo was etched on the door in a sort of gold leaf and was done up in a typeface that looked as if one of the Ls were going to take flight at any moment.

She opened the door and started up the stairs to the second floor. When she was halfway up she heard two men talking. There was something familiar about their voices, but she couldn't quite place them.

And then the two men appeared at the top of the stairs and it all came together for her. The man on the left was tall and thin and still quite handsome. If she remembered right, his name was Robert Carroll and he had been the host of the television show *Funniest Moments Caught on Tape,* which had been a big hit in the mid-1990s but had been off the air the last two years. The other man was shorter, blond and quite muscular. He'd grown out his hair, but even without his trademark crew cut, she recognized him as Gil Belfontaine, who'd had his own syndicated exercise show for years, but who had recently been eclipsed by the next wave of younger, better-trained, better-looking, and more knowledgeable television fitness hosts.

"I don't know," Carroll was saying. "Coming out is a big step. It might kill any chance they have to sell *Funniest Moments* in syndication."

"You can't think like that," said Belfontaine. "Nobody cares about that anymore. It's actually cool to be gay these days. They'll still be able to sell the show to all the regular markets . . . *and* once you're out they can sell it to the new gay channels, too. Who knows, you could even audition for a job on one of their new shows."

Carroll seemed to consider this, nodding slightly.

Jody stopped on the stairs, moving over to the right to let them pass. They both nodded a polite hello to her, but continued on with their conversation as if she weren't even there.

"And for me," Belfontaine said, "it would be so liberating not to have to pose with all these women and pretend that I like it." He shook his head, as if thinking of the possibilities. "I just know we'd really make some news if we came out."

"I'll think about it," Carroll said, opening the door at the bottom of the stairs.

"That's my man," she heard Belfontaine say just as the door closed behind them.

What the hell am I getting myself into? Jody wondered.

She reached the top of the stairs and found herself standing in front of a huge lime-green desk, staffed by a very young raven-haired man with a stylish five o'clock shadow, and wearing a silky blue and teal short-sleeved shirt over his rather buffed frame. At first Jody thought he was talking to himself, but soon realized that he was actually having a lively conversation with a friend through his sleek black headset.

"Oh, just a second, hon," he said, then looked up at Jody. "And you are?"

"Jody Watts, I'm here for—"

"Have a seat. Matilda will be with you in just one sec, okay?"

Before Jody could respond, he was back talking on the phone. She sat down and tried not to listen to his conversation, but couldn't help it, especially since the man didn't seem to mind her hearing him talk about someone's new implants.

"They didn't *really* squeak when you rubbed them. . . ." A pause. "You mean like a balloon?"

Thankfully the door of one of the offices opened just then and an attractive middle-aged woman in a tailored gray business suit stepped into the reception area.

Jody hadn't noticed at first, but the young man behind the desk had stopped talking the moment the door had opened, as if he had some sort of radar that told him his boss was in the area.

"You must be Jody," she said.

"Are you Miss Lester?"

"She's off today, I'm Matilda Loew and I've been assigned the job of prepping you."

"Prepping me?"

"Come into my office and I'll explain."

She followed the woman back to her office and as she did the young man opened and closed his hand and mouthed the word "Bye."

Jody waved to him.

"Have a seat," the woman, Matilda Lowe, said when Jody entered her office.

Jody sat down in the big leather chair that faced the woman's desk.

She went around the back of her desk and without sitting down opened up a blue file folder and began studying it. "You're the farm girl, right?"

"My name happens to be Jody, not 'the farm girl.' But I did grow up on a farm, if that's what you mean."

The woman smiled, but it was a fake, forced smile, as if she knew how to make it look as if she were smiling without ever having experienced joy or happiness in her life. "Those are nice highlights in your hair. Where'd you get them done?"

"Uh, they're natural, I guess."

She looked at Jody a long time, as if studying her.

Jody took the time to study the woman, as well. At first she'd thought she was somewhere in her early forties, but now in the different light, Jody realized she was probably closer to fifty, maybe even over the half-century hump. Her face was caked with makeup and the skin seemed unnaturally taut, as if it had been nipped and tucked a few too many times.

"Have you ever considered pigtails?" she asked.

"Uh, no."

"A ponytail?"

Jody ran a few fingers through her shoulder-length hair. "Not since I was twelve."

She paused a moment, and pretended to make a notation in Jody's file. "Have you ever been on television before?"

"Well, once when I was sixteen I went to an Iowa football game and me and a friend ended up on camera for about five seconds. Everybody in town saw it, even wrote it up in the local paper."

"What a charming anecdote. You should use it every chance you get."

"Use it? For what?"

Several creases appeared on the woman's forehead and for a moment her eyes grew dark, like the double barrels of a shotgun. "Didn't anyone explain to you why you're here?"

"Not really. They just told me you were a media consultant, whatever that is, and that I had to make an appointment."

She smiled again, this time causing crow's-feet to form at the corners of her eyes. "Well, in a nutshell, we reinvent people here. Someone needs a career change they come to us for advice and direction. A news anchor needs a new look to sharpen his image, we design it for him. Some actress slips up and talks about how she's actually someone from another dimension, we come up with a spin that minimizes the damage . . . that sort of thing."

Jody was confused. "But I thought I got this job because the Gowan brothers liked me for who I am."

"Of course you did, and of course they do, but there's always some room for improvement. Besides, the network has a lot of money invested in the show and they have a say on what goes out on their airwaves. Basically they just want you to be a little more media savvy in the days leading up to and after the show."

"For what?"

"Well, television and print interviews for one. The network media relations manager already has a dozen interviews lined up for all the contestants . . . and the winner—whoever that might be—has been booked on *Oprah* and *20/20* and a couple other shows like a reality television winners episode of *The Weakest Link.*"

"Wow!"

"So, it's my job to help you get prepared for all that."

Jody really couldn't picture herself on any of those shows, but she nevertheless felt herself starting to dream. *Oprah* and *20/20*. You are *The Weakest Link.* "Okay, what do I need to know?"

The woman smiled yet again, and this one was the phoniest of them all. Her cheeks were pulled way back exposing two rows of perfectly white teeth, the kind Jody had only ever seen in toothpaste commercials.

"Well, first of all—"

Jody paid close attention, readying herself for an inside scoop, an industry secret.

"—and probably the most important thing to re-member is to always be yourself."

What?

That was it?

Jody wondered how much this woman was charging the network per hour just to tell people to be them-selves. Whatever it was, it was way too much.

"Okay," Jody said slowly. "Seems easy enough."

"Second, and equally important, is to never tell a re-porter a lie."

Jody did her best not to laugh.

Here was a fifty-, maybe sixty-year-old woman who'd had twenty years surgically removed from her face, who was wearing a pound of makeup, extensions in her hair, false eyelashes, fake nails, and was flashing teeth that were as white and perfect as her dentist could make them, telling Jody to be herself and to never tell a lie.

And she was able to do it all while giving the impres-sion she was being sincere.

Apparently there was a lot Jody didn't know about the entertainment business.

And somehow she was glad for it.

Six

"Where is this guy?" Ike said, glancing at his watch.

Olsen shrugged. "I don't know. He was supposed to be here at nine."

The two men stood on the weedy grass in front of the house, still sipping coffees that had gone cold long ago. After a few rough patches, preproduction on the show and preparations on the house were going more or less smoothly and it looked as if they might even be ready a few days ahead of schedule. But, as with any production, there were always tiny glitches and problems that needed to be sorted out on a daily basis.

Like this morning's meeting.

They had arranged to meet with a man named Feroze Mohammed, a parapsychologist who had written several-best-selling books on the subjects of hauntings and poltergeists and currently served as the public information and media consultant to the American Society of Psychical Research. All he was supposed to do was drop by the set, take a tour of the house, act as if there were some real ghosts haunting the place, and then say as much in an on-camera interview.

At first Ike hadn't been crazy about having a so-called real-life "ghost buster" involved with the production because it would make it seem as if they were desperate to give the project some credibility. But the network had insisted on using a parapsychologist so they could market the show as a kind of documentary after its initial run as a reality television show was over. Eventually, Ike came around to the network's way of thinking, realizing that having a known parapsychologist appear on camera to tell people that the house was genuinely haunted was exactly what the show needed, especially if they could convince the man that he'd look best surrounded in shadows and lit from below. That would make him look creepy enough, and then all they'd have to do was add the right music and a few quick inserts from inside the darkened house, and they'd be able to convince people about anything they wanted.

Ike glanced at his watch again. "He's already on the payroll as a consultant, right?"

"Yeah, for the past five days."

"And he knew we were meeting him here today?"

Olsen nodded. "I spoke to him last night and he assured me he'd be here by nine."

"Well, it's after ten."

Olsen sighed.

"How long will it take you to find another expert?"

"Well, there's a graduate parapsychology program at John F. Kennedy University in Orinda. Maybe I can get a professor from there to come out and have a look at the house."

"Fine. Do that," Ike said. He poured out the rest of his coffee onto the grass and started heading for his trailer.

"Gentlemen."

Ike and Olsen turned around and saw a midsized middle-aged man with dark skin, a thin beard, and a head of graying hair cut with a number two all around, standing on the front porch of the house. He wore a short-waisted leather jacket, tan pants, and suede soft-soled shoes. He removed his wire-rimmed glasses, then took a cloth from the black bag that was slung over his shoulder and gave the lenses a wipe.

"Who are you?" Ike asked.

He stepped off the porch, pocketing the cloth and returning his glasses to the bridge of his nose. "I'm Feroze Mohammed." He shook Ike's hand first, then Olsen's. "I've been spending some time in the house . . . . you know, to get a feel for it."

He spoke with a slight accent that Ike couldn't place. From his name and complexion it should have been Middle Eastern, but he sounded almost English. And he was fairly cheerful, which wasn't what Ike had expected considering that the man's area of expertise was investigating and communicating with the dead.

"How long were you inside?" Olsen asked.

He glanced at his watch. "Oh, six or seven hours."

"Why didn't you let someone know when you arrived?" Olsen asked. "We could have put you up in a trailer for the night."

Feroze shook his head. "Oh, no, no. . . . You see I needed to wander the house alone. If you knew I was here you would have been looking over my shoulder the entire time, wanting me . . . no, *willing* me to find something in the house, and that's no way to do my job."

"Okay, fair enough, but now that you've spent half the night in the house, can we at least get you a coffee or something to eat?"

"Oh, yes, thank you. That would be wonderful."

"Never mind that right now," Ike cut in. "What I want to know is . . . do you think the house is, you know, haunted?"

Feroze nodded. "Oh, most definitely."

Ike turned his head to one side in disbelief. He almost couldn't believe what he was hearing. "What?"

"Yes, the house is haunted by several spirits. I can't be sure how many, but they're definitely inside there. Maybe even outside, too."

Olsen gently clapped his hands together. "All right."

Ike still didn't believe it. There had always been a fear in the back of his mind that the parapsychologist would determine that the grounds weren't haunted at all and there was nothing to fear inside the house, but this . . . this was exactly what he wanted. It was almost too good to be true. "You sure?"

"Oh, yes." Feroze nodded. "In fact, the spirits seem very disturbed by all the activity that's been going on in the house."

Ike smiled. "Really?"

"Yes. And if I might make one suggestion it would be that you cancel this production right away and find another house—one with more receptive spirits—in which to film."

The smile was gone from Ike's face in an instant.

Olsen looked incredulous.

Ike put a hand on the man's shoulder, then said, "Let's get you that coffee. I think we need to talk."

"You do this for a living then, Doctor?" Ike asked, pushing a cup of coffee across the table in the catering trailer they had set up on the site.

"I'm not really a doctor of anything."

"But you do make your living from this, right?"

"Yes, it is my profession. But, my living is derived more from books I've written and talks I give across the country. There's really no money in haunted houses . . ." His voice trailed off and he laughed. "Maybe there is for movie producers, but not for parapsychologists like me."

"So you're a real-life ghost buster," said Erwin, who had joined his brother and Olsen in the trailer.

"A funny movie, but an unfortunate label to be stuck with. I prefer the term parapsychologist."

"Sure, okay." Ike nodded. "That's what we'll put on the super . . . *Feroze Mohammed, Parapsychologist.*"

"That would be fine, thank you."

Olsen slipped a plate with a danish in front of the man.

"Now," Ike said, "tell me about the house."

Feroze took a bite from the danish and sipped his coffee. "Well, first of all let me say that the job you wanted me to do was very unlike my normal investigative work. When someone first calls me to investigate a poltergeist or haunting, there is a five-step procedure I usually go through, the very last step being an on-site investigation. . . ."

"This is television. We like to work fast," Ike said.

"And cheap," added Erwin.

Ike shot his brother a harsh glance.

"Well, since last Friday I've been researching the history of the house, and as you probably already know, there are several reasons why this house could be haunted."

Olsen slid into the chair next to the parapsychologist. "We've documented the back story pretty well."

"Yes, I'm sure you have. And you wouldn't be here if there hadn't been some reports of hauntings in the house over the years . . . so that basically took care of step one." He took another sip of coffee. "Step two requires that I question about why you might want me to investigate the house. Well, that was obvious, but sometimes people *want* their home to be haunted by loved ones, or they're looking to get rich with a story about a ghost and need someone like me to give some credibility to their claims."

"Like *The Amityville Horror.*"

"Precisely," said Feroze. "A complete and utter hoax."

"You mean that never happened?" asked Erwin.

"That was a terrific franchise." Ike nodded, ignoring his brother's put-on. "I think there were at least four of those movies."

"More like eight," offered Olsen.

"Exactly why people in my profession must be careful." A pause. "The third step requires that I determine if there is a need for an on-site investigation. Now, since you boys paid me, of course I had to come out here, but then comes number four in which I contact witnesses to any strange events that have occurred in the house."

Olsen looked surprised. "Did you find any?"

"One—a woman named Wallace Calverley. She lived in the house as a teenager, and, well . . . I have copies of her statement for you." Feroze pulled a few photocopied sheets from his bag and handed them out. "Basically when she turned sixteen she awoke each night with the feeling of a great weight on top of her. At first she would merely shake it off and go back to sleep, but the weight would always return, until she eventually opted for sleeping on the floor . . . sleeping quite comfortably through the night."

"This is great," Ike said, picking up one of the papers and giving it a quick scan. "Where did you find her?"

"She's a patient at the Saybrook Institute in San Francisco—and I must say, quite mad."

"Really?" Ike was thinking they might be able to interview her for the show. "How crazy is she?"

"She drools from the corners of her mouth, is prone to using foul language as a child might use baby talk, and she bites anyone who steps inside her 'danger' zone, the boundaries of which only she knows."

"Oh, okay, never mind."

Feroze let out a sigh. "All of which leads me to my being here today. Step five, which is the very first, and perhaps only thing you wanted from me, an on-site investigation."

Ike stopped reading. "Tell me about it, what did you find?"

"Well, first of all, understand that my own abilities of psychokinesis are rather limited, so I might not be getting the whole or even an accurate assessment about what's going on. If I had more time . . . say six months to a year, I would bring in a few of my colleagues and do a proper study of the house."

Ike leaned forward, closer to Feroze. "What *did* you find?" he repeated.

"As you know, there were several grisly murders committed in the house. That's fact, so it's not outrageous to think that there might be a few apparitions roaming the halls."

"You mean ghosts."

"Not exactly ghosts, not at the moment at least. They're . . . apparitions, the unsettled spirits of those who lost their lives on the property—"

"Where's Dunbar?" Ike looked around the room. At some point the writer must have entered the trailer because he was there, standing in the corner like a part of the furniture. "Are you getting this?"

Dunbar lifted his notepad so Ike could see it.

"They're here in the house, because their energy will always be here. And for some of them the events of their lives—and deaths—are being replayed over and over again night after night, like a movie on a continuous reel."

"Oh, this is great," Erwin said, leaning forward over the table to get as close to the parapsychologist as he could.

"Go on," Ike said.

"What you're doing with this production is disturbing their world, entering their time and space . . . and they don't like it."

Ike smiled. "They don't?"

"No, they don't and they're asking to be left alone."

Ike sat up straight. "You're kidding me, right?"

Feroze shook his head. "I assure you, I am not."

"Do you have any idea how much money is riding on this production? What's at stake?"

"I imagine several million dollars, the entire assets of your production company, and the filmmaking careers of you and your brother."

"Exactly, that's why we're doing this show a week from now. Rain or shine . . . ghosts or no ghosts."

Feroze's shoulders slumped slightly. "That's truly unfortunate, and I'm sorry you feel that way. This house has been vacant for decades and in that time the apparitions have built up strong levels of psychokinetic energy. *Strong levels*—" He stopped abruptly and looked Ike directly in the eye. "I understand a worker was injured here several days ago."

"Work-related injury. Nothing to do with the house."

"Perhaps, but I propose to you that the work being done on the house has awakened a set of spirits that have been dormant for many years. They are not pleased about the intrusion and they wish that you would go away and leave them alone. Furthermore—and I don't say such things lightly, so pay very close attention—if there are raw emotions unleashed in the house, such as anger or hate, or if these emotions manifest themselves in the form of violence, or if there is a physical reminder of the atrocities that have been committed inside the house—such as the spilling of blood—then it might very well fully awaken the spirits, and rekindle their desire for revenge and retribution. Obviously I can not be certain exactly what affect all these things might have on the spirits, but whatever it is, I assure you that it will be bad. Very bad."

The inside of the trailer was silent for the longest time.

"Whoa," Erwin gasped.

"That's fantastic!" Ike said, feeling a chill travel down the length of his spine. He rubbed his hands over his forearms to get rid of the goose bumps that had bubbled up onto the surface of his skin. "Would you mind saying all that again for us on tape, just they way you said it now?"

Feroze nodded. "You are going on with the production then, despite my warning?"

"Well, yeah." Ike managed to stop himself from giving the man a "Duh!" thinking it might offend him.

Erwin, on the other hand, had no such reservations. "Duh!"

Feroze inhaled a deep breath and let out a long sigh. "Then I absolutely insist that you record my words for posterity."

Seven

The office of Dr. Sheldon Katz, the show's psychiatrist, had fairly modern, perhaps even space-age decor, seeming to have more glass, steel, and aluminum on the floors and walls than the Space Shuttle *Atlantis*. Still, it all somehow felt safe for Jody, maybe even a little cozy.

The chairs in the waiting room were made of leather, and were overstuffed and comfortable. The rush and excitement of preparing for the show were taking their toll on her, and so while Jody waited to be called into the doctor's office, she felt herself getting more and more comfortable in her chair . . . drifting off into a light sleep.

The leather chair and the drone of the radio coming from the receptionist's desk reminded her of the time when her father took her into Cedar Rapids on her birthday to see a rerelease of *The Wizard of Oz*. It was a long drive into the city, but the excitement of the trip had kept her awake and talkative. On the way back, with Oz and all of its marvels dancing around inside her head, she curled up into a ball and fell asleep in the backseat of her father's Chrysler. When they arrived back at the farm, her father tried to carry her up to her bed, but she'd been too big for him to lift out of the car.

So he'd had to wake her up.

"Jody," he said, poking her arm with his finger. "Jody . . ."

She opened up one eye, then the other. There was a woman kneeling before her, smiling.

"What?" she said.

"You must have dozed off," the woman said. "I'm sorry for keeping you waiting so long, but the doctor's last patient needed a bit more time."

Jody blinked several times to clear her head and eyes. "Oh, that's okay."

"The doctor will see you now."

Jody got up from the chair, feeling a slight chill down her back, and followed the woman into the doctor's consultation room. There was a large art deco desk at one end of the room and a full-length overstuffed couch on the other side, complete with a small chair next to it for the doctor.

"Make yourself comfortable, the doctor will be right—"

Before she could finish, a diminutive man with a balding pate and a slight comb-over entered the room. "Jody?" he said.

"Yes."

He introduced himself, then proceeded to explain why she was there. "I've been hired by the Gowan brothers to ask you a few questions in order to help them figure out the kinds of things that really scare you."

"Well, I don't like spiders," she said.

"Yes, of course," he answered. "Most people don't, but that's not the sort of thing I'm after. . . . Do you mind if I ask you a few questions?"

"No, not at all."

"Has anything really horrific happened to you in your life?"

"Not really, I'm only in my twenties, so I haven't been around all that long. . . ."

"Of course, but you don't have to live a lifetime in

order for something bad to happen. Bad things can happen in an instant."

Jody knew that. She'd been around when things had gone wrong, but she didn't feel like going over it all with a man she looked upon as more of a total stranger than a doctor. "I guess I've been lucky, then," she said.

"Indeed. . . . Let me tell you what I'm getting at. I once treated a young man who, when he was eight years old, was roughhousing with his father . . . you know, the way kids will do. Well, after about ten minutes of this, his father suddenly let go of him and sprawled out on the floor. He'd had a heart attack right then and there, and for the rest of this young man's life, he felt as if he'd *killed* his father."

Jody smiled. "I never killed my father."

"No, of course not," Dr. Katz said. He paused a moment, as if selecting his next anecdote. "Another patient of mine, an older man, was out hunting with his fourteen-year-old son. It was the boy's birthday and he'd given him a brand-new shotgun to celebrate the occasion. So they were walking through the woods on their way to the hunt, with the father explaining to the boy the basic rules of gun safety and care. The boy was an excellent student and did everything his father told him. But as they headed down a slight hill, the father stumbled on a rock. He took several steps to try and right himself, his arms flailing in all directions. Amid the chaos, the father's gun went off. The shot blasted the boy's head clean off his shoulders."

Jody felt hot and uncomfortable. Why on earth was this man telling her these awful, awful stories?

"Has anything like that ever happened to you, Jody?"

She took a breath and thought about it. Yes, things like that had happened to her, or at least while she was around. *If that's the sort of stuff he wants to hear, then maybe it would be better just to give him what he wants and be done with it.* "Well, something like that *did* happen to me, or at least to my cousin. He lost his arm in a farm accident."

"And you were there when it happened?"

"Yes."

"You saw him being dismembered? You saw the blood spurt from his arm?"

"Yes, I did."

"Then what happened?"

"My father sent me to call for help while he stayed with my cousin to try and keep him from bleeding to death."

"I bet that was a phone call you didn't enjoy making."

"I don't mind making calls," she said. "It's answering the phone I don't like."

The moment the words were gone from her lips, she wondered why on earth she had told him. Maybe he was a better psychiatrist than she gave him credit for.

"Why don't you like answering the phone?"

She shrugged. "You never know who's going to be on the other end. Might be someone with bad news."

"Persistent wrong numbers?"

Jody smiled. That was silly. "No."

"News about the death of a loved one?"

She had heard about her grandmother's death that way, but it hadn't been traumatic or anything like that. "No, not really."

"Bill collectors, then."

"Sometimes, but only since I moved to Los Angeles."

The doctor nodded as if he understood, then scratched a few notes onto his pad. "Have you ever been stalked?"

Jody hesitated. She hadn't really been stalked, but if she answered with anything other than a no she'd be opening a door for the doctor she really didn't want explored. "No."

"Someone harass you over the phone, then?"

Again, she felt herself hesitate. Did he think he was on

to something? "No!" she said again, this time with a little more emphasis.

The doctor spent several long moments writing in his notepad. Jody couldn't see what he was writing, but it looked to be fairly in-depth, whatever it was.

After a while, the door opened and the doctor's secretary came into the room.

"I'm afraid that's all the time we have," the doctor said, smiling politely.

"That's it?" Jody said, surprised they were done, but happy for it to be over before he'd dug any deeper into her past.

"The Gowan brothers only paid for a couple of hours of my time and I'm afraid most of it was taken up by the previous contestants. I didn't really have enough time to interview you all properly, but . . ." He raised his hands as if the amount of work he did was totally out of his control.

Jody rose to her feet. "If they don't give you enough time to do the job right, then why do you do it?"

He flashed her a smile, this one appearing more genuine than the previous one. "Having the Gowan brothers as a client, well, any studio for that matter, is good for business. It brings a lot of their actors in for therapy."

Jody was a little confused. Weren't psychiatrists supposed to be like doctors, choosing their profession because of a strong desire to help people? This man was running his practice like a business, and a very successful one at that. She wondered, though, if he'd ever helped anyone with their problems.

"Well, break a leg on the show," the doctor said.

Jody had been wondering if people still said that anymore. Apparently, some did. "Thanks," she said.

She left the office feeling good about herself and about her chances on the show.

Thank God the doctor only had the time to scratch

the surface. If he'd gotten to the heart of the matter, there was no telling what the Gowan brothers would have done with the information.

Eight

They had originally planned to have the director of photography, Steve Bottin, tape the special effects tour of the house, but when the brothers realized that the tour might take more than two hours to complete, they decided to use a younger and stronger man to carry the camera through the house.

"So what we're looking for . . ." Ike said, hesitating as he looked at the cameraman. "What's your name again?"

"Bruno," he said. "Bruno Roper."

Ike nodded. "What I want, Bruno, is a few good shots no more than ten or fifteen seconds each that I can cut to when we're introducing the contestants or explaining what's in store for them inside the house."

"Got it," the young man said, hefting the camera onto his decidedly broad shoulders.

"So it's not all that important that you get the tour in one smooth take, but when we get into a new room I expect you to get into position, set yourself, and get a steady shot."

"How close do you want me to get?"

"My brother will guide you on that stuff. I'd think wide shots would be safe to begin with, but zoom in when you feel it's right."

Bruno nodded, then said, "Speed," to let everyone know he was taping.

Ike turned to special effects coordinator Andy

Matheson. "You don't have to explain *everything* you've got in the house, but I do expect you to point out some of the best stuff. And I want to see you get excited about it, 'cuz I know you do."

Andy smiled. "Sure, no problem."

"And, Erwin?" Ike twisted around to find his brother.

"Over here." Erwin stepped out of the shadows.

"Bruno will be looking to you for instructions, so let him know if there's anything special you want. After that, you'll be providing a bit of color for Andy so feel free to show everyone how demented you are, just don't overdo it."

"You got it, my brother."

Ike nodded with satisfaction.

He was the producer of the show, and he had a bunch of ideas about how the entire package should look in the end. Still, he was happy to set things in motion and then let Erwin take care of the details. It was an arrangement that had served them well so far, and Ike wasn't about to go messing around with success. "All right, then, let's do it."

"Well," Andy began, "we should go into the basement first and work our way up to the top level of the house. So walk this way."

Erwin immediately emulated Andy's walk, which wasn't all that distinctive, but was different enough so that people watching would get the joke.

The stairs leading down to the basement were narrow and the basement itself was only dimly lit. When Bruno was set up in one corner, Andy began to explain a few of the basement effects.

"We've got a couple of air conditioners hidden in the basement windows so we can make cold spots anywhere down here we want."

"What's so cool about cold spots?" Erwin asked, as if he were a bad actor in a high school instructional film.

"A drop in temperature signifies the presence of a spirit or ghost, so we can put 'cold air' ghosts into any part of the room we want."

Erwin had pasted a couple of thimbles to his chest and was now pulling his T-shirt tight against his skin as he stepped in front of the camera. "Wow, it *is* cold in here," he said, thrusting his chest out, "but I like it."

Ike just shook his head. It was such a stupid gag, but they'd probably still end up using it in the show.

Andy moved to another spot in the basement, then adjusted his position slightly to the left, as if searching for his mark. "We've also got tiny blood reservoirs located throughout the house, which are hooked up to a control board in the production trailer. Anyone standing in the right place . . ." Blood began to drip down onto Andy's forehead and face. ". . . will find themselves being bled upon."

Erwin put his hand out to catch a few drops of blood. Then he cried out, *"Blood! Mother!"* echoing the famous cry Norman Bates uttered in both versions of *Psycho*.

Everyone in the basement laughed.

When the laughter died down, Erwin said, "Whose blood is this supposed to be anyway?"

Andy raised an eyebrow. "We'll just have to leave that up to the viewers' imaginations."

"Cool," Erwin said, nodding.

"Best of all, a few of the reservoirs hold more than a liter each, so there will be blood drips, blood spatters, and a few real gushers over the course of the night."

Erwin made a fist, flicked his thumb into the air, and moved in close to the camera lens. "Cool!"

Ike shook his head slightly upon hearing Erwin's dialogue. They had a writer on staff for this sort of stuff.

Andy looked around the room as if wondering if he should talk about anything else. "Let's head up to the main floor and show you a few of the other tricks we've got in store for our contestants."

Erwin and Bruno headed upstairs. Andy stayed behind to ask Ike what he thought so far. "Well?"

"That's fine," Ike said. "Just clean your face before you go upstairs."

Andy touched a hand to his face and wiped off the blood as best he could. "How do I look?" he asked.

"Jesus Christ!" came a shout from upstairs.

The two men hurried up to the main floor.

Ike got there first. "What happened?"

"I was walking by this bookcase and a book fell off the shelf and hit me on the head."

"Yeah, it's supposed to do that," Andy said with a bit of a smirk.

"Oh, isn't that hilarious," Erwin whined, gingerly rubbing the lump on the top of his head.

"There's a pad on the floor in front of the bookcase. . . ." Andy took a few steps, looking for it, then placed his foot deliberately onto the floor. There was a soft hiss and a book was pushed off the top shelf of the bookcase. Andy easily caught the book in his hand.

"How come when you do it, it's a little chapbook, but when I do it, it has to be a friggin' tome?"

"Just lucky, I guess."

Ike beamed. Erwin was turning out to be the star of this little piece and the humor would play off the somber tone of the rest of the show rather nicely.

"I'll show you the kitchen now, but first let's just look in that direction."

Bruno panned the camera into the kitchen and held the shot. Smoke began to billow out of the doorway.

"We've got six smoke machines in the house, so we can smoke any room we want. But best of all, we've also got some projectors set up that can project images onto the smoke . . . like holograms."

"Or ghosts," added Erwin.

A light came on somewhere behind them and for a moment, there was an image of a woman projected onto the smoke. An attractive woman for the most part, except for the bloody gash that had been opened up across her chest and belly. There was a scream then, too, and the image of the woman disappeared in a flash of light.

"Nice," Erwin said, nodding approvingly. "Very nice."

Ike had to agree. It was a creepy enough image when you knew what it was and how it got to be there, but the contestants wouldn't have that knowledge and would likely jump back and scream the moment the woman appeared.

When the smoke in the doorway cleared, Andy led them into the kitchen. "We haven't quite finished in here yet, but we've got a few neat tricks set up in the cupboards."

"Which were the ones you rigged?" Erwin asked.

"I can't remember," Andy said.

Erwin smiled. "So you want me to open one up and show everybody what happens, right?"

"It would be a good demonstration."

"Okay, I'm game. Ooh, I'm hungry," Erwin said in his instructional video voice again, this time playing the part of a contestant. "I wonder if there's anything to eat—"

He opened up a cupboard on the wall and as he did so a blast of compressed air shot a blob of green goop at his head. It bounced off the right side of his forehead, then hit the camera lens dead center.

"Cut!" Ike shouted, even though he wasn't actually directing the shoot.

Erwin fell to the floor, dazed.

Bruno staggered and almost went over backward with the camera.

Andy and Ike grabbed the man to keep him standing. "What the hell was that?" Ike asked.

"Ectoplasm," Andy said, as Erwin rubbed a hand over the welt on his head. "It's supposed to spatter on whoever opens the cupboard door. I think the mix must have dried out a bit, and we've got a bit too much air pressure on the compressor."

"You think?" said Ike. "Let's get that fixed before it takes someone's head off."

"Good idea," Erwin agreed, getting to his feet and looking none the worse for wear. "And maybe we can put some slime on the handles. You know, leaving them feeling all icky."

Ike turned his attention to Bruno and the rented camera that had a deductible on it that was just about equal to the camera's entire worth. "You okay?"

Bruno nodded, putting down the camera. "Had me spooked."

Ike took a closer look at the lens. "Does this stuff clean off?"

"Should be able to peel if off in one piece," Andy said.

"Okay, let's take five. We'll start up again once the camera's clean."

Ike knelt next to Bruno, who was beginning to peel the green goop off the camera lens, and asked, "How did it all look?"

"Picture was good. The sound is going to be a bit spotty, especially going up and down the stairs."

"That's okay. After we get what we need for the inserts, I'll only need ten or so minutes of decent tape for the DVD."

Erwin looked at his brother with a strange expression. "I didn't know we had a DVD deal."

"We don't. Well, not yet, anyway," Ike answered. "But I want to be ready for when we do."

Erwin scowled. "Why am I always the last to know?"

* * *

"Okay, that should do it," Bruno announced five minutes later, after he had the lens clean.

"Anything else in the house that's going to wipe out my cameraman?" Ike wanted to know.

"Your cameraman?" Erwin said.

"Okay, *our* cameraman."

Andy shook his head. "No, that was a fluke. But you know as well as I do that that shot is a keeper."

Ike couldn't disagree. "Just keep him and the camera out of harm's way for the rest of the tour."

"Will do," Andy said. "Now let's head upstairs." He led the group to the bottom of the stairs, then held back Bruno and Ike while Erwin went up the stairs ahead of them.

Erwin made it up five, six, seven steps when—

One of the steps broke away and Erwin stumbled.

He let out a shriek and grabbed the railing as if his life depended on it.

"I thought we fixed these damn steps," Erwin cried.

"We did," Andy said, moving up the stairs. "But one of my assistants thought it would be a great gag to have a few of the steps be breakaways." He pointed to the broken step. "But it only drops an inch, so it's just enough to jostle you, but not enough to seriously trip you up."

"How many steps are there like that on these stairs?"

Andy shook his head. "I'm not telling," then hurried up the stairs, avoiding any other broken steps along the way.

The rest of them followed Andy, doing their best to copy his footsteps exactly.

When they were all safely at the top of the stairs, Andy took an exaggerated step to the left . . .

And the house was suddenly filled by the haunting scream of a woman.

It was so loud and long and absolutely terrifying that Ike could feel the hairs on the back of his neck stand up on end.

And when it was over, Andy was smiling proudly. "Sounds good, doesn't it?" He looked into the camera. "That's a shriek by a mezzo-soprano from the Los Angeles Opera Company. We've also got similar screams from a tenor . . ."

Andy stepped on the pad again.

"A bass . . ."

Another step.

"And a soprano, tenor duo."

Andy lowered his foot one last time.

Erwin grinned like a kid who had just been let out of school for the summer. "This is going to be so cool!"

After a few moments of silence, Ike half instructed, half asked, "Moving on."

Andy led them into the nearest bedroom and when Bruno was set up, he began talking. "Each one of the contestants will be instructed to enter one of these rooms . . . and that's where the serious shit happens. We've still got some work to do on the other rooms, but this one is pretty much finished."

He moved close to one of the inside walls. "It's got a combination of live-action and animatronic effects that will be sure to strike fear into anything with a heartbeat."

Spiders began falling from the ceiling on the ends of strings made of clear filament.

One landed on Erwin's shoulder and he jumped.

At the same time, live spiders were released from a rigged box on the floor. Andy slowly moved out of the frame and came up behind Bruno, placing three spiders onto the camera lens.

Then, as the spiders crawled back and forth over the lens, a dead body fell from the shadows on the ceiling.

The body arced down toward the floor as if it were

strung up by its feet and then swung back and forth like a pendulum until it came to an uneasy rest, hanging upside down from the rafters.

"Damn, that looked good," Erwin commented.

"And it'll look even better once we get the face right. We've had one of the actors make a mold, so it'll be his face on the mannequin during taping."

Erwin smiled at the camera. "That's going to be killer."

"And the wounds in the thing will all be dressed up to look wet and fresh."

"I love the sound of that," Erwin said, poking his finger into the eye socket of the mannequin. "Wet and fresh."

Andy led the group back out into the hallway.

"I could show you the rest of the rooms up here, but they're basically variations on the same theme and I don't want to spoil any of the surprises. . . ."

Just then, over Andy's shoulder, Ike saw a shadow moving in one of the bedrooms, as if someone was in there working.

"What was that?"

Andy looked behind him. "What was what?"

Apparently, Erwin had seen it, too. "In the bedroom at the end of the hallway," he said. "Something was moving around in there." He turned around to look at Andy. "Have you got someone up here?"

Andy smiled nervously, probably thinking the brothers were playing a gag on him. Turning the tables. "No. I had the house cleared for the tour."

"It was a dark shape floating about a foot or two off the floor," Erwin said. "Something like a ghost, only it was dark."

Andy shook his head, laughing. "You guys are full of it."

"No, there was something inside the room," Erwin insisted. "And I want to see what it is."

Ike wanted to see what was there, as well. However, the thing wasn't the dark floating ghost that Erwin had described, but rather a shadow that had darkened the air, much like a swarm of insects might do.

Erwin led the group down the hall, but stopped just short of the door to the bedroom.

"What is it?" Ike said.

Erwin was silent.

"Go on inside," he prodded.

"No," Erwin said. "I don't want to anymore."

Ike opened his mouth to say something, but Andy beat him to the punch.

"You're not *chicken,* are you?"

"No, it's just that . . ." Erwin's voice trailed off. For a few moments everyone expected him to say something funny, but he said nothing, his mouth remaining open and silent. He stood in the doorway without moving.

Ike knew they were taping material that could be used for teasers and other inserts, but this was becoming too staged for his liking. "For crying out loud, Erwin," he said, "move out of the way." Ike grabbed Erwin's flowered shirt and pulled him back from the doorway. With Erwin out of the way, Ike started into the room, but stopped just a step or two inside it.

He felt . . . cold.

More than just cold.

He was freezing.

Ice seemed to be flowing through his veins and a chill gnawed at his skin as if it were being pricked and prodded by a million icy needles.

"What's the matter, Ike?" Erwin said, putting enough emphasis on his name to give it two syllables.

"Nothing, I, uh . . ." He was finding it a little hard to breathe and his heart was racing. He looked for the shadow in the room, but it wasn't there.

There was *nothing* there.

It was just an empty room that Andy had rigged to run cold, to give people a chill.

That's all it was.

Nothing more.

Whatever he'd seen, it had to have been a shadow cast through a window by something outside the house. Yeah, that was probably it. And to think, for a minute there he'd actually thought the house might be haunted.

Ike turned around and looked at Bruno. He was about to say, "Cut!" when a noise originating from outside the house caught everyone's attention.

"Now what's going on out there?" Ike said.

Just then the front door opened and William Olsen stepped into the house.

"What the hell is that?" Ike asked him from the top of the stairs.

"People from town," Olsen answered.

Erwin had gone down the stairs and was looking out one of the foyer windows. "There's a lot of them out there."

Ike came down the stairs to join his brother. "How many?"

"Ten or twelve."

"That's a lot?" said Ike.

"We're out in the middle of nowhere." Erwin shrugged.

Ike turned to Olsen. "What's their problem?"

"They want you to shut down the production and leave."

"Oh, is that all?"

"Yeah, basically."

"Tell them to get lost."

Olsen shook his head. "They want to talk to a Gowan."

Ike looked over at his brother. "Why don't *you* go out there?"

Erwin laughed. "Me? Uh-uh, I'd fold like a deck

chair. . . . This is the kind of situation that calls for a real asshole."

Ike shot his brother a contemptuous look, even though everyone in the room seemed to agree with him.

"Okay, but at least you guys have to come outside with me. Okay?"

Erwin nodded. Olsen and Andy Matheson, too.

Ike went out onto the porch and found that his brother—in true Hollywood fashion—had exaggerated the number of people in the crowd. There were only six of them standing on the lawn, and four of them were old, old ladies.

"Hi," he said. "I'm Ike Gowan. Is there a problem?"

A gray-haired woman dressed in a lavender and green track suit stepped forward. "You can't do this!" she cried, shaking her walking stick at him.

Ike smiled. "I assure you, ma'am, I *can*, and we *will* be taping a television show in this house. I've got all the permission I need from the state of California, your town council, and the owners of this property. In fact, if I was so inclined, I could call up the sheriff's office and have the lot of you arrested for trespassing."

Ike hated to come down so hard on these people right out of the starting gate, but this was an unnecessary delay when there was still plenty of work to be done.

"Well, you *shouldn't* be here," the old woman said, amending her position and losing the anger from her voice.

Ike made himself comfortable, sitting on the porch railing and leaning his back against one of the heavy white posts holding up the wooden overhang. "Now why is that?"

"People died in this house. Things happened inside there that we'd rather forget about. There's spirits in there, too, that have been dormant for years. We've left them alone and they've pretty much left us alone. . . ."

An old man wearing a pair of tan coveralls and a base-ball cap from the local Legion hall stepped to the front of the crowd. "You go messing around in there"—spittle flew from his mouth as he spoke—"and God only knows what sort of evil will be unleashed. I'm not ashamed to tell you that I was scared to death of this house when I was a kid, and I'm still scared to death of it today—and believe me, sonny, I've seen some pretty frightening things in my day."

"That right?"

"You betcha."

"That's a fact," the others all chimed in.

"You're playing with something you don't know any-thing about." It was the gray-haired woman again. "You might as well be playing with matches and gasoline. . . ."

Ike turned away from the crowd and glanced over at Bruno. "Are you getting all this?"

Bruno gave Ike the thumbs-up, then pulled his head away from the eyepiece a moment. "But I don't think you're going to get a release form from any of them."

Ike laughed under his breath. "Are you kidding? *Every-one* wants to be on television." He turned back around to face the crowd, flashed a smile, and turned on the charm.

"I appreciate you all taking the time to come out here and warn us about the house, and I do think it's an im-portant message to get across, one that we definitely want to include in our broadcast."

"Us?" said the gray-haired lady.

"Of *course,* you people," said Ike. "Who knows this house better than you do?"

A few of the women had obviously taken to the idea judging by the way their expressions had just trans-formed from sour to golly-gee.

"Now, why don't we go to my trailer? We can have coffee, something stronger if you like . . . and then we can talk."

Ike stepped down off the porch headed for his trailer. The group followed closely behind him.

Like lemmings.

Nine

Andy Matheson entered the house through the front door, grumbling every step of the way. "This is the last job I ever do for these assholes," he muttered under his breath. "Unless I need the work."

He tried the light switch on the wall by the door and two desk lamps set on either side of the foyer came on. One of the lamps flickered slightly for a moment, then flashed intensely before burning out.

"That figures," Andy said, wondering if the light had been rigged to come on for a few moments, then burn out. It would be a good effect if it did. Simple, creepy . . . and cheap.

But the burnt-out light didn't matter. All Andy needed was enough light to turn on one of the television lamps—sun guns, they called them—that they'd been using to work on the house at night. Those lamps would be removed tomorrow morning since the show was going to be shot in available light or with cameras equipped with night vision. So, like it or not, this was the only chance Andy had to give the brothers the effect they wanted.

He aimed a sun gun at the spot on the ceiling where he'd be working and switched on the big light. The room suddenly came alive with light and the white ceiling was almost too bright to look at. When his eyes adjusted to the brightness, Andy studied the hole in the ceiling he'd have to work with. Seemed straightforward enough, and with any luck he'd be able to get the job done in time to join the rest of the crew at the party they were throwing at the six-room fleabag motel just outside Kettleman City.

Andy went back outside and dragged a twelve-foot aluminum stepladder into the house. He set the ladder up in the middle of the foyer under the large empty spot where the bigger of the two chandeliers had been removed.

"Wouldn't it be cool if that chandelier could suddenly fall from the ceiling?" Andy said in a mocking falsetto meant to sound like Erwin Gowan. He shook his head in disgust.

They had made a final tour of the house, just to make sure everything was in place and in working order. The brothers had approved it all, had seemed genuinely pleased with all the work he and his crew had done, but then just as they were about to leave, Erwin came up with another one of his brilliant ideas.

Brilliant, sure. If there'd been money for a proper winch and two or three days in order to set it up right. But no, the show was taping in a couple of days and he had to have something rigged up by morning when the big chandelier would be brought back from the shop where it was being rigged to hold two tiny cameras.

Andy adjusted the ladder under the empty spot in the ceiling and when he was satisfied it was in the right place, he put on his tool belt. He checked everything in the belt twice since he didn't want to be left wanting for something while he was at the top of the ladder and have to go all the way back down just to get it. When he was sure he had everything he needed, he checked that the ladder would be steady, then began the climb to the top.

It was just as well they didn't have the budget for a proper winch setup since that would have meant cutting a hole into the ceiling, installing the winch, and then closing up the hole to hide the installation. That was a lot of work for an effect that wouldn't produce more than a few seconds of usable videotape. So, as with all of the other effects in the house, Andy had come up with a compromise. He'd install a geared spool that would unwind slowly and let the chandelier fall at a controlled rate of about two feet per second. That would make the effect last somewhere around five seconds and give the director time for a couple of quick-reaction shots. The only downside was that the effect could only be used once, because after the spool was unwound it would take a crew of three to wind it back up again. So instead of using the effect on each contestant, they could only use it on one, or once when all the contestants were in the foyer.

Not the best setup, but not bad either, considering he'd rigged the spool from stuff that had been lying around the shop.

At the top of the ladder, Andy checked to see which step would be the most comfortable to work from. He decided to stand on the third step from the top, which allowed him to rest his shins and the lower part of his thigh against the top of the ladder while he worked.

The spool was about the size of an apple juice can and was mounted inside a sturdy steel frame. There was a release on the spool that could be sprung from the control trailer, and the spool had been tested to one hundred and eighty pounds—twenty-five pounds more than it needed to be.

The mount was a perfect fit and the job turned out to be a simple matter of putting four screws into the beam that usually supported the chandelier. In the morning, technicians would hook up the chandelier, leaving enough loose chain and video cable to allow the fixture to fall without any problem.

Andy was about to drive in the final screw when it slipped from his fingers and clanked against the ladder on its way to the floor. He watched to see where it fell, then fished around inside his tool belt for a spare screw. When he found one, he slipped it onto the end of his screwdriver. Then, setting himself on the ladder again, he looked up in search of the final hole when—

The sun gun went out.

"What the—"

The effect was like day and night.

One of the desk lamps was still on, but it hardly provided enough light for Andy to see, and there was nothing he could do until his eyes adjusted to the darkness.

He grabbed hold of the ladder and waited.

As the seconds ticked away, Andy became aware of *something* below him.

A presence in the foyer.

"Is somebody there?" he asked.

No response other than a soft, swaying sort of sound, the kind sheer drapes might make as they billow and furl in front of an open window.

Andy looked down at the foyer floor and, although his eyes were slowly becoming accustomed to the dimmer light, he still couldn't make out anyone, or anything, down there.

"Is someone there?" he asked again.

Nothing.

He began to climb down off the ladder.

And that's when he saw . . .

It.

That was the only word he could think of to describe what he saw. *It* was little more than a wispy shadow in the darkness. It glided effortlessly across the floor, then rose into the air until it was level with where Andy was on the ladder.

For the briefest moment, Andy wondered if this was another trick, a special effect the brothers were going to introduce on this project, but the thought was dismissed just as quickly as it came. If this was an effect, it was brilliant. There was nothing supporting the shadow, no wires, no strings, no pedestal. It was as if it were actually floating in the air, like a hologram, only the brothers didn't have any equipment that was capable of doing that. This was just too good an effect for the Gowan brothers.

And then all at once the breath went out of Andy's lungs as he realized that this was no trick.

This was the real thing.

A real ghost.

He began crawling back up the ladder to get away from the thing, but it rose up alongside him, matching his progress on the ladder rung for rung.

When he reached the top, Andy clutched the ladder tightly against his body to keep himself from shaking. His breath had become ragged and labored, and his clothes had suddenly become damp with sweat.

The shadow moved slowly around his body, then over him and under him, as if examining him from every angle.

Andy breathed a little easier. Curious, that's all it was, just curious. The thing had given him a fright, but it was basically harmless. He would get off the ladder, leave the house, and have a great story to tell everyone at the party. No one would believe him, but the brothers would probably want to work the story into the show somehow.

Andy began moving down the ladder again—one small step at a time—when the shadow figure darted down to the floor and came to a stop at the ladder's base.

Andy stopped on the middle rung, wondering if it was safe to continue, if the thing would allow him to get off the ladder. But the dark shape remained below him like a big black dog who'd just run someone up a tree.

"Please, God," Andy muttered, "let me get out of this

mess alive and I swear the next project I work on will be something right out of the Bible."

A dark tendril rose up from the figure, then transformed into the shape of a hand. The hand reached up for his leg as if to touch it, forcing Andy to scramble back up to the very top of the ladder.

And that's when he felt the first spikes of pain shoot down the length of his left arm. The pain was intense—as if his arm had been run through with a very dull knife—and caused him to let go of the ladder with his right hand so he could use it to clutch his arm.

The sudden movement made the ladder teeter onto two legs, forcing Andy to reach out with his right hand to keep his balance. The pain seemed to jump from his arm, stabbing straight into the center of his heart.

Andy let out a scream.

But there was no one around to hear it.

He closed his eyes and tried to catch his breath, hoping that the pain would pass. But when he opened his eyes again, the shadow was floating in the air in front of him, mere inches from his face.

Andy couldn't move. Immobilized by pain and fear, he stared into the darkness suddenly aware of the thing's smell—burnt almonds mingled in with the stench of rot and decay.

It moved closer.

Andy tried to back away from it, but there was nowhere for him to go.

Closer still.

Andy felt the ladder starting to go over again and he quickly righted it . . . bringing himself back toward the thing in the process.

He turned away to try and avoid contact with the darkness but it was no use because the thing reached out and touched him.

No, more than just touched him . . . it *entered* him.

And Andy felt pain.

The ache in his arm had been nothing compared with what he was experiencing now. His very being was wracked by terror. Every nerve ending in his body was alight with searing pain. His mind was suddenly sliced and scarred, and his heart filled with agony and anguish, and then seemed to break apart into a million bloody pieces.

And then the thing was gone, passing through him as if he weren't even there. But while *it* was gone, the pain remained.

Andy's chest felt as if it had been impaled with a railroad spike. He clutched at his heart with both hands . . .

Letting go of the ladder.

The fall was only twelve feet, but it seemed to last forever.

Andy put his arms out to break his fall, to save himself, but the attempt was futile.

His heart had already stopped.

And he was dead before he hit the floor.

The ladder rocked back and forth on its legs, almost toppling over, then came to rest. Solid and still.

The dark figure floated over the lifeless body at the base of the ladder like a fog, circling it several times before gliding away and becoming one with the shadows.

Ten

It was just after six in the morning and the sun was beginning to top the snowcapped summits of the Sierra Nevadas in the east. It was a cold morning, even for early autumn, and William Olsen blew directly down into his coffee cup so the rising steam would warm his face and nose.

He took a sip, enjoying the infusion of heat, then glanced around at the people who were milling about the catering trailer. It was possible he hadn't shown up for work yet, but it wasn't like Andy Matheson to be late, even for six A.M. calls. He was usually the first one on the set in the morning and the last to leave at night, running his assistants and underlings ragged just trying to keep up with him. But even if he'd worked late last night, Andy wasn't the kind to miss out on a party, especially one where drinks were charged to the production.

"Hey, Morty," Olsen said, grabbing a young grip by the sleeve as he walked by.

"My name's Walter."

"Sorry, Walter. . . . You were at the party to the end last night, right?"

"Yeah." Walter squeezed his eyes shut as if trying to rid himself of some pain. "Didn't hit the sack until two."

"Did you see Andy there last night? Andy Matheson, the special effects coordinator."

Walter thought about it, then shook his head. "No, I don't think so."

Maybe Andy had worked so late he went straight to sleep in one of the trailers instead of heading into town for the party. But even so, he would have been up by now. The location was starting to come alive and Andy couldn't lie in bed while everyone else around him was getting ready for work.

"Do me a favor, check the trailers and see if he's still asleep." But then Olsen hesitated, and shook his head. "No, if you find him sleeping, just come back and let me know. All right?"

"Sure, no problem."

As Olsen watched the kid run off, he was struck by another thought. Maybe Andy was already working inside the house. That would be more his style. While all of his technicians and assistants were grumbling over their morning coffee, Andy was already in the house, working away.

Olsen headed off for the house.

He found the front door ajar, but didn't think anything of it. It was still early, but there might be people already inside. People like Andy, trying to do as much as possible in the small amount of time they had left. Then again, maybe Andy or somebody had left the door open last night after they were done. The doors were always being left open, or unlocked. . . . Hell, even that parapsychologist had been able to walk into the house as he pleased.

Olsen pushed open the door and noticed that the lamp on the table on the left side of the foyer was on. There was some light shining in from the front windows, and there was a twelve-foot ladder standing in the middle of the room.

He looked up.

There was no one on the ladder.

He looked down.

"Oh, shit!"

Olsen rushed forward, ending up on his knees next to the body.

"Andy?" he said, as much a statement as a question.

He reached down and touched one of the body's mangled, upturned hands. It was cold, and everything inside it was so broken it felt like a fleshy sack of stones.

Suddenly someone was in the doorway.

The kid, Walter.

"He's not in any of the trai—"

Olsen let the hand fall back to the floor.

"Get Ike and Erwin."

"Is he dead?"

"Now!"

"What are we gonna do?" Ike said, running a hand hard over his head.

Ike and Erwin had joined Olsen in the foyer while the crew had gathered on the lawn in front of the house. News of Andy Matheson's death had spread quickly and it wouldn't be a surprise to anyone if reporters for the trades in Los Angeles were already making calls trying to confirm the rumor.

"What do you mean, 'What are we gonna do?'" William Olsen echoed. "We have to call the police."

"Not that," said Ike. "We're going to lose at least a day of prep time, maybe more. And when they hear about the worker who got hurt last week, we might even get shut down by the labor people for bullshit safety violations."

"Ike, I don't want to seem insensitive to *your* problems." Erwin's voice was even, and unusually serious. "But Andy died, you know . . . he's dead."

"That's right, and there's nothing we can do about it."

"Jesus, Ike. Andy worked with us on a lot of our movies . . . he was like a friend. I don't think it would be such a bad thing if we shut down for a day to, like . . . you know, make a note of the fact that he died."

Ike looked at his brother, saw the sadness in his eyes, and a smile suddenly broke across his face. "You haven't got the stomach for this, have you? You're working to make people look dead all the time, but you can't handle it when it happens in real life, can you?"

"Aw, c'mon, let's not get into this," Olsen said, putting an arm on Ike, only to have it shrugged off.

"Big-shot horror movie director." Ike laughed. "Blood and Guts Gowan, can't deal with the real thing."

"Fuck you!" shouted Erwin. "I worked with Andy for eight years, and I'm sorry if his death has affected me. You just told him he couldn't do things, 'That would be great, Andy, but there's no money in the budget to make it look that good,' but I actually worked with him . . . he was my friend."

"We don't have any friends," Ike responded. "They'd all steal the food off our plate if they could. They'd stab us in the back if they thought they'd get ahead because of it. Andy was just like all the—"

Erwin lunged forward at his brother, "Don't say that!" he said, pushing both hands hard against his brother's chest. "Don't even think it!"

Ike pushed back and suddenly the brothers were shoving each other and about two seconds away from coming to blows.

Olsen jumped between them, and tried to keep the brothers apart.

"Andy was a good guy," Erwin spat. "He didn't care about getting ahead. Shit, that's why he worked for us. He *liked* working for us, liked working with me."

"Guys, that's enough!" Olsen's voice was authoritative, his words commanding. "We're calling the police. I'm the location manager and I'm shutting down the production, at least for today."

The brothers both turned their heads, as if they couldn't stand to look at each other anymore.

"In the meantime, I suggest you two settle down. I don't believe that parapsychologist's bullshit any more than you do, but it wouldn't be such a bad idea to get along with each other while we're inside the house."

Ike looked at Olsen, then at his brother, and felt a small tingle of fear trickle through his body.

Then all three of them looked over at Andy's body.

"Is there any blood?" Ike felt stupid for asking, but he wanted to know.

Erwin was on his knees next to the body, his face close to the floor trying to see underneath it. "No, doesn't look like it."

Ike sighed in relief.

At that moment the front door opened and Ike could feel a push of cool air against his back. It was noisy outside, too, as if the entire crew were lined up and wanting a tour of the death scene.

"I told everyone to stay outside," Ike said, without looking over his shoulder.

"I'm Deputy Borden, Kings County Sheriff's Department. We got a call about a . . . Oh."

The house was sealed off and access to the foyer was restricted to sheriff's deputies and people from the county medical examiner's office. So even if they had wanted to work inside the house today, the cops wouldn't have allowed it. They were treating the foyer like a crime scene.

Deputies were also interviewing every member of the crew, especially those people who worked either with Andy or for him.

As one of the producers, Ike Gowan was at the top of the list of those to be interviewed. Deputy Borden caught up with Ike in his trailer, just as Ike was pouring a shot of brandy into a paper coffee cup.

"Ah, Deputy," Ike said, as the man stuck his head into the trailer. "Join me?"

The deputy hesitated a moment, then said, "And I bet that's really good stuff, too."

"St-Rémy . . . it's a Napoleon brandy."

"It's tempting, but I'm on duty."

Ike nodded, finished pouring, then took a sip. "So this isn't a social call."

"I want to ask you a few questions about Mr. Matheson."

"Go ahead."

"He worked with you before, didn't he?"

"Only on six or seven of our movies."

"So you knew him well."

"Well enough. My brother knew him better than I did. Maybe you should be talking to him."

"We'll get to your brother in time."

Ike emptied the cup in a gulp, then poured himself another shot.

"Did Matheson have a drinking problem?"

"No, he liked having a drink or two at a party, but I never saw him drunk, especially on the job. Wouldn't have been working for us if he had."

"Did he have any medical problems, like diabetes?"

"No."

"I understand last night he was working late, and by himself. Isn't that unusual?"

"Not really. Andy was like that."

"But working by himself?"

"He might have asked one of his assistants to help him, he might not. Hooking up that spool was a one-man job. There was a party that night and Andy probably didn't want any of his crew to miss out on the fun. He was a hard worker and didn't mind doing extra stuff like that. That's why we used him."

"*Used him,* that's an interesting phrase."

"Just an expression." Ike felt himself becoming uncomfortable and wasn't sure why. "We can use anyone we want on a job, we liked him, so we used him. No big deal."

The deputy nodded, smiling faintly. "You and your brother have a reputation for doing things on the cheap, don't you?"

Ike was suddenly forced to go on the defensive, like he was a suspect or something. "We're independent film producers, so we do a lot of *low-budget* productions. Cheap suggests we have money we don't want to spend. Low budget means we just don't have any money."

"I see, so it's vitally important that every one of your projects succeeds . . . turns a profit."

Ike didn't know exactly what the deputy was getting at, but he didn't like the direction things were heading. "What are you trying to say?"

"I've been reading about your show in the local paper. There's not a day goes by when there isn't something about this production in there somewhere."

"They've been kind to us."

"And from what I've gathered, this is the kind of show that might actually benefit from having someone die on the set. I bet that by tomorrow morning news of this man's death will be in every paper in the country . . . along with the name of your show."

"Yeah." Ike sighed. "I suppose."

"Publicity like that's got to be worth millions. Hell, you couldn't buy that amount of advertising even if you wanted to."

Ike was getting confused. "What are you *getting* at?"

"Well, until we hear otherwise from the M.E. we're treating Mr. Matheson's death as suspicious. So, one of my first thoughts has to be toward motive. Why would somebody want the man dead—"

Ike got up from his chair. "Whoa, wait a second. I'm a

bit crazy, and you can find all kinds of people who'll swear I'm an A-one asshole, or even worse, but there's no way I'd kill anyone for the *publicity*. That's just . . ." Ike paused, thinking. "No, I could never do something like that. I've done a lot of things to make sure my movies made money—some of them I'm not very proud of—but I gotta draw the line somewhere."

The deputy smiled. "Fine, thanks."

Ike let out a deep breath. "What? That's it, you believe me?"

"Basically, yeah. It was a long shot, but I had to check it out. Suggest it to you and see what you'd say."

"Oh, okay, good." Ike was breathing easier, but unsure if he'd just been screwed over.

"Now, I've got other people to interview."

"Sure, no problem."

The deputy didn't move. "I thought maybe I'd be able to use this trailer as an interview room." Judging by the deputy's tone of voice, he was telling Ike what he wanted rather than asking him for a favor.

"Yeah, sure, okay . . . just, uh, let me get what I need and I'll be out of your way."

"Thanks. I appreciate it."

Then the deputy tipped his hat, and showed Ike the door.

Reporters from the newspapers in the neighboring towns had shown up first, hoping to get a few quotes from the Gowan brothers themselves. Hours later, stringers from Los Angeles arrived on the site with video cameras looking for *anyone* willing to talk about what had happened.

Ike had tried to keep the lid on things as long as he could, but the less he was willing to talk, the more likely it was that some assistant dolly grip would end up on television saying something stupid and putting the whole production in jeopardy. So the brothers scheduled a press conference for three in the afternoon, giving everyone enough time to get some tape, do an interview, and then head back to the city in time for the six o'clock news.

By two-thirty it was obvious that there were too many people to hold the press conference in one of the trailers, so they set up a makeshift podium on the hill on the west side of the house. The location was chosen by the director of photography because it was the best angle to shoot the house from, and having the house in the background while the brothers talked about their good friend would be both creepy and respectful at the same time.

Carl Dunbar wrote up an official statement, signed by both Ike and Erwin, but which only Ike would read at the press conference. They had also prepared a bio and filmography of Andy Matheson, from which Ike had been amazed to learn that Andy had worked on an even dozen Gowan Brothers films.

". . . Andy Matheson's death on the set was tragic," Ike concluded, reading the statement with a surprisingly sorrowful voice. "And I know I speak for every member of the crew when I say, he will truly be missed."

After a few moments of silence William Olsen, who was coordinating the press conference, allowed for a few questions.

A tall, thin, and very attractive black woman was first. Ike thought he'd seen her on a tabloid show, something like *Inside Edition* or *Etalk*, but couldn't be sure. "Have there been any charges of negligence made against you, your brother, or any members of your crew?"

Ike felt as if a few years had just been shaved off his life. "No, there have been no charges laid, and there's been no mention of any negligence or wrongdoing in regards to Andy Matheson's death."

Hands went up again, but the woman wasn't finished

asking questions. "But this is the second incident inside the house—"

A sound coursed through the crowd of assembled reporters, as if this was the first time they'd heard this little bit of news.

"—three weeks ago a carpenter was injured while doing some renovation work inside the house. Isn't that right?"

Ike did his best to smile. "First of all he was a laborer, not a carpenter." Somehow that hadn't sounded right. "And he was hurt out on the porch, not inside the house. And while it's true he suffered some serious injuries none of them were life-threatening, and I've been told the man is going to be fine."

"Were his injuries caused by your negligence, as well?"

Christ! thought Ike. This was a far cry from the press junket interviews he was used to where reporters would get a few minutes to ask a few questions, and maybe tell you how much they enjoyed your last film, while a team of publicists lingered in the background ready to cut a reporter off the moment he or she asked a forbidden question. This was like being attacked by a pack of angry pit bulls. He felt his knees go a little soft and he grabbed the sides of the podium to help keep himself upright and steady.

This was going to be one of the longest afternoons of Ike's life. . . .

Ike skipped dinner that evening, substituting a few snifters of brandy for his regular meal. It didn't make him feel any better about the fate of the production, but at least he didn't care as much about it anymore.

People died in the middle of productions all the time and those projects still got completed. How many times did you see movies dedicated to the memory of so-and-so in the end credits, and it was the first you ever heard that somebody had died during the production? They'd get over this . . . somehow, and the show would be a big hit. Furthermore, the movie they'd make after this was going to be their best one yet. That was the way great horror movies got made anyway—through adversity, improvisation, and ingenuity. They'd coped with the last two of those things plenty of times before; now they had some adversity to deal with, and they'd get through it, and in the end they'd be better filmmakers for it.

Ike poured himself another drink.

He'd retreated to the production trailer, which Olsen had transformed into a sort of communications center. Olsen was there, his brother, Erwin, too, even the writer Carl Dunbar, all of them fielding calls from print reporters too lazy to drive up to the site of the shoot. A phone call, a couple of quotes, some speculation, some stills from previous Gowan Brother films, and bingo! a special feature on the perils of shock horror on a budget.

No such thing as bad publicity, they say. Well, *fuck that!* Here was all the bad publicity you'd ever want . . . and more. Sure, Gowan Brothers videos and DVDs were selling well right now, but try and find someone to invest in the next production.

Didn't somebody get killed the last time you guys made a movie? . . . Sorry, guys, I need the work and all, but I want to live, too, you know.

Shit!

Then over the din inside the trailer, Ike heard the electronic *Psycho* theme coming from his cell phone. He searched his pants pockets for it, but in his slightly drunken haze he couldn't find the phone.

Erwin rushed over and took the phone out of Ike's jacket—which was hanging over a chair—and flipped the phone open.

"Erwin Gowan."

A pause. Erwin looked over at Ike, then said, "He can't come to the phone right now."

Ike made a halfhearted attempt to take the phone from his brother but Erwin stepped back out of his reach. He was probably right. In his condition Ike would probably say something he'd regret later, and it wouldn't be so bad to let Erwin handle some of the fallout from this thing.

Knock yourself out, thought Ike.

"Who's this?" Erwin said.

Another pause.

"Hey, it's good to hear from you." Erwin put his hand over the phone and said, "Shut up, everyone! It's Bartolo from the network." He took his hand away. "No, it's okay to talk now, sure. I can tell him for you." Erwin began pacing the trailer. "It was an accident. . . . You know as well as I do that these things happen all the time." He stopped pacing a moment. "The network's first in ten years. . . . Really? I didn't know that."

Then Erwin resumed pacing again, only now he was circling the table in the center of the trailer. He went around it three times before stopping in front of Ike. "No, I know you've been in our corner from the start. And we appreciate it."

A pause, and Erwin's face changed expression, as if he'd eaten something bad and it had suddenly hit him.

"Okay, I'll tell him. And you'll let us know if there's any change, right?" One final pause. "Okay, bye."

Erwin closed the phone.

The inside of the trailer was silent.

Ike was the first to speak. "Well?"

"They're having a meeting on Monday morning to decide what to do about the show."

Ike tried to stand, but his body wasn't responding to

his wishes as well as he'd hoped. "What do you mean, 'what to do about the show'?"

Erwin slid the phone back into the pocket of Ike's jacket. "Whether they still want to go through with the project or not."

"Go through with the project?" Ike looked around the room as if the words he was looking for might be pasted up on a wall somewhere in the trailer. "You mean they might cancel us altogether?"

"I got that impression, yeah."

Ike slumped back in his chair. "Shit!" he said out loud, just managing to stop himself before articulating his next thought.

How could Andy do this to us?

Eleven

Jody struggled with the weight, trying to do one more rep before the muscles in her arms and chest finally gave out on her. Parts of her body felt as if they were on fire as her oxygen-starved muscles begged for the chance to relax and recover. She had about an inch to go before her arms could lock, but before she could manage it a handsome young face appeared above her and helped her with the rest of the lift.

She was relieved to be free of the weight, but she was angry with the man for helping her. She wanted to know if she could do it by herself, know if she was getting any stronger, but now she'd have to wait until tomorrow to find out if she was making any progress.

She let the weight back down and it clanked onto the stack of steel slabs below it.

"Wow, you're really working hard," he said.

Jody didn't respond. She took a moment to catch her breath and feel the pain in her arms, and across her shoulders and chest. There was a nice feeling of fatigue in there. She had to be getting stronger.

Finally, she sat up on the bench and looked over at the guy who'd helped her. Only then did she realize it was one of the Crunch trainers, a man named Armand Zeman, whose job it was to make sure no one pushed themselves too far or otherwise risked an injury. The annoyance she'd felt quickly left her and she managed to show the young man a smile. "Thanks for noticing."

"It's like you're on a mission or something," he said. "Most people come in wanting to lose some weight or to firm up their buns, but you look like you're trying to make yourself strong . . . you know, sort of like Linda Hamilton in *Terminator Two*."

Jody could live with that. Hamilton looked pretty buffed in that film. Buffed and tough. "What tipped you off?"

"Most women aren't all that interested in the bench press . . . unless they think it will give them a bigger chest."

"Does it?"

"Firmer maybe, but not all that much bigger."

Jody snapped her fingers. "Darn."

"Hey, from where I'm standing it doesn't look like you need any improvements."

Christ, she thought, *how many women have fallen for this guy's crap over the years?* But the longer she looked at him the more she thought he was cute. "Thanks."

"You got a competition coming up or something?"

Jody wondered if she should tell him about the show. She wanted to, but she knew that if he—or any of the other people in the gym—caught wind of what she was preparing for, she'd lose what privacy and anonymity she enjoyed in the place. She wasn't a star. Hell, she hadn't even been on television yet—and no, a five-second shot of her in the stands at an Iowa football game didn't count as an appearance. It was merely—as the consultant woman had said—an interesting anecdote or bit of trivia.

Question: Which two blonde bombshells were discovered cheering in the stands at football games?

Answer: Pamela Anderson, at a British Columbia Lions Canadian Football League game in Vancouver, Canada; and Jody Watts, at an Iowa Hawkeyes Big Ten game in Iowa City, Iowa.

Yeah, right.

"Let's just say . . . or something," she said, answering his question with a coy little shrug.

"Okay, that's cool." He nodded absently. "But if you need to work on something specific, you know, like speed, strength, or endurance, I can help you. I mean, it *is* my job and all."

"That'd be great, but I'm all done for today."

"Oh, well, I was just heading downstairs for a cup of coffee. . . . Maybe you'd like to join me."

Doesn't this guy ever quit? Jody wondered. Then again, he was cute, maybe even handsome in a boyish sort of way, and of course he was in great shape. "Sure, why not?"

"Excellent," he said. "I'll wait for you out in the lobby."

"Give me a few minutes."

"Take your time. I'll be waiting."

After a hot shower, Jody took her time getting dressed. She'd gone to Crunch in an old pair of sweats and an Iowa Hawkeyes shirt she'd bought on campus. They were okay for going to the gym, but not for going out for coffee with a good-looking guy afterward.

Maybe he won't notice, she thought. *Or maybe he won't care. If he just wants to get into your pants, who cares what obstacles are in the way?* And from that perspective, sweats were about the easiest pieces of clothing to slip out of, so why should he mind?

As she came out of the locker room, she found him sitting on one of the couches in the lobby reading a copy of the *Times.* When he saw her he folded the paper carefully and tucked it under his left arm, presumably to read in the coffee shop if things didn't go all that well between them.

"As you can see I dressed for the occasion," she said.

"What?"

Jody suddenly felt dumb. Why did she draw attention to her clothes when he hadn't noticed anything wrong with them? "Uh, I'm sorry I took so long to get dressed."

"Oh, no problem." He held the door open for her as they left the gym.

The sun was still hot in the cloudless sky and the heat, along with her little faux pas, had Jody feeling as if she might need to shower again by the time she got home.

They went down the stairs and ended up out on the sidewalk. Luckily, Buzz Coffee was situated right below Crunch and it was *the* place to go for bottled water or coffee after a workout.

As they entered Buzz, he opened the door for her again. *What a gentleman,* she thought. *Either that, or a lady killer.*

"I'm getting an iced cappuccino," he said. "What do you want?"

"Just a regular Colombian coffee is fine."

"Cream or sugar?"

"Both."

He headed off to the counter, taking his newspaper with him. Jody made herself comfortable at one of the tables by the window and watched the mix of glamor girls, buffed boys, and Hollywood bums make their way along Sunset Boulevard.

He joined her a few minutes later, trying to glance at the newspaper while he carried their coffees on a tray. When he got to the table, his interest in the paper almost caused him to spill hot coffee onto Jody's lap.

"Hey!"

"Oh, I'm sorry," he said, righting the tray and sliding it safely onto the table.

"What's so interesting?"

"There's a casting call here in the paper for a new western starring Harrison Ford."

"Are you an actor?"

He grinned. "Isn't everyone out here?"

Jody thought about that. She was going to be in a television series, but she wasn't really an actor. At least she didn't think of herself that way. "Not everyone."

He glanced at the paper again. "Hell, I might go and try out for a part." He did his best to give himself a western-sounding accent, but it wasn't at all convincing. Sounded stupid, actually.

She turned the paper around and read the article. They were looking for actors who could ride. "You ever been on a horse before?"

"No, but I'm not going to let that stop me."

And all at once, a little bit of the young man's shine was gone. You couldn't fake riding a horse. You either knew your way around the animals or you didn't and no amount of chutzpah was going to fool anyone.

She read the rest of the article, thinking that maybe she'd try out for a part. After all, she'd grown up around horses and could ride them as well as anyone on the farm. But then she read how they were looking for men between the ages of forty and fifty.

Obviously there wasn't a part for her in the film. Him either, for that matter.

"You're too young for this part," she said.

"Hey, I can play older."

Yeah, in your dreams, maybe. Jody sipped her coffee, no longer interested in the man across the table from her after realizing he was just as phony and full of himself as everyone else in Hollywood seemed to be.

She shifted her attention entirely onto the newspaper, and as her eyes scanned the rest of the page, a pair of words caught her eye—*Gowan Brothers.*

She found the article . . .

DEATH HALTS PRODUCTION ON GOWAN BROTHERS LATEST.

. . . and began reading.

Apparently someone had died working on the set. And, since another crew member had been seriously injured a few weeks before, they were calling the production a cursed set and were making all sorts of comparisons to the original *Crow* feature in which Brandon Lee lost his life.

It was a silly notion, but the thought of it still sent a chill down the length of Jody's spine. If nothing else, she was intrigued. While she'd done her best to prepare herself for the show physically, she hadn't done anything to get herself mentally prepared for the night she was going to spend in the house. From the sounds of it, there was a chance the house might actually be haunted. And if that was the case, she wanted to do all she could to be ready for whatever it might throw at her.

"So what do you say?"

"What?" Apparently he'd been talking to her while she'd been reading the newspaper.

"After we're done here, we take in a movie . . . or, I don't know, maybe rent something and watch it at my place."

Wow, he's fast, Jody thought. But she wasn't interested anymore.

"No, thanks, I've got plans to head over to the library."

"You a student?"

"No, but there's some research I need to do."

He nodded, as if to say *That's cool.* "How about I give you a ride?"

"Uh, no, thanks," she said, flashing him a smile similar to the one the consultant had shown her days earlier. "I'd rather walk."

The public library was midway between the gym and her apartment. She had visited it only a few times, checking out a few videotapes when money was tight and she couldn't afford to go to Blockbuster.

Jody really didn't know what she expected to find in

the library, but considering what had happened on the site, she figured it wouldn't be a bad idea to take the haunted house part of the show a little more seriously.

Most of the nonfiction was shelved on the second floor and although she had a rough idea where to look for what she needed, Jody felt it would save time to ask one of the librarians at the information desk to help her out.

That was what they were there for, wasn't it?

There was a man and a woman sitting at the desk and although the man was free at the moment, Jody waited until the woman—an older lady in her late fifties, early sixties wearing a blue flower-print dress that was accented with lace—was finished with a patron before approaching the desk.

"Yes," the woman said. Her name tag read DOROTHY.

"I'm interested in reading up on some ghosts."

"Ghost stories . . . real-life accounts . . ."

She was obviously going to go on with her list, but Jody knew what she wanted. "Real-life accounts."

"Historical or contemporary?"

"I'm interested in stories about real ghosts. Ones in California mainly . . . and over the last hundred years or so."

The woman looked at Jody with a bit of a snarl and Jody prepared herself to receive a sharp reply, but the woman's face slowly brightened with a smile.

She stared at Jody for several moments, still grinning.

"What is it?" Jody said, feeling self-conscious.

"Forrest J. Ackerman once visited our library and asked for help on the exact same subject."

"Really." Jody didn't know who Forrest J. Ackerman was, but judging by the librarian's excitement, he must have been some sort of celebrity.

"Yes." She nodded. "It was either 1980 or 1981."

Jody smiled, not sure if she should be more impressed by Forrest J. Ackerman, or wary of the old lady because she was obviously a psycho. She remembered the man had come to the library more than twenty years ago, for crying out loud. "Were you able to help him?"

"Of course, and in fact he mentioned my name and thanked me in the article he wrote."

"That's great, congratulations."

She got up from the desk and walked out from behind it. "Follow me," she said.

Jody followed the old woman and in minutes they had a stack of books on the subjects of California ghosts and hauntings with titles like *The Realms of Ghosts* and *ESP, Hauntings and Poltergeists*. There was also a thin hardcover book with a faded red cover and worn spine. There was gold lettering on the front and spine, but much of it had been worn away over the years. The title of the book read: *For   den   laces of S. Cal forn   a.*

"Forbidden places," she said, filling in the letters that appeared like faded ghosts on the book's cover.

That sounded like a good place to start.

She gingerly cracked open the book and began reading.

Twelve

"So we've got two more months on the lease of the house and property, right?"

William Olsen, the location manager, nodded. "Yeah, I didn't know how long it was going to take to clean the place up, so I opted for an extra month. Why? What do you have in mind?"

"Well, we've got the house rigged. We've got all kinds of cameras set up, and even if the network pulls the plug on us, they'd have to pay a few penalties to us to do it."

"Right," said Olsen. "So you walk away from this with a bad taste in your mouth and few hundred grand in your pocket for your trouble."

"Or . . . we get Dunbar to write us some haunted house thing that makes use of all the effects and goofs we've set up inside; then we get a few starlets with nice tits, and the kid from that sitcom—you know the one I like . . ." Ike snapped his fingers a couple of times.

"House Arrest?"

"Yeah, that's the one. . . . We get that kid, and just like that we've got ourselves a movie." Ike stared off in the direction of the mountains lining the eastern horizon, thinking they'd make a great opening shot, panning down slowly until the leafless autumn trees filled the screen. Then flash, *Gowan Brothers Entertainment Presents* . . . followed by the house, looking all ominous and creepy in the moonlight . . .

Olsen nodded. "It could work, but you think Dunbar can deliver on such short notice?"

"What deliver? We just tell him we want something like *Night of the Living Dead*, or maybe like *Cujo*, but in a house instead of a car. And the house can still be haunted, so the people trapped inside are being attacked from inside and outside all at the same time—two times as scary as either of those movies."

"Okay, I'll see if I can find Dunbar, see what he says."

"Right, and let my brother know what's going on . . ." Ike hesitated, feeling that that might cause some tension between him and Erwin. "On second thought, I'll tell him and make it sound like it was his idea."

Olsen nodded, then turned to head off in search of the young horror writer when Ike's cell phone went off. "Hold on," he told Olsen as he took the call.

"Ike Gowan."

"Hello, I'm calling to speak to one of the Gowan brothers," said the voice on the other end.

"This is Ike Gowan."

"One of the producer brothers?"

"How'd you get this number?"

"My name is Miriam Schapp," she said, enunciating every syllable carefully and sounding like some eighty-year-old stroke victim.

Ike rolled his eyes. He didn't have time for shit like this. Not now.

"I work for the King's County medical examiner."

Ike stood up straighter and held the phone closer to his ear. "Oh, hi."

"Deputy Borden said I should call you. He said you might want to hear the autopsy report from me personally."

"Yes, of course. That was very thoughtful of the deputy." He covered the phone and whispered to Olsen. "It's the medical examiner."

Olsen's eyes widened slightly at the news and he was no longer in a hurry to find Dunbar.

"You see, even though Mr. Matheson's death appeared to be an accident, we're required to perform a medical-legal autopsy on the body to determine the cause of death."

"Yes, we understand that, ma'am. . . ." Ike struggled to remember her name. Miriam, that was it. "We understand that, Miriam, and we appreciate your diligence, but—"

Ike wanted her to get to the point, but she didn't seem to have one. "I'm glad to hear that because a lot of people don't understand how the coroner's office works. . . ."

She paused a moment as if waiting for Ike to say something. But he really couldn't think of anything appropriate, so he opted for something safe and meaningless. "Oh, I'm sure."

"You'd be amazed by the work we do here."

Ike looked over at Olsen and shrugged. "I bet I would."

"In fact, I've written down a lot of my experiences and I think they would make for a good television series, or maybe even a movie of the week."

Ike sighed. It was becoming clear to him now. Rather than have her drop by and tell him the news, Deputy Borden had Miriam call him directly. Probably even egged her on, you know? "Sure, I was talking to him yesterday and he told me he's always looking for good material for the movies." Ike could picture the deputy standing within earshot of Miriam right now, barely holding back his laughter.

"Well, I'll give that some thought, Miriam. And in the meantime I'll have one of my assistants get in touch with you about your ideas."

"When would I need an agent?"

"Not for a while yet," Ike said, shaking his head.

"Oh, okay."

The line was silent for several moments.

"Uh, was there something *else* you needed to talk to me about, or was that it?"

"Oh, I'm sorry. I got so carried away there I almost forgot the reason why I called . . . which is the results of Mr. Matheson's autopsy."

"Yes . . ."

"Well, my first inclination was to rule the cause of death to be a severe fracture to the skull, which Mr. Matheson suffered when his head hit the floor. After all, twelve or so feet is quite a height." A pause. "But the internal examination revealed something else."

"Yes." It was all Ike could do to keep himself from screaming into the phone, "Get to the fucking point!"

"A cursory examination of the heart revealed that there was some necrosis of the tissue because of obstructions to the vascular supply to the area."

What was it with everybody from around here, speaking in riddles all the time? "What does that mean?"

"It means that Mr. Matheson fell off the ladder because he had suffered a myocardial infarction."

"Which is . . ."

"A heart attack, Mr. Gowan. Andy Matheson had a heart attack. That's why he fell off the ladder."

"Really," Ike said, glad that the M.E. couldn't see the smile on his face.

"What is it?" Olsen whispered, but Ike waved him off.

"Yes, but it gets a little more curious than that."

"Oh?"

"We did a few routine toxicology tests on his bodily fluids and found an abnormally high amount of epinephrine in his blood, and that's what likely caused the ventricular fibrillation of the heart, which in turn brought on the heart attack."

The line was silent for a long time.

"Epinephrine?" Ike said. "You mean he had a cold and he was taking something for it, some kind of drugs?"

"No, epinephrine is a hormone. It's also known as adrenaline, and it's released by the body in moments of great stress . . ." she hesitated. "Or fear."

"Fear?"

"Yes."

"That's incredible!" Ike could barely contain his excitement.

"Not that incredible. It happens more often than most people think."

Ike struggled to contain himself. "Yes, of course. . . . And thank you so much for the call, Miriam. I'll have my assistant get in touch with you about your ideas. They sound like real winners." He hung up without saying good-bye.

"What is it?"

"Only the best thing that could have happened to this damned production."

"What?"

"Andy Matheson died of a heart attack."

"No," Olsen said in disbelief.

Ike pumped his fist into the air. "Yes!"

After breaking the news of the latest development to his brother, Erwin, Ike called for a meeting of everyone on the set. Then while Ike was busy getting in touch with Bartolo from the network, Olsen headed out to round up everyone he could find.

Less than an hour later the production trailer was filled with about two dozen people. The majority of the crew were still in town, had taken a few days off to go hiking in the mountains, or had gone home to look for other work. Ike had instructed Olsen that this last group of people— O thee of little faith—were not to be called back.

"Welcome, everyone," he said.

The group gave a halfhearted greeting in response.

They'd either been out drinking the night before, or they were still depressed about the production being postponed.

"I've brought you all together to share a bit of good news."

Some of the faces around the table brightened, a few other people leaned in closer to Ike, rolling forward on their chairs.

Ike cleared his throat and said, "Andy Matheson died of a heart attack!"

The trailer remained silent. Ike had been expecting a cheer or something similarly rousing from the group, but there was hardly a ripple.

Then Erwin stepped forward. "What my brother means is that while we're both deeply saddened by Andy's death, at least we can all take some comfort in the fact that his death had nothing to do with the production."

The room seemed to have suddenly come to life. Ike looked at his brother with a mix of admiration and jealousy over his ability to be compassionate at a time when all Ike could think about was getting everyone back to work.

"Andy had a heart attack," Erwin continued. "Maybe working on this production helped him along a bit, but let's face it, if he had a heart attack, he could have had it anywhere. At least we can take solace in the knowledge that Andy died doing something he loved."

Damned if there wasn't a good warm feeling floating around the trailer.

Ike looked at his brother wondering how he knew what the word *solace* meant, but the thought was fleeting. Now that everyone was feeling better about Andy's death, it was time to get back to business. "Right, thanks, Erwin. And so, because Andy died of a heart attack and not through any sort of negligence, the network has decided to green-light us again."

This time there was a mild cheer from the group.

Now that's more like it, thought Ike.

"So let's get back to work, and make this the best Gowan Brothers production ever . . ." Ike paused, feeling as if he was losing them again, then added, "For Andy's sake."

Slowly, people got up from the table and began filing out of the trailer.

"Dunbar," Ike called out. "Hold on a minute, I want to talk to you."

The young writer nodded and sat back down.

When the trailer was cleared, Dunbar pulled up a chair between Ike and Erwin.

"I want you to do up a press release telling everybody we're back in production."

"I've already been working on something like that."

"Good . . . but there's something I want you to put in it . . . something *special.*"

"Sure, whatever you want."

"I want you to hint—" He shook his head. "No, I want you to say that Andy Matheson died of fright."

"What?" said Dunbar.

"Ike, we can't say that—"

"Oh, yes, we can. This morning I got a call from the coroner's office, and the woman there told me that while it's true Andy died of a heart attack, there was a drug in his system . . . epinef-something."

"Epinephrine?" said Dunbar.

"Yeah, that's it. And this drug—"

"Uh, it's a hormone, actually."

"That's right." Ike was beginning to like the young writer more and more. "And this hormone is released by the body when it gets scared. So we can say that he died of fright, and it'll be true."

Erwin wasn't convinced. "What if she denies it?

Reporters are going to call her and she might say we twisted her words."

Ike smiled, shaking his head. "No," he said, confidently. "She's going to play ball."

"How can you be so sure?"

"She told me she has an idea for a television series, maybe even a movie of the week . . ."

Erwin groaned.

". . . so we keep her strung along until we're done here and then feed her a line about the idea not being commercial at this time, but we'll keep it in mind for next season. You know, the usual bullshit."

"You really want to do that?" Erwin asked.

"Hell, yeah."

"All right, whatever," Erwin said, getting up and heading out of the trailer.

That left Ike and Dunbar in the trailer alone.

"So we're really back in business?" Dunbar asked, probably still reeling over the thought of his first television writing credit suddenly reappearing out of the ether.

"Not only are we back in business, kid," Ike said, putting a hand on the young man's shoulder. "But thanks to Andy Matheson, we're going to be one of the hottest properties in town."

PRODUCTION

Thirteen

Jody rode in the black Dodge Caravan along with Erwin Gowan and two of the other contestants. It was late afternoon and the sun was just starting to fall out of the western sky, painting the horizon in a wash of purple-tinted orange. Growing up on a farm surrounded by plains and flatlands as far as the eye could see, Jody had often spent afternoons gazing out at the setting sun and contemplating what the sun meant to her family and friends.

The sun was a symbol of happiness and a life giver, but like everything else in the world, too much of a good thing was ultimately bad. So the sun needed to work in conjunction with the rain in order to make life flourish. But no matter how much or how little rain the farmers got, there could be no life without the sun.

And the same would be true here.

When the sun was gone from the sky there would be no joy. Instead of life, Jody would be surrounded by death, or at least by the ghosts of the dead. Sure there would be other contestants in the house, but the ghosts would be her real companions throughout the night, never leaving her until the sun returned to bring the light back into her world.

There was a tap on her shoulder. "What are you thinking? Are you nervous? Scared?"

It was Erwin Gowan, the show's director. His face

was stolid for the most part, but there was a hint of a smile at the corners of his mouth, as if he were bursting with glee on the inside and couldn't wait for things to start happening.

Jody shrugged. "Just looking at the sun . . . wondering what the situation might be like when I see it again tomorrow morning."

Erwin glanced over at the cameraman who was sitting in the passenger seat next to the driver and taping everything that was happening in the back of the van.

The camera was trained on Jody.

Erwin seemed pleased. "Well, *somebody* will be a winner in the morning."

"That's right," said a voice from the back. "And that winner's going to be me."

The camera swung off Jody and found the source of the voice.

Jody turned around and saw one of the two male contestants, Radko Arruda, looking directly into the camera. He jabbed his thumb into his chest, then pointed an index finger at the camera. "If those ghosts think they're going to put the scare into Radko Arruda they are mistaken. Radko Arruda fears nothing in this world . . . or any other world."

Jody couldn't help but smile.

Radko Arruda was a blue-eyed, ruggedly handsome, and neatly chiseled block of a man who originally hailed from Romania. Jody thought she'd seen him in a local commercial or two, but couldn't be sure since his hair had obviously been the victim of a recent chop job. At the mixer they'd put on for all the contestants the night before, he'd told her he was working on an acting career. He'd asked her to call him "Rad," but the name hadn't struck a chord with her. "Rad" was the sort of name you gave to blond-haired, suntanned surfer dudes, not muscle-bound Romanians. With Radko's pale brown crew cut, square jaw, and sculpted muscles, she couldn't help thinking of him as a future professional wrestler whose name would be Radko "the Eastern Block" Arruda. If it weren't for the fall of Soviet communism, the name might have had some legs.

"Do you think it's wise," said a female voice, "to dismiss the ghosts so easily?"

Jody turned to look at the other contestant in the van, Vonda McNair, and did her best to hide her displeasure. She'd known the woman less than twenty-four hours and she already disliked her with a passion. There was a saying Jody had heard a few times when she was growing up that described people like Vonda— *She was born on third base and grew up thinking she'd hit a triple.* That was Vonda McNair all right. Vonda's mother was Jennifer McNair, the Emmy Award–winning star of a string of nighttime soaps and a frequent guest on most of the big daytime game shows. Vonda McNair showed up on the screen every once in a while playing her mother's daughter on things like *Murder, She Wrote* and *Matlock.* She'd also appeared on a few talk shows—always with her mother—and had even co-hosted some preaward show party with her mother where the two of them described the outfits that everyone in attendance were wearing, as if it were radio and people couldn't see the outfits for themselves on their television screens. But even if Jody hadn't recognized Vonda from her television appearances, Vonda wasn't one to wait around for people to make the connection. She'd been able to work in the fact that she was Jennifer McNair's daughter less than five minutes into their first conversation.

Radko smiled at Vonda. "What's there to be afraid of?" He smiled. "Sticks and stones will break my bones, but ghosts will never hurt me."

Jody smiled. Radko did have a certain amount of charisma.

Vonda rolled her eyes, then said, "When I was in Hungary filming a movie-of-the-week with my mother, we saw a live show by a mentalist who claimed he could stop bicycles and cars with the power of his mind . . ."

Her voice trailed off and the inside of the van was quiet for several moments.

"And?" Radko said.

Yes, Jody thought. *And?*

"A week later he was killed trying to stop a freight train outside of Budapest."

"That's not the same thing," Radko said, looking a bit confused.

Jody laughed under her breath, also wondering what the story had to do with anything other than being an opportunity for Vonda to mention her mother.

Jody thought she might be able to relate one of the experiences she'd had with the ghost of her grandfather and said, "Back on the farm we had a ghost—" only to be cut off in midsentence.

"We're here," the driver said, sounding a lot like the young Heather O'Rourke from *Poltergeist.*

Jody turned around and felt a chill crawl over her skin.

The house was still a few hundred yards up the road, but even at a distance it looked dark and mysterious, everything a haunted house should be. In fact, Jody thought it looked more like some Gothic castle than a southern Californian farmhouse. After just a single glance at the house and its surroundings, Jody had no trouble believing that ghosts lived there.

And as the van drew nearer, and the house loomed larger and more ominous through the windshield, Jody actually began to feel anxious about going inside. A strong feeling of dread began to well up inside her, and although she couldn't quite be sure why, she was certain there was some sort of evil living inside the building.

Inside it, and all around it.

And so, regardless of the rationale her mind had provided for her the past few weeks, explaining away ghosts as figments of people's imagination, and reasoning that it was a television show and no one would ever be seriously hurt during taping, Jody decided she would try and remember to take nothing for granted.

"Ooo, very scary," said Radko, with a sort of Lugosi-inspired accent.

"It only looks that way," Vonda added. "You'd be amazed what lighting directors and set decorators can do with a decent budget."

Jody crossed her arms and rubbed her hands over her shoulders. "Well, whatever they did to the house, they sure did a good job of it."

"Yeah, it's amazing what a half dozen brutal murders will do to a house's appearance," offered Erwin Gowan, ignoring the mention of his crew and reminding everyone about the show's tone, which was deadly serious.

The driver pulled to a stop just past the front door of the house. Behind them, a second black Dodge Caravan pulled to a stop, followed by a black Chevrolet pickup that had a pair of cameras set up in back of its box. Those cameras had recorded the drive up to the house, and would now be taping the contestants on the front lawn as they got out of the vehicles and awaited their final briefing.

When the sliding door of the van rolled open, Jody was struck by how chill the late afternoon air had become. At this rate the night was going to be a cold one and she'd be shivering uncontrollably by morning. Jody chided herself for not bringing along an extra sweater, but of course there was nothing that could be done about it now.

Radko and Vonda joined Jody on the lawn and a few seconds later the door of the second van opened up and the three other contestants slowly spilled out of the vehicle.

Of the three of them, Jody only really liked the guy. His name was Forrest Thorpe, a young man on a football scholarship to Rutgers University who reminded Jody a lot of a young Denzel Washington. His face was beautiful and he was certainly buffed, but he also had a gentle quality to him that she hadn't found in a lot of men, not growing up on the farm, and certainly not while she'd been living in Los Angeles. At the mixer, Jody and Forrest had talked for hours until one of the producer's assistants noticed them off in a corner and encouraged them to mingle so they could get some footage of them at the party. Like everyone else in California, it seemed, Forrest had been considering a career in television when he was done playing college football, but he didn't have his heart set on it. There were a lot of things he was thinking of doing, but Jody knew that whatever he ended up choosing, he'd probably be pretty good at it.

"Hey, Forrest," Jody said.

"Joe-dee!" he responded.

"Enjoy the ride?"

He shook his head. "Like riding in a chicken coop."

"Those vans aren't that small."

"No, not that." He threw a thumb over his shoulder. "Those other two wouldn't stop talking. It was like sitting between a pair of hens the whole way. *Cluck-cluck-cluck-cluck-cluck.*"

Jody looked over in time to see Tamisha Robinson stepping out of the van.

"That's all right," she said, looking up at the house. "I seen worse than this in the city."

Jody looked over at Forrest and he just shook his head. Like Forrest, Tamisha Robinson was black, but unlike

Forrest, she seemed to wear her color out on her sleeve as if it were some sort of badge.

And that didn't make sense.

From what Jody had pieced together from the press kits and from talking with Tamisha herself, the woman had grown up in a middle-class family in Reading, Pennsylvania, and had earned a master of fine arts degree in motion pictures from UCLA. After graduation she'd managed to get a job producing a Saturday morning kids' show in San Jose, and was currently using that job as a platform from which to search for something bigger farther south, preferably in Hollywood. Yet, for all her success, the woman seemed to talk as if she had grown up in the projects, and invoked the name of Oprah Winfrey as if it were the title of some minor deity. Jody didn't care for the act, but it had obviously been working for the woman so far, and Jody wouldn't be surprised if Tamisha Robinson wound up running some network or studio within the next ten years.

After Tamisha, the sixth and final contestant got out of the van, smoothing out her jeans and adjusting her top so that her breasts hung off her chest just so.

Jody wasn't crazy about Melanie Menendez either, but of all the women in the group Melanie was the only one that Jody understood. Melanie Menendez was a tall, shapely, olive-skinned beauty who had a body that was to die for, and who, not surprisingly, worked as an exotic dancer. Melanie had obviously had a hard life growing up in Los Angeles, but she never seemed to complain about anything. Instead, she exuded an assertive quality that Jody begrudgingly admired. And while Melanie, like the other two women, was always looking for ways to get ahead, she seemed to prefer relying on herself rather than trying to ride along on someone else's coattails. She knew she was good looking and sexy and had no trouble using those attributes to her advantage, even if it meant going for a ride on the casting couch to get a part. Jody wasn't impressed by that part of Melanie's character, but she still couldn't help but be a little jealous of Melanie's shoulder-length curly black hair and centerfold's body that always looked fantastic, even in a pair of jeans and black pumps.

After the contestants were out of the second van, Ike Gowan climbed out of the passenger seat. Jody wasn't all that crazy about Ike Gowan either. If the Gowan brothers had been policemen, doing a "good cop/bad cop" routine with the contestants, Ike would be cast in the role of the bad cop, coming down hard on everyone as if the only way he knew how to get results was to threaten and bully everyone around him. Erwin, on the other hand, was kinder and gentler, and acted as a friend to the contestants and crew. Jody imagined that on their own, neither of them would have had much success in Hollywood, but together their styles complemented each other perfectly, making them a winning combination.

"All right, everyone," said Erwin, "I want you all to take a good look at the house. Contemplate what's inside it and what the night might have in store for you. . . ."

The six contestants lined up in a ragged line about twenty yards from the house.

"And don't move until I give the word," Erwin instructed. "Because we want to get footage of all of you before you go in."

Jody looked up at the second floor of the house, finding the slight glow emanating from the windows on the upper floors especially creepy, like the eyes of some demon that had just been roused from a deep, deep sleep.

She was aware of the cameraman moving back and forth along the line of contestants, first from behind—probably getting some shots of the house over their shoulders—then moving around to shoot them from the front.

He started at the left end of the line where Vonda Mc-Nair was standing. When the camera was on her she seemed to go through a range of facial expressions, as if she didn't know what they were looking for and gave them every one she knew just to be sure.

Then the camera moved onto Radko, who remained impassive.

Tamisha tried to give the house an inner-city sneer, like this thing was going to be no problem and she should be signing the movie contract right now since that was the way it was going to work out anyway.

After Tamisha, the camera strolled past Forrest, who seemed to be studying the house like a scholar.

And then the cameraman stopped and held his position on Melanie. The camera seemed to be stuck on her, moving up and down her body several times without carrying on down the line toward Jody.

Jody turned her head to take a closer look at Melanie and realized that the woman's nipples had become erect in the cold late-afternoon air and were poking through her top like a pair of thimbles. Melanie didn't seem to mind the attention and stood with her chest slightly thrust out so the cameraman could get the best view possible.

Jody glanced down at her own chest and saw that the cold wasn't having nearly as much effect on her.

The camera moved on, pausing a moment on Jody's face, then panning past her and taking in the brilliant twilight sky.

"Okay," Erwin called, "let's get the closing shot for this scene."

The cameraman set himself at the end of the drive, away from the contestants.

The vehicles were restarted, then drove away slowly.

Behind the two vans, the two cameras were rolling in the back of the pickup truck, one trained on the vans driving away, the other on the contestants, who were now alone with the house.

Jody felt the chill night air pressing against her skin and for the first time since her audition she felt . . .

Fear.

Fourteen

When the two vans and pickup truck were gone, a second cameraman appeared out of the shadows to join the contestants on the front lawn.

Ike and Erwin Gowan were whispering words back and forth to each other, almost as if they were rehearsing something. The contestants remained loose, laughing and talking amongst themselves but always being wary of one another, since this was as much a competition as it was a television show.

Jody positioned herself next to Forrest, sizing up the others and figuring she had as good a chance as anyone to last the night, maybe even win the whole damn thing.

"What do you think your chances are?" she said in little more than a whisper.

Forrest looked over at her and gave her an odd smile. "You remember on the original *Star Trek* series how Kirk, Spock, and McCoy would beam down onto the planet along with a couple of guys in red shirts?"

"Yeah," Jody said, wondering what this had to do with anything.

"Well, that's how I feel right now. Like a red shirt beaming down onto the planet just to take the bullet for the real stars."

"What are you talking about, real stars?"

"The show's called *Scream Queen*, not *Scream King*."

Jody didn't understand. She was about to ask Forrest what he was talking about, but never got the chance.

"Over here," Ike called out, motioning with his arms for everyone to gather around him.

The contestants made a rough semicircle in front of both Ike and Erwin Gowan so that they were looking at the brothers and the house at the same time.

The sun was minutes from falling below the horizon.

"I know that by now all of you are familiar with the rules, but I want to go over them one last time so there can be no mistake or misunderstanding about what you will be required to do inside the house."

"First of all," Erwin said, taking over for his brother. "You can't win unless you stay inside the house the entire night. Leaving the house at any time before the sun comes up will automatically disqualify you no matter how short a time you spend outside."

"Second." Ike this time, as the brothers traded off hosting duties. "You will be expected to explore the house, which means you can't just find a comfortable spot to stretch out and sleep through the night. You will have to move around . . . go down into the basement and up into the attic, to give the audience a chance to see you in action in different kinds of group situations."

Erwin moved forward until he was standing in front of his brother. "And about midway through the evening, you will each be given an envelope. Inside the envelope will be specific instructions about visiting a room in the house. When you reach that room you will be required to act out a classic horror movie scene."

Jody didn't like the sound of that. Knowing the Gowan brothers, each room was going to be loaded with more than enough surprises to scare the hell out of each and every one of them.

Erwin continued speaking as Ike had momentarily disappeared from view. "There's food and drink in the kitchen if you want anything during the night and there is a working bathroom on the main floor."

Jody smiled at that. She just might need to make use of the bathroom at some point during the night, but she had a feeling that she probably wouldn't feel much like eating. She just knew there was going to be a lot of gore in the house—maybe even a severed head in the refrigerator—and food was going to be one of the last things on Jody's mind.

Ike reappeared with several assistants in tow. "There are thirty-six cameras set up throughout the house covering every room inside from two or more angles. About half of the cameras will provide a direct feed into the production trailer. The rest are mini digital video cameras hooked up to motion sensors that will start recording if and when they detect that one of your are nearby."

Vonda put up her hand to ask a question—

"And no, there are no cameras in the bathroom."

—then quickly brought it down.

Ike began to move down the line, followed by an assistant.

"These are Digital Handycams provided to us by Sony." He gave the first camera to Vonda. "There are all sorts of technical reasons why we're giving each of you one of these cameras, but all you need to know is that there is a switch that reads *Nightshot: on/off* and you will want this to always be in the *on* position, which will allow you to record images in complete darkness. They do have a light, but using it will drain the battery three times more quickly than regular taping, so we advise that you use the light sparingly. Also, although the camera has an image-stabilizing system, I ask that when you're taping you try to keep the camera as still as possible."

Melanie and Radko now had their cameras and had slipped them onto their right hands.

"You'll have plenty of spare cassettes, and infolithium

batteries, each one good for about four hours of taping. So, feel free to keep your cameras running the entire time you're inside the house. Tape what you see, and don't be afraid to turn the camera on yourself every once in a while for a comment, observation, or . . . a plea to God begging him to please let you get out of this nightmare alive."

A gentle laugh made its way through the line of contestants. Jody took her camera from Ike with little more than a smile and immediately began to refamiliarize herself with its controls. She had been given a quick lesson in the camera's operation a week ago in a meeting with the show's director of photography, but this would be the first time she'd been able to hold one in her hand for any length of time. It felt comfortable strapped into her palm, and the controls seemed simple enough with clearly marked *Power*, *Record*, and *Zoom* buttons. There was also a light on the camera that could be used like a flashlight . . . at the cost of extra battery power. She figured she'd be using that, a lot.

Jody put the viewfinder to her right eye and took a look around through the camera lens and saw that Radko was already zooming in on Melanie as if he were some sort of fashion photographer, and Vonda had turned her camera onto herself and, *ugh!*—Jody could hardly believe it—had already said, "Hi, Mom!" into the lens.

"Okay," Erwin called out to get everyone's attention. "Before you head inside for the night, we want to give you a bit of the history and background of the house . . . just to set the stage for tonight's show."

Jody shut off her camera. There were cameramen shooting the brothers at the moment and she figured that shooting a lot of unnecessary footage would just give the show's editors more work than they needed.

A soft light suddenly appeared at Erwin's feet, held by a technician that lit his face from below and gave his whole upper body an eerie, otherworldly sort of glow. It was an effective bit of lighting, especially now that the sun was gone from the sky.

"As you already know, this is the Shields house," Erwin said, waving his left arm in the direction of the house.

Behind him, several floodlights slowly came on, casting light onto the house from below and covering the sides of it with the shadows of leafless branches and other jagged black lines. The shadows looked like veins, throbbing and pulsing with the movement of the wind.

"It's gone by other names over the years, such as the House of Horrors or the Slaughter House, but how could one possibly describe a place in which countless unspeakable acts have been committed with just a few short words? It's an impossible task. . . ."

Erwin Gowan continued talking, more for the benefit of the camera than for that of the contestants.

Jody nervously shifted her weight from one foot to the other. Because of the research she'd done, she was already pretty familiar with the history of the house, but there was a big difference between reading a chapter in an old book in a brightly lit library and standing in the cold in front of a scary-looking house while a man who was lit to look like a monster recounted the numerous violent deaths that had occurred on the property over the years.

". . . Karen Misfeldt, a young woman of twenty-three driving down to Los Angeles to take a job as a secretary in the office of her uncle's metal shop. She never made it. Two days from home she met up with Marcus Shields, who abducted her and brought her back to this house, where he bound her hands and feet and hung her by a leather thong from the upstairs landing. But for all of Shields's depraved acts, he spared the woman the humiliation of a gag. Was he being kind? Hardly. He only neglected to gag her because he wanted to hear her screams, to hear her beg him to let her go. And so for three days and three nights, he tortured her, telling her again and again that if she cooperated and promised not to tell anyone about what he had done, he would allow her to walk out of the house when he was through with her."

A pause.

"Well, she might very well have been allowed to walk away, but when the time came she was hardly able to stand because Shields had cut off both her feet at the ankles." Erwin shook his head. "No, like so many others before her, once Karen Misfeldt entered the Shields house she never left it, never saw daylight again. She was savagely tortured and brutally murdered, and when Marcus Shields was done performing his heinous acts on her cold, dead body, he cut that body up into countless little pieces, making trinkets from the bones, feeding the fleshy bits to his dog, and burning the other parts on the hearth. Then, what little remained was buried out on the property."

Several of the contestants looked at the ground beneath them and lifted their feet as if they'd just stepped in something.

Jody laughed slightly under her breath. She had done enough research on the house to know that the story Erwin Gowan was relating was most likely fabricated. Since Marcus Shields had never been charged with any specific murders, the identities of his victims were pure speculation. It was possible that a woman named Karen Misfeldt had disappeared sometime in the late 1950s on her way to Los Angeles, but it would be impossible to link her death with Marcus Shields, especially nearly sixty years after the fact. And of course, the gruesome details about her death were pure fiction.

And yet—

And yet knowing that didn't stop Jody's skin from turning into gooseflesh upon hearing how the woman's body had been cut up and disposed of.

Her reaction to the tale brought a smile to her face.

If she'd been frightened by Erwin's words, then what

was it going to sound and look like to the audience when the stories were interspersed with dramatized scenes portraying the murders, creepy music, and slow pans of the house looking all shadowy and ominous against the black night sky?

This show, Jody realized, was going to be a huge hit.

"But while Karen Misfeldt's body is gone and has long since turned to dust," Erwin continued, "her spirit . . . her life force, still walks the stairwells and hallways of the Shields house, looking for a way out, perhaps even for redemption and revenge. Of course, she'll never have it, and will instead be condemned to relive the horrifying final days of her life, over and over again, now and till the end of time."

At that moment a light flickered in one of the upstairs windows and a shrill woman's scream cut through the night air like an arrowhead.

Jody was startled by the intensity of the scream, feeling as if it had cut her straight to the bone.

Tamisha let out a scream of her own.

Vonda gasped.

Melanie look troubled, but managed to maintain her cool.

The two men laughed out loud, giving each other a spirited high five.

Ike Gowan smiled. "That was just a small taste of the kinds of surprises that are waiting for you inside."

He turned and began walking toward the house, his brother slightly behind and to the right of him.

The contestants followed, walking single file in a ragtag line.

The brothers stopped at the front door, then took up a position on either side of it.

Jody had managed to control the butterflies fluttering around in her stomach, but she could do nothing about the weakness in her knees. They had all the strength of wet noodles and her feet felt as if they weighed upwards of ten pounds each.

"You okay?" Forrest asked in a whisper.

"This is going to be a lot harder than I thought," she said over her right shoulder.

She had expected Forrest to comfort her, to tell her not to worry about it, that she was going to be fine, but he didn't say a thing.

The Gowan brothers opened the two front doors, letting the contestants in.

And as they entered the house, the brothers gave them a few final words of encouragement.

"Good luck," said Erwin.

"You're going to need it," said Ike, laughing.

Then the doors closed behind them, and they were inside.

And alone.

Until morning.

Fifteen

Jody was the last of the six contestants to enter the house. She was relieved to find that the inside was well lit and she could easily see into every corner and doorway.

"Wow," Tamisha said, looking around the foyer like a tourist. "This is really nice."

Jody agreed. It was a beautiful house with thick dark wood framing the doors and windows, a gorgeous wooden staircase leading up to the second floor, and plenty of space for people to move around in. Back home, such houses were reserved for doctors and men who ran the marketing boards, and for Jody they had always indicated an atmosphere of strength and tradition. This house, however, for all its stately decor, still had the feel of a place in turmoil. The longer you looked at the house the more you came to realize that things weren't as wonderful as they seemed.

All around there were signs of age, with cracked windows, bits of framing and trim rotted out, and pipes that leaked almost as much as they carried water. Sure there were a few signs of renewed life—fresh paint on the walls, new stain on the stairs—but seeing those things, Jody couldn't help but wonder if the house's temporary rejuvenation might have also reinvigorated the spirits haunting it.

"It looks like a set from one of my mom's soap operas," Vonda said.

Melanie turned her camera on herself and laughed. "It's big enough for four families to live in."

Jody thought of turning her camera on herself to make a comment as well, but knew it would look as if she were following Melanie's lead. So instead, she opted to focus on Forrest. "What do you think, Forrest?"

"It doesn't look so rough." He smiled, showing off his perfect white teeth. "I could get used to living in a place like this."

And at that moment the lights went out.

Jody, like everyone else in the room, let out a cry.

For several moments the room was completely dark and Jody was unable to see even her own hand. That was probably due to the sudden change from light to dark and surely she'd be able to see once her eyes adjusted to the change. But as the seconds stretched out into minutes, she was still unable to see anything.

"Oh, this is great," Tamisha said. "How are we supposed to do anything if we can't see?"

"It's a trick," Radko said. "They are playing tricks on us already." He raised his voice. "Very funny, Misters Gowan."

"So?" Vonda asked. "Do we just sit around and do nothing until the lights come back on or what?"

"The lights aren't coming back on."

Jody couldn't be sure, but she thought that the last voice had belonged to Melanie.

"Just sit tight everybody," Forrest said, his tone firm and commanding. "Don't move! You'll just bump into something, or trip over somebody. There's going to be lights, there has to be—"

A sound from upstairs cut Forrest off in midsentence.

"What was that?" one of the women asked. Again, Jody wasn't sure which one had spoken.

"There's somebody upstairs," Radko suggested.

"You stop that, you hear!" cried Tamisha. "There's no

one in the house but us. And I don't need you putting thoughts in my head. There's enough going on in there already."

No one said a word for several moments.

The silence was broken by a muffled cry of pain coming from the second floor.

"Oh, shit!" someone said.

And then the table lamp on the right side of the foyer came on, bathing the room in a soft yellowish glow.

Everyone breathed a sigh of relief.

Tamisha shook her head. "And we've got twelve hours of this kind of shit to look forward to."

"Watch your language," Forrest reminded. "You won't end up on the screen much if you keep using four-letter words."

Tamisha cleared her throat. "And we've got twelve hours of this *stuff* to look forward to."

Radko chuckled. "Yeah, isn't it cool?"

"Oh, shut up!"

"Hey, hey," Forrest said. "Let's not start that already. We've got a long time to go in this house and we don't need to get started out on the wrong foot."

Tamisha shook her head and looked away as if to say she knew Forrest was right, but couldn't bring herself to admit it.

"Now, from what we've seen already, the Gowan brothers are going to make this night hard for us, so we've got to come up with a plan."

"What do you have in mind?" Vonda asked.

Forrest shrugged. "I don't know. I was hoping somebody else might come up with something. . . ."

He paused, and nobody said anything for the longest time. Forrest was about to offer a suggestion when Tamisha said, "I think we should stick together for a while."

Radko looked at her and smiled. "You want to win this thing, or do you just want to make it through the night?"

Vonda shrugged. "I want to win. Of course, I want to win."

"Well, you aren't going to win anything hanging around with five other people. The winner gets the *starring role* in the next film, not a job as an extra. If you want to stand out, you have to be on your own."

"Are you crazy?" Forrest replied, stepping out of the shadows and into the light. "We have to stick together. We've got twelve hours in this house and there's no reason we have to spend all of them alone . . . or weren't you paying attention when they went over the rules? They need us in group situations as well as on our own."

Radko took a step, moving closer to Forrest, as if confronting him.

But Forrest turned to his left, choosing instead to talk to the rest of the group, ignoring Radko completely. "We stick together as a group for the first little while until we're more comfortable inside the house. Then, later on, we can go off and explore the house on our own and do our auditions, but for now we've got to stick together."

"Okay, then what if we just split up into groups of two? We can still explore the house, and it will be safer because there'll be two or more of us together, instead of just one," Radko suggested from behind Forrest's back.

"Why do you keep pushing this on us?" Forrest answered. "We don't have to decide anything right now. We just got into the house, for crying out loud."

Radko said nothing for a while, then began snapping his fingers in Forrest's direction.

"Wait a minute. Wait. Wait. I know what you're doing. . . . You're part of the show, aren't you? Someone gets an idea about what they want to do inside the house, and you're here to tell them that their ideas are no good, and to guide them along so we do what the Gowan brothers want us to do. Right?"

"Would they do that?" Vonda wondered aloud.

"Damn right they would," offered Tamisha. "Anything to throw us off."

Jody wanted to say something in Forrest's defense, but his earlier comment about being one of those expendable crew members from *Star Trek* was still echoing in her ears. Maybe he *was* in on the show, or at the very least he knew something the others didn't.

"Sorry, man," Forrest said, shaking his head. "It's a nice theory, but I'm just trying to get through the night in one piece and I figure I've got a better chance of doing it if we don't all get freaked out in the first couple of hours."

Forrest paused a moment to let his point sink it, but the silence was cut by the sound of a door creaking open somewhere in the house.

By now the contestants had come to expect such sounds, or at least had learned not to be too alarmed by them. With the exception of Vonda, hardly anyone seemed to pay much attention to the noise, yet Jody still found it unnerving.

So a door had swung open in the house. So what? Doors swing open and closed all the time. And yet, long after the sound of the door had faded many questions still remained.

What opened the door?

What was moving through the doorway at this very moment?

Thinking about it sent shivers through Jody's body.

"I suppose we could stay together for a while," Radko said at last. "But we're going to have to split up sooner or later."

"Agreed," said Forrest.

"What do you want to do right now, then?"

"Well, we could take some time to check out this part of the house, or interview each other about how we feel so far. . . . That will at least give us a chance to get more familiar with how these cameras work."

Jody didn't exactly feel ready to start roaming the

house, so Forrest's suggestion seemed like just what she needed at the moment. "That sounds good," she said.

"Okay," said Radko. "We can stay on this floor for a while."

"Great." Forrest nodded. "Then we're all in agreement."

"Yeah."

"Sure."

"Whatever."

Jody breathed a sigh.

Then Radko approached her slowly, holding out his right hand, the one that held his camera. "Do you know how to turn this on?"

"Sure," Jody said, showing him the *Power* button.

"Thank you."

Jody put the camera to her eye and said, "Go ahead."

"Go ahead, what?" Vonda asked.

"What are you feeling so far?"

"Well, I'm not afraid, if that's what you mean."

"I wasn't implying that at all."

"Good. 'Cuz I'm not."

Jody said nothing.

Vonda looked quickly to her right. "What was that?"

Jody panned her camera to the left, but there was nothing there.

Forty-five minutes later, everyone had done at least one interview—recorded either by themselves, another contestant, or both—and they were all familiar enough with the cameras now to start venturing through the house.

The only room they could examine on this floor without moving into another part of the house was the living room. It was a large room, probably twenty feet by thirty, which featured a large fireplace on the right wall, a rounded reading nook in one corner, and bookcases and paintings lining the remaining outside walls. The room was lit by the small amount of light shining in from the floodlights outside. The light created great long shadows that seemed to vault upward along the walls and ended in smoky tendrils that looked like splayed fingers on the ceiling.

Jody followed the others into the room, being careful not to knock anything over. A few of the others were taping, so Jody decided to shut off her camera and look and listen instead.

There was a hard thump at the other end of the room.

Followed by a scream.

Jody held her breath.

Then someone cried out. "Ow, damn it!" It sounded like one of the women.

"What is it?"

"What happened?"

"Are you all right?"

Jody rushed over to the far wall where the others were already huddled around someone who was down on the floor.

She peered in between Radko and Melanie and saw Tamisha on her knees rubbing her head. "I was just walking by the bookcase and this book fell off the shelf and hit me on the head."

"What book was it?"

Tamisha's eyes narrowed. "What the hell difference does that make?"

Vonda picked up the book. "Maybe it means something."

"Yeah, it means that you're a stupid bitch!" Tamisha snarled, picking herself up off the floor.

"Hey, hey," Forrest said, keeping the two women apart. "We're still together on this."

"I got a lump on my head and she wants to know the title of the book." Tamisha's head was moving from side to side on the end of her neck as if she were talking to her friends out on some street corner.

"It's only a paperback."

"Yeah, but it's a thousand pages long!"

Vonda hesitated a moment, then said softly, "Are you okay?"

And all at once all the fire in Tamisha's eyes seemed to be gone. "I'll be all right," she sighed.

"What is the title of the book, anyway?" Jody wanted to know.

Vonda turned the book over in her hand. *"In the Dark* by some guy named Richard Laymon." She looked at Jody. "Mean anything to you?"

Jody shrugged.

"Are we done here?" Melanie said, using the light from her camera to inspect some of the darker corners of the room.

"Maybe it's time we head down into the basement," Forrest suggested.

"Good idea," Vonda said. "After you."

Forrest led them out of the living room and to the small door under the stairs leading to the second floor. When they were all gathered around, he opened the door and stared down into the blackness. "Okay, go ahead."

Vonda smiled nervously. "It was your idea. . . . Why don't you go first?"

Forrest hesitated.

"What's the matter," Vonda chided him, "you scared?"

"Damn straight, I'm scared." Forrest peered through the door and into the basement. "I can't see a thing down there."

Melanie let out a little laugh. "Maybe we should draw straws to see who goes down first."

"Maybe we should," Forrest said.

Jody admired the man for admitting his fear. It made him more human in her eyes, especially since she herself was deathly afraid of drawing the short straw and being forced to be the first one into the basement.

"Don't worry, you little babies," Radko said, moving in front of the small doorway. "I'll go down first and chase away all the bad ghosts for you."

"Okay, sure."

Radko looked the group over. There was disdain on his face as he shook his head. "What a bunch of little babies."

Then he turned, switched on the light on his camera, and headed down into the basement.

The rest of the group relaxed.

But the respite was short-lived.

Radko couldn't have gone more than two or three steps when he tripped.

Light flickered and danced in the doorway.

A series of loud crashes and bangs echoed up from the basement, followed by a long scream of pain.

And then silence.

No one said anything for a second.

Finally, Forrest stuck his head through the doorway. "Radko!"

No answer.

"Radko, are you okay?"

Nothing.

Forrest switched on the light of his camera, then headed down. Jody followed closely behind.

One of the steps had broken.

There were several fresh scratches and cuts on the rest of the steps leading down into the basement.

Radko's camera was lying on the basement floor a few feet from the bottom of the stairs. The light was still on, illuminating a pie-shaped section of the floor in front of it.

Dust floated and swirled in the beam of light.

But there was no Radko.

"Where do you think he went?" Jody said.

"I don't know," Forrest replied. "He's just . . . gone."

Sixteen

"What do you mean he's gone? He can't be gone."

Forrest shone his light around the basement, taking extra time to check out the farthest corners. "He's just gone," he said. "As in, not here, as in somewhere else, as in vanished."

"He couldn't have disappeared," Jody said. "Maybe he's hiding somewhere."

"Hiding from what? Ghosts? He's not going to run from any ghosts."

"Maybe he's hiding . . . from us."

"Why would he want to do that?" someone behind her asked.

"I don't know, maybe he's part of the show."

Forrest turned around to look at Jody. She could feel the other contestants coming down the steps behind her, suddenly making the stairway rather crowded.

"I knew it," said someone at the very top of the stairs, most likely Tamisha.

"He was pretty quick to volunteer to be the first downstairs. Maybe that was part of the plan. He could be hiding in some closet, or maybe there's some way to get out from the basement that we don't know about."

"That makes sense," a voice said behind her.

Just then a light came on in the basement. It was a naked bulb in the middle of the room, giving off just enough light so they could see where they were going.

"Where'd that light come from?" Forrest wondered.

"There's a switch on the wall here," Melanie said.

One by one, the camera lights were turned off and the five contestants continued down into the basement.

Forrest picked up Radko's camera, shut off its light, then rewound it to see if he could find out what had happened to him. As he replayed the tape, the others gathered round and watched on the camera's small LCD display monitor.

Radko entered through the doorway, switched on his camera light, took three steps, and then the image went wild, twirling and spinning, then blacking out twice—presumably from a couple of hard hits—before coming to rest on the basement floor. Jody held her breath trying to listen for the sound of footsteps, but there was no sound at all.

A couple of the contestants had seen enough and rose up from their crouch to take a look around. Jody remained where she was, watching the continuous shot of the basement floor illuminated by the camera light. At one point a spider crawled past the lens, causing Jody to gasp, but after that it was the same unchanging view of the basement.

Forrest shut the camera off.

"Well, doesn't that beat all," he said.

"What do you mean?"

"Just a little while ago Radko was trying to split us up, accusing me of being part of the show, and here it turns out that he's the one who's actually trying to screw us all up."

"Yeah, but at least now he's gone and we have an idea about what to expect, right?" Melanie said.

Forrest laughed under his breath. "You really think so?"

Melanie didn't respond, but Vonda shook her head and said, "Oh, God. We're screwed."

* * *

"Okay, pull back on camera two," Erwin instructed. "Ready, two . . . Two. I want a wide shot of the basement with all of them in the middle. Good."

Ike slid into the chair next to Erwin and put a hand on his brother's shoulder. "How are you liking it so far?" Ike asked.

Erwin took his headset off and ran his fingers through his long, shaggy hair. "The living room stuff was a bit lame, but we probably won't have to use much of it. The fall down the stairs was excellent and we got some great reaction shots from the foyer cameras. Even the stuff in the basement afterward was pretty good."

Ike nodded. "I didn't expect there would be so much tension between the contestants so early on."

Erwin shrugged. "There's no way we can predict how each of them is going to react once the cameras started rolling."

"But we tested them all."

"Yeah." Erwin laughed. "But now there's some real money at stake."

Ike nodded. "Yeah, all right. That, I can understand."

Erwin glanced up at the wall of television screens. Most of them were blank since the only feeds they were interested in at the moment were the ones coming from the basement. A couple of contestants were just sort of mulling around, checking out tools and looking behind curtains, while the others were reviewing what they'd taped, or were doing interviews about the disappearance of Radko.

Downtime.

"Where are those files?" Erwin asked.

An assistant brought over five file folders, one for each of the remaining contestants. He shuffled through the files until he found the one he wanted, then opened it up and quickly flipped through it to refresh his memory.

"What's up?" Ike asked.

"I'll give them about five more minutes to relax and finish their interviews," Erwin said with a mischievous smile on his face. "Then I'm going to turn up the heat."

"Going after anyone in particular?"

Erwin tapped the file folder on the top of the pile. "She's gonna freak out."

Ike clasped his hands together and rubbed the heels of his palms against each other. "That's why we're here."

There was a sound, like something scraping against the cement floor, coming from a dark corner of the room.

"Did you hear that?" Vonda said.

"Came from over there," Jody said, gesturing toward the corner with a flick of her head.

"What was it?" Vonda wanted to know.

Melanie casually looked over at the corner, then turned back around. "Whatever it was, it's not there now."

Tamisha let out a scream, then jumped off as if the chair she'd been sitting on was on fire.

"What is it?"

"What's wrong?"

She looked down at the floor. "There was something at my feet, crawling over them like . . . like . . ."

"Like rats?" offered Forrest.

"Yes, like rats."

"What's the matter, girlfriend?" Melanie asked. "You never had any rats in your hood?"

Tamisha just glared back at Melanie.

Jody was also startled by something touching her left foot. Her body jerked in surprise but she made sure not to cry out. "They're on the floor," she said, trying to keep her voice as steady as steel.

"Oh my God, I can't stand rats!" Vonda shrieked. "Ow, get it off me." She kicked out her leg and a ball of dirty grayish fur sailed across the room.

"Relax," said Melanie, "there's only a few of them. And they're not even that big." She picked one up by the scruff of the neck and held it out to Vonda.

"No, get it away from me," Vonda cried, backing away from Melanie and the rat.

"Oh, he's so cute."

"No, they're not cute." Vonda was still backing away. "They carry filth and disease. . . ."

"Oh, come on. They let them loose down here just to scare us," Melanie insisted. "I've seen wild rats before and these aren't them. These little guys came out of a pet shop."

Vonda shook her head, and seemed to be having trouble breathing. "About ten years ago my mom got a part playing a homeless woman in a Christmas movie-of-the-week. The network wanted her to research the part so we went and brought meals to a bunch of homeless people living in San Francisco's Tenderloin." She took a moment to catch her breath. "When we met this one homeless family they were so happy to see us, they called for their daughter to come see my mother, but the girl never came. We started to look for her and after a while I found her in one of the back rooms of this abandoned house. She was sleeping, or I thought she was. . . . She wouldn't wake up, and when I pulled the blanket back, there were three rats gnawing on her toes. She was just a little girl, same age as I was . . . and she bled to death in her sleep . . . because of the rats."

The rest of the contestants were silent.

Melanie slowly put down the rat she was holding, a bit of the self-confidence gone from her face.

As soon as the rat was on the floor, it started moving toward Vonda, as if it wanted something from her.

"Get them away from me." Vonda was pleading now.

Jody looked around for a broom or something to sweep the rats away, but there was nothing like that lying around the basement. So she began clapping her hands and shouting to try and scare the rats away . . .

"Shoo! Go away! Scat!"

. . . but the rats seemed interested solely in Vonda.

Vonda backed up the stairs slowly, her wide eyes locked on the rats climbing up the risers after her.

"Make them stop!" she cried, now on the verge of tears.

"Come down," Forrest said, extending his hand to her. "I'll help you."

"No," Vonda replied. "I want out!"

She tried the door at the top of the stairs.

It was locked and wouldn't open.

The rats kept ascending, sniffing in Vonda's direction between steps.

Vonda pushed and banged on the door a few more times; then she stopped and slumped down on the top step.

The door wouldn't open.

She was trapped.

And the rats just kept on coming.

Vonda curled up into a tight ball, making herself as small as she could, and began to sob.

Seventeen

"What's wrong with the door?" Erwin asked.

William Olsen, the location manager who had been watching from the back of the trailer, stepped up next to Erwin and said, "Don't know. It never got stuck before."

"You mean we didn't set that up to be locked?"

"Not that I know of."

"It's a great bit, but"—Erwin threw up his hands—"it's over now and she wants to get out of there."

Olsen looked over to Roger Kettyls, one of his assistants who was standing by the door to the trailer. "Go and check it out!"

In a moment the young man was gone.

While they waited for him to get inside and open the door, Ike pointed to one of the screens. Vonda was sobbing uncontrollably as the rats continued to move farther up the stairs, closer to her feet. "How'd you do that?" he asked.

"Do what?"

"Make all the rats ignore everyone else and concentrate just on her?"

Erwin let out a giggle. "The animal wrangler, Ryan Mayhew . . . he dabbed a bit of rat pheromone on her shoes before they came out to the house."

"It's working great."

"Of course it is," Erwin said, his slight grin turning

somewhat devilish. "Those rats will follow her anywhere. They think she's in heat."

"Oh, Christ!"

There was a crackling sound on Olsen's two-way radio.

"Yeah," Olsen said, holding the radio close to his ear. "Door works fine."

"Then get out of there."

All eyes moved to the screens where the assistant was hurrying through the foyer and out the front door.

"Okay, Vonda McNair," Erwin said to the bank of screens, "the door's open, what are you going to do now?"

Roger Kettyls closed the door to the house as silently as he could. He couldn't be sure what was happening inside now that the door to the basement was open, but he didn't want the sound of the closing front door to be caught by any of the mikes in the foyer.

He turned to head back to the trailer, but stopped when he heard the sound of something moving in the bushes at the end of the porch.

"Somebody there?" he whispered.

He waited for a response, but heard only the gentle *shhh!* of the wind brushing past the trees.

"Is there a problem?" he tried again.

Nothing.

There were countless sound and video cables lying all over the place, so it was possible that there *was* someone out here doing some troubleshooting. *It would be nice if they answered me, though,* he thought.

Roger waited another few moments while a growing sense of unease began to wash over him. He took one last glance down the length of the porch, then dashed back to the production trailer before Olsen would start to wonder what had happened to him.

Moments later he was stepping back into the trailer.

He wasn't sure why, but it felt good to be back with the rest of the crew.

One of the rats, a persistent black and gray one, had grabbed hold of the toe of one of Vonda's Reeboks. She didn't see it at first because she had her eyes closed tight while she cried. But then she opened her eyes, and through the blur of tears saw this rat sniffing her shoe as if it were something to eat.

"Get away!" she said, kicking out her foot and sending the rat flying through the air where it hit Tamisha square in the chest.

Tamisha swatted at the rat, jumping and dancing about as if her blouse were on fire.

Vonda began pounding on the door, screaming to be let out. Finally she tried the handle again and . . .

It turned.

The door opened up to the main floor.

Vonda scrambled to her feet, ran into the hallway, then through the foyer and out the front door.

She stopped out on the porch, one hand against a post as she struggled to catch her breath. She wiped her face with the inside of her elbow, then stood up straight and cleared the tears from her eyes with her hands. Her fingers came away smudged with mascara.

"Oh God, I must look like Tammy Fay Bakker," she said, using the tips of her fingers to wipe the mascara more delicately from beneath her eyes. "And I bet I looked really good down inside. . . ."

The last word seemed to echo off the outer walls of the house.

Inside.

She'd been inside.

And now she was *outside*.

Outside and out of the game.

"No," she said, stomping a foot down onto the porch.

She was out of the game. She knew that. It was one of the rules they'd talked about before they went in. But she was Vonda McNair. . . . Her name was going to help sell the show. That's what they'd told her when they'd interviewed her. Surely they wouldn't want her out of the show already. And how far out of the house was she? Still on the porch. That was still part of the house. And she hadn't been outside for very long. A minute? Two?

There weren't even any cameras out here. . . .

And the door was still open.

She could sneak back in, say she just went out for a breath of fresh air, to clear her head. Surely they wouldn't begrudge her that after what happened down in the basement.

She took a tentative step toward the door.

Only to see it slam shut in her face.

"Scratch one *Scream Queen* contestant," Erwin said as he watched the door slam shut on the screen in front of him.

Ike shook his head in disbelief. "She can't be out. We need four contestants for the viewers to vote on."

"Ike, we're taping this live. What do you want me to do, call her back in and have her redo it?"

"They do stuff like that on *Junkyard Wars* all the time, don't they?"

Erwin folded his arms across his chest. "You really want to give Vonda McNair another chance to be the star in our next feature film?"

Ike was silent a long time.

"I didn't think so," Erwin said, turning back around to face the screens. "Besides, judging by the way she slammed that door, I don't think we could drag her back inside with a team of Clydesdales."

"Yeah, I supposed you're right. Still, we should send someone out to get her. I don't want her wandering off into the woods and tripping over a log. The last thing we need is Jennifer McNair taking us to court for letting something bad happen to her baby girl."

"I'm on it," said Olsen.

The location manager looked over at Roger Kettyls and flicked his head in a gesture that would send the young man outside to fetch Vonda McNair.

Roger hesitated a moment, took a deep breath, then slowly exited the trailer.

"Let me in," Vonda cried. "I didn't mean to go outside, I swear." She pounded on the front door of the house and tried the handle, but it was locked, just as the door to the basement had been.

She stood up straight and took a long look around her.

Thankfully, there were no cameras here. But they'd already got a great shot of her running out of the house as if her hair were on fire, and then the door slamming shut behind her like there was no way she was ever going back inside.

"Bastards!" she spat. "They know I can't stand rats and—"

There was something, or somebody, over in the bushes. Probably a production assistant come to get her and bring her to some trailer where she could sit out the night in comfort.

"Okay," she said. "I guess that's it, then. I'm done."

There was more movement in the bushes.

She looked out into the darkness, but couldn't see anyone there. "I said, you can take me away now. . . . I could use a cup of coffee anyway."

More rustling, this time across the lawn, but still no sign of there being anyone there.

"Look, this isn't funny. You don't have to try and scare me anymore. I'm out of the game, I couldn't hack it, okay? There aren't even any cameras out here."

For the first time since she stepped outside, Vonda began to feel the cold night air pressing against her flesh.

She also felt fear.

But not the same fear as when she'd seen the rats. That had been a panicky and irrational sort of thing that came over her in a flash and burned white hot until it was done. This, on the other hand, was a dull ache of fear that wrapped its arms around her and squeezed her tight until she felt trapped and afraid to move.

"Is someone th-there?" Her voice was cracking, and her mouth was suddenly very dry.

She stepped off the porch and turned right. There were supposed to be people out that way, soundmen and grips.

"Hello?"

She glanced back at the house. It seemed so far away now, as if the entire building were shrinking from view.

Vonda gasped as something touched the back of her neck.

She turned around quickly, but there was no one there.

"Where are you?" she said.

For several moments there was nothing, and then movement again. It was hard to discern at first, a shadow in the darkness. But as the seconds passed, a dark form began to take shape.

It moved toward her without effort, gliding over the grass as if riding along on a cushion of air.

Vonda opened her mouth to scream, but no sound escaped her lips.

And so she stood there, unable to speak and unable to move as the dark figure approached, then swirled around her.

Vonda could feel a warm wetness beginning to run down the inside of her right leg, and for the briefest of moments, she was glad there were no cameras out here to record her moment of shame.

The thing was behind her now. She could feel the coolness radiating from it, like the open crack of a refrigerator door on an hot California day.

It moved in close to her, sliding over her shoulders and around her neck like a cool stream of water.

And then it was inside her, passing through her body as if she weren't even there.

Vonda struggled to catch her breath.

Her body was wracked by needle-sharp shards of pain and suffering.

Screaming men.

Crying children.

Dying women.

And then it was outside her.

She suddenly felt old and tired, and for the first time in her life she wanted to tell the world that she didn't *want* to be in show business anymore. Never wanted to be in it in the first place. She wanted a family and a career of her own, something that was hers and had nothing to do with her damn mother.

She opened her eyes and it was there in front of her.

A figure of shadow and black.

She turned to run.

Run away.

But a cold, dead hand reached out from the darkness, grabbed her firmly by the hair, and violently pulled her backward, almost knocking her off her feet.

Something *zinged* in the air.

Then searing heat across her neck, starting from the left side and burning straight through to the right.

She could feel the warm fluid, her blood, flowing over her shoulder, down her back, and across her chest.

It was a pleasant feeling, and then it was gone . . .
As her head came away from her shoulders.

All was quiet.
Except for the wind in the trees . . .
And the hum of a few distant generators . . .
And the sound of the dark figure retreating into the shadows, a headless body in one hand, and a severed head in the other.
A few moments later, footsteps.
And then a voice called out.
"Miss McNair? Hello. Are you there?"
No answer.

Eighteen

"Well," said Forrest, looking up the stairs where Vonda had been just moments before, "that's one way to get yourself noticed."

Melanie laughed. "Yeah, right, hysterical is definitely the way to go."

"I didn't say it was the way to win this thing, only a way to get noticed."

"That kind of attention I can do without."

"You think we should go after her?" Jody asked. It didn't seem right to let someone as terrified as Vonda be alone in the house.

"To hell with her," Tamisha cut in. "She's on her own now as far as I'm concerned. She don't need to win this thing anyway. When this is all over, she'll be just fine back home poolside in Beverly Hills with her mother."

Jody couldn't argue with that logic. Of all the contestants, Vonda McNair's lifestyle was the one that would be least affected by the winning of *Scream Queen*. But then Jody was struck by another, more sinister thought. Maybe Vonda was also more savvy about the way Hollywood worked and she had used the rats to help her play out a big terror scene that would show her vulnerability. And now that she'd gotten that out of the way, she was wandering the house, giving herself all kinds of solo time in front of the cameras.

"What if she did it on purpose?" Jody said.

"What?" Melanie said.

Tamisha tilted her head to one side. "What do you mean?"

"She's from an acting family. What if she was just pretending to be scared so she'd have an excuse to get away from the rest of us?"

The others were silent, thinking about it.

"And now she's off on her own, exploring the house by herself with all kinds of chances to play the hero."

Tamisha put her hands on her hips and looked critically at Jody. "You think we've been had?"

Jody shrugged. "I don't know all that much about Hollywood, but if I've learned anything so far it's that nothing is really what it seems. She might have been scared to death, or she might have just been acting."

Tamisha threw a hand up in the air. "Oh, that's just great," and turned away from Jody.

"Hold on, hold on," Forrest cut in. "We've still got all night ahead of us. And remember that the winner isn't going to be doing a monologue on Broadway, but a horror movie with a large ensemble cast. So if she is off by herself, she's no closer to winning this thing than any of us are right here."

"That's right!"

Tamisha and Melanie both nodded, as if they liked the sounds of what Forrest was saying.

Jody, however, still wasn't convinced.

"Enough downtime," Erwin said. "We need to put some life back into this show. What have we got down in the basement we can use?"

One of Andy Matheson's assistants handed Erwin a handwritten list.

"All right, then . . . let's give them all a little chill. Turn on the cooling units down there and send the cold air through the middle of the room."

A technician at the other end of the room passed on the direction, then reported back. "It's on."

"Good, now let's see what kind of goose bumps we can get out of these girls."

Just then the door to the trailer opened up and Roger Kettyls stepped inside, a little winded and obviously alone.

Ike looked at the man for several seconds, waiting for a report.

"What?" Roger asked.

Ike shook his head in disgust. "Where's Vonda?"

"Oh, that." Roger took a breath. "I couldn't find her."

"What do you mean, you couldn't find her?" Ike said.

"She wasn't anywhere outside the house."

"You called out for her?"

"Yes."

"And she didn't answer?"

"No."

"Where could she have gone?"

Erwin turned away from the wall of screens a moment. "There are some woods out on one side of the house, maybe she's in there."

"And what would she be doing out in the woods in the middle of the night?"

Erwin looked up into the corner of the trailer and put his hand up as if he were putting words up on a marquee. "TV star's daughter lost on set of reality television fright fest—reappears with fantastic story on morning after final episode gets record ratings."

Ike looked at his brother in disbelief. "You don't think she's sharp enough to pull something like that off, do you?"

Erwin shook his head. "No, but her mother sure is. And if her mother isn't, then the team of publicists she might have hired would be."

"Aw, fuck!"

"It's just a thought, Ike."

"Yeah, but what a thought."

"Look, we've got her on tape running out of the house like a crazy woman. If she wants to keep running into the woods, that's her problem. I don't think we're liable for something like that."

The production's lawyer was there with them, sitting in one of the seats at the far end of the trailer, watching the show along with the parapsychologist Feroze Mohammed. Ike glanced over at the woman, raising his eyebrows as if to ask, "Well, how about it?"

She nodded. "Your brother's right. If she was scared, it would make more sense for her to run to the trailers . . . where there are people."

That was all Ike needed to know.

"Fuck Vonda McNair, then. Let's get on with the show."

"Still . . ." the lawyer said.

"What is it?"

"It wouldn't hurt to have someone keep looking for her, you know, just in case she is lost and in trouble and a judge asks you what effort you made to find her."

Ike sighed. "Right." He looked over at Roger Kettyls. "Keep looking for her."

"Is it just me, or has it gotten cold in here all of a sudden?" Melanie said.

Jody looked over at her and noticed the woman's nipples were hard and jutting up from beneath her clingy top. Then she glanced down at her own chest and was pleased to see that her own nipples were trying to garner a little attention of their own. "It's cold in here," Jody said.

"But it's been warm up till now, even down here in the basement."

"Maybe it's the ghosts," Jody suggested.

"Oh, come on . . ." Tamisha moaned.

"No, I'm serious, that's what they say drafts and cold spots are in haunted houses like this one. The spirits of the dead traveling from room to room. If the cold is in the same spot all the time, then it's either the ghosts' favorite spot in the house when they were alive, or the place were they ended their life."

"Who says that? Who's they?"

"Paranormal researchers, parapsychologists, experts on the occult . . . That's why they rely on thermometers so much when they investigate haunted houses. A sudden drop in air temperature is a good indication of the presence of a ghost or spirit."

"That's very interesting," Tamisha said, moving about the basement trying to find someplace warm. "Now stop it, all right? You're freaking me out."

"Sorry. I'm just trying to let you know what's going on."

"No, you're not trying to let us know what's going on, you're trying to throw us off. I feel cold, and Melanie feels cold, and all of a sudden you're telling us that it's the ghosts. And just a few minutes before that you're trying to tell us that Vonda McNair is some kind of smart-ass white girl who's playing us all for the fool."

"But I didn't—"

"Let me tell *you* something! Vonda McNair is just some spoon-fed, milquetoast piece of white trash that was lucky enough to be born into a family with money. She's probably off in some corner right now with crap in her panties wondering how she's going to come out of this looking good."

Tamisha stopped a moment, but only to take a breath.

"And the cold we're feeling ain't no ghosts or spirits or anything like that. I've never been in a basement that didn't get cold at night, and that's all that's happening here. All right?"

Jody was taken aback by the woman's confrontational tone, but thought that maybe this was Tamisha's attempt to show the tougher side of her personality. Or maybe something Jody had said had touched a nerve and Tamisha was just venting some of her frustration. Or, maybe she was just scared, like they all were, and this was the only way she was able to handle the emotion.

"Hey, come on now, she's just playing the game," Forrest said, a bit of a smile forming at the corners of his mouth. "I thought a street-smart girl from the hood like you would have seen that right off."

"Yeah, what do you know about it?"

"Well, I know that this is basically a popularity contest. And the name of the game is making yourself look good while making the other guy look bad. So what if she tells you the cold is from the ghosts? How you handle that suggestion is how you're going to be judged by the viewing audience."

"I don't believe this," Tamisha said, throwing up her hands in despair. "You're taking her side instead of mine. Siding with her instead of giving a sista a break."

Forrest just shook his head. "How long you plan on playing that hand?"

"What are you talking about?"

"You keep talking about black and white like somebody owes you something."

Tamisha didn't say anything.

"Well, that's not going to work here. Not with me it isn't."

"Is that right?"

"That's right, because the people voting are going to be all colors," he said, "and they aren't going to look at you and see a black bitch, they're going to look at you and just see a bitch."

Tamisha lunged forward, as if she might try to hurt

Forrest, but she was halted by a cry coming from the far corner of the basement.

Everyone turned to look at Melanie, who was over by the eastern wall, where the house's boiler sat.

There was blood on her face, and a bright red spatter down the front of her top.

Melanie ran a hand over her face and it came away smeared with blood. "Am I bleeding?" she said, the fear evident in her voice, and on her face.

Jody and Forrest hurried to her side, looking for any cuts or wounds.

They found nothing.

"You're fine," Jody said.

"Then where's the blood coming from?"

Jody felt a drop strike her shoulder. She stepped back and noticed a pool of blood had formed on the concrete floor next to where Melanie had been standing. Then she looked up and saw that the blood was dripping down from the floorboards and wooden beams over their heads.

"There!"

The blood was leaking out from the cracks between the boards, running over the beam and then dripping onto the floor a few feet away from the source.

Tamisha gasped. "Where is that coming from?"

Forrest looked up at the growing bloodstain. "Maybe Vonda had a little accident up on the main floor—"

"Oh my God," Melanie cried out, doing her best to wipe the blood from her face, neck, and hands.

"—or maybe it's just a goof."

"What do you mean?"

"You know, maybe it's rigged. A special effect. A trick."

Jody put her right hand against the wall to steady herself, then went down on one knee to check the blood on floor. She ran her left index finger through the puddle and brought the finger close to her face for a closer look. Even though the light was dim, it still appeared to be real blood. She brought her finger in front of her nose and sniffed at it. Something about it didn't smell right. Jody held out her left hand and waited for the next drop to fall. When it spattered onto her palm, she brought her hand to her mouth and tasted the blood with her tongue. It was sweet, not at all like the coppery taste real blood usually has.

"It's a fake!" she said.

"What?"

"It's fake blood." She brought her hand to her mouth again to taste the spot on her palm. "It's sweet, like it's made out of sugar or something."

"Damn it!" Melanie exclaimed angrily, probably because she'd really been terrified by the blood . . . and everyone had seen her.

Tamisha smiled. "Wow! That was a good one."

"Had you going there, didn't it?" Forrest said to Melanie.

Melanie was in no mood for laughter. "Shut up!"

"It would have scared the hell out of me," Jody said, trying to keep the peace.

Just then Tamisha pointed to Jody's right hand. "What about that blood?"

"What?"

"On your other hand," she said, pointing. "It's covered in blood, too."

Jody brought her right hand up so she could see it and sure enough, it was covered in blood, as well. Jody didn't understand. She'd traced her left-hand fingers through the puddle on the floor and she'd put her right hand up against—

Jody felt herself go faint.

The wall was bleeding.

"Whoa!" Tamisha said approvingly. "Now *that* is cool."

Jody stared at the wall in terror. She could understand how blood might drip through the cracks in the wooden floorboards, but she couldn't see how the special effects people could make the walls bleed. And the blood wasn't leaking out of holes in the bricks, or running down from the crevice at the top of the wall where it butted up against the floor above. . . . The wall itself was *bleeding*, the crimson liquid seeping out of the bricks like sweat from skin.

"That is an awesome effect." Forrest nodded approvingly. "They ever use that in one of their films?"

Jody felt herself trembling.

She brought her right hand to her face and before it even got close she could smell the foulness of the blood. She didn't want to taste it because real blood, she knew, carried disease. So instead, she held her hand in front of her face, opened her mouth and inhaled deeply through both her mouth, and nose at the same time.

The smell of it made her want to vomit.

It was if she were holding a handful of dirty pennies.

Dirty copper pennies.

Somehow, this blood was real.

"Freaked me right out," Melanie said.

Forrest clapped his hands together. "Nice try, Gowan brothers."

"Didn't scare me one bit," Tamisha said.

"Yeah, right."

"Sure," the others said.

Jody said nothing, having already decided that trying to convince the others the blood was real wouldn't be worth the effort.

Besides, knowing that the house was either truly haunted or that the Gowan brothers were capable of even more complex levels of deception would make her more wary, and the knowledge just might give her an advantage over the others.

That, and she didn't want to let anyone know she was more afraid than she'd ever been in her life.

Nineteen

"Can we get a close-up of the wall?" Erwin asked.

The camera operators on his right began to fiddle with the zoom and aperture of the cameras mounted in the basement.

Meanwhile on-screen, several of the contestants were taping the bleeding walls with their own handheld Digital Handycams.

"Okay, that's good, but is there any way we can get it looking more red?"

"Can't we do that afterward in post?" Ike asked.

"Sure," Erwin answered. "But if we can get the right color here, it'll look way more real."

"Looks pretty real as it is."

Erwin turned halfway toward his brother, an ear-to-ear smile on his face. "It does, doesn't it?"

"Did you do it?"

"I'd love to tell you it's mine, but it's not."

"Then whose effect is it?"

"I don't know," Erwin said, glancing down at the sheet of paper in front of him. "The effect's not on this list." Erwin looked up and turned to his right. "All right, whose idea was it to make the walls bleed?"

No one answered.

"It's a great effect, maybe even worthy of a performance bonus."

Suddenly, there was no shortage of people willing to take the credit for it.

"It's mine."

"I did it."

"My idea."

"I'm the one."

"All right, you guys, very funny."

Ike tried to recall budgeting the money for the effect, but couldn't. "But if you didn't know about it, and no one else is taking credit for it—"

"Andy," Erwin said at last. "It had to be Andy. He probably set it up the night he died and rigged it so the walls would bleed when we cued the overhead drip in that corner."

"Yeah, that makes sense."

Erwin dragged his fingertips lightly across his forehead as if he felt pain there. "Andy was good at coming up with stuff like that. . . ." He shook his head. "Man, I miss him."

Ike put a hand on his brother's shoulder. "He's going to be pretty hard to replace, that's for damn sure."

"I think we're about done down here," Forrest said.

Melanie looked at Forrest with a bit of a sneer on her face. "Who died and made you boss?"

"Okay, fine by me," Forrest said, sitting down and making himself comfortable. "We'll stay here for as long as you like; just let me know when you want to leave."

Melanie nodded her head slowly as if she was more than satisfied with Forrest's response. It was obvious that she thought she'd just wrested some control from him, but Jody felt that just the opposite had happened. Forrest seemed too sure of himself to let someone else be in control. And for the first time since they'd entered the house, she wondered if *he* might be the one who was a part of the production. It sure was a nice fit with everything he'd said so far, and all she knew about him—as little as that was.

But before she could articulate that thought, she heard a low growl coming from the corner of the basement where a workbench and washbasin stood gathering dust. It was a soft sort of sound, like the breathing of some great beast. And it was wet, too, as if whatever it was had a slobbering tongue, a great wide maw, and rows of jagged, deadly teeth.

It was obvious to Jody that the sound was artificial, initiated by the crew in the production trailer to convince them to start moving on through the house. Even so, it was very effective in making the basement one of the last places any of them wanted to spend any more of their time.

"I think we've seen everything we need to see down here, don't you, Tamisha?" Jody said, trying to get them moving.

There was a hint of fear in the woman's eyes. "Yeah, back upstairs is a good idea."

Melanie looked as if being the one in charge no longer held an appeal for her. "All right, all right. What can I do?" She shrugged, as if things were absolutely out of her control. "I'm outvoted three to one." She seemed eager to leave, especially since the suggestion to leave had come from someone other than Forrest.

Forrest got up from his chair without a word, ready to join them.

As Jody headed for the stairs, Melanie gave her a sideways glance and Jody knew right away that the look was meant to say, *Thank you.*

Jody smiled back at her, just happy they were on the move.

They headed up the stairs in single file and then stepped one at a time into the foyer. It was just as they'd left it, except now a desk lamp against one of the walls was on, giving them just enough light to see.

"Vonda?" Forrest called out as the four contestants gathered in the foyer.

Jody wondered where she'd gone, as well. "Vonda, are you here?"

Tamisha and Melanie didn't say a word.

"Vonda," Forrest tried again. "We're all here now. It's okay. You can come out and join us if you want."

"Yeah, there's no rats here," Tamisha said under her breath.

Melanie laughed. "At least not very big ones, anyway."

The two women cackled and gave each other a high five.

"Quit foolin' around, you two." Forrest went down the hall and poked his head into the kitchen, then came back and checked the dining room.

"What's the matter?" Jody asked.

"She's not here."

"Maybe she went upstairs."

They all looked up the staircase at the darkness of the second floor. There were several rooms up there, all of them dark and ominous and scary as hell. They'd have to visit those rooms before the night was done, but no one in their right mind would head up there before they had to, especially if they'd run out of the basement scared out of their minds.

That left just one possibility.

"You think she went outside?" Jody asked.

Forrest didn't answer right away, but then he said, "It sure looks that way."

"I knew she couldn't handle it," Tamisha said, barely able to contain herself. "That girl's been spoon-fed all her life and the minute things start getting rough, she's running home to her momma."

Jody had her camera focused on Tamisha, making sure

she got a good close-up of the woman while she talked. Jody's mom had always told her that you never got ahead by bringing others around you down. Tamisha's little rant about Vonda might go over well with some in the viewing audience, but Jody was willing to bet it was going to lose her more votes than it won. So what if Vonda had bailed early? She probably had her reasons, especially if that story she told about the rat was true. Just the thought of it chilled Jody, and it made her wonder about what the Gowan brothers might have in store for her.

"I hope she's all right," Jody said, sitting down on the second-to-last step of the stairs heading up to the second floor. It made sense to remain as rested as possible before they ventured farther into the house.

"Don't worry, she'll be taken care of." Forrest sighed. "Who knows, maybe she even did it so she could do all the talk shows during the week between the first and second episodes."

Jody just shook her head. There seemed to be no end to the number of angles in which something could be played out in Hollywood. The trick wasn't so much figuring out an angle, as deciding on the right angle to choose, the one that would be the next stepping-stone down the path to success.

"Well, whatever happened to Vonda McNair," Melanie said, the spikes of her heels clicking hollowly against the wooden floorboards, "it's obvious that she's not in the house anymore, which means she's no longer in the game."

Tamisha's face brightened. "That's right! There's only four of us now. And only three of us are women, so we all just had our chances of winning the game and getting the part in the movie improved by twenty-five percent."

"Actually, it's just eight percent," Jody said.

"What?"

"Well, if there was a part for a female lead, we had a one-in-four chance before, which is twenty-five percent. Now our chances are one in three, and that's thirty-three percent, eight percent better than our chances were before."

"Sure," Tamisha said. "Whatever."

Melanie laughed. "Actually, your odds are still the same, girlfriends. Vonda McNair wasn't winning anything."

"I'm with that—"

Something snapped above them.

The smaller of the two foyer chandeliers fell from the ceiling.

Jody looked up, saw the ornate fixture coming toward her, but couldn't do anything but watch it fall.

Crash!

It sounded as if a car had smashed into the side of the house. Glass and metal broke apart, sending pieces and shards flying in all directions.

Jody jumped back and brought her hands to her face to shield her eyes, but still felt something strike her leg.

"What the hell was that supposed to be?" Tamisha cried.

Forrest pointed to the empty space on the ceiling. There was a blank, almost dumbfounded look on his face. "The chandelier fell from the ceiling."

"I can *see* that," Tamisha sneered.

Melanie was brushing glass crystals off her jeans. "I think she means something like, *Are they trying to fucking kill us now or what?*"

"Exactly. I signed up for a reality television show that's supposed to scare me, not kill me. I ain't being paid enough to take these kinds of chances."

Forrest went to Tamisha's side. "But everyone's okay, right?"

"I'll live."

"Me, too."

Jody wanted to answer positively, too, but there was a

pain in her leg that didn't feel right. "I think I'm hurt," she said.

Forrest was on the stairs a moment later. "Let me see."

She looked down at her leg and saw that one of the glass crystals from the chandelier had cut into the muscle next to her shinbone. The muscle was called the *Tibialis anticus,* and why that bit of trivia came to her mind, Jody had no idea. All she knew for sure was that it hurt like hell.

And she was bleeding.

Bleeding all down her leg.

Onto the steps . . .

And floor.

"What the fuck happened there?" Ike shouted.

Erwin looked down the line of technicians to his right. "Who cued the chandelier?"

Every head was shaking.

"Well, *somebody* did." Erwin stood up, pushed his chair aside, and began to pace back and forth in what little room he had inside the trailer. "And whose bright idea was it to have the chandelier *fall* from the ceiling? Christ, any one of those people could have ended up dead . . . which would have been perfect since we've already had one person die setting the damn thing up!"

Someone cleared his throat. "Uh, that wasn't the chandelier that was rigged."

Erwin stopped in midpace. "What?"

"That wasn't the chandelier that was rigged to fall. Andy was working on the rig for the big chandelier when he died."

"Then how did that one fall?"

"Uh . . . I'm not sure. As far as I know that one wasn't rigged to do anything but light up."

"What the hell is going on here?" Erwin said, slamming

a fist on the desk in front of him. "How many other things are going to happen tonight that I don't know about?"

Nobody said a word.

Erwin took a deep breath, then turned back toward the wall of screens. "Is everyone okay in there?"

"It looks like one of them is hurt."

"Which one?"

"The blonde. Jody."

"Oh, great. We're going to be a huge hit, but we won't have a pot to piss in when the contestants sue our asses for trying to kill them on national television."

"You wanted to try the small screen," Ike said. "People die on movie sets all the time and you hardly ever hear a thing about it. If it happens on a TV show, on a network that has its own news division . . . you never hear the end of it."

"Oh, you're being a real help, Ike."

"Uh, Mr. Gowan?" The voice belonged to the show's lawyer.

Both Ike and Erwin turned to face her. "What?" they said, almost in unison.

"You don't have to worry about being sued."

"No, why not?"

"Well, the waiver signed by each of the contestants was quite comprehensive. It protects you personally, as well as Gowan Brothers Entertainment and the network, against any and all civil suits relating to injuries, or even deaths, that occur during the taping of the show."

"So what you're saying is we're in the clear?"

"Not exactly. The police can always lay criminal negligence charges against you, but as far as being sued goes, you're fine."

"Thanks," said Erwin. "That's good to know."

"Yeah, thanks," echoed Ike. "I feel a whole lot better knowing that."

"There's something else." This time it was the voice of the parapsychologist.

Ike was in no mood for whatever it was. "What is it?"

"You might want to consider halting the production, I mean, just until you can be sure that the house is safe."

"What!"

"Blood has been spilled inside the house. Real blood. The spirits will be fully awakened now, both inside and out."

"Give me a break."

"I am trying to do just that, Mr. Gowan. The spirits will become stronger as the night goes on. You should get those people out *now,* because if they remain, there is no telling what might happen to them by morning."

Ike smiled and glanced around the trailer. "Can somebody get that on tape?"

"This is no laughing matter," Feroze persisted. "If you ignore my warnings, I will have to seriously consider disassociating my name from the show."

"Fine, fine, whatever. . . ."

Feroze sat back in his chair, arms crossed. He was shaking his head and muttering softly under his breath.

Ike and Erwin turned their attention back to the screens. It was looking as if the girl wasn't too badly hurt.

"Andy Matheson," Ike muttered.

"What?" asked Erwin.

"Andy Matheson," Ike repeated. "He must have done something to the chandelier."

"To make it fall?"

"Maybe, or maybe he touched it while he was working on the other chandelier. You know . . . made it loose or something."

Erwin shrugged. "It's hard to think Andy would be that careless, but I suppose it's possible."

"That asshole," Ike hissed. "Putting us in a spot like this.

If he wasn't already dead, I'd kill him right now with my own bare hands."

Erwin ignored his brother's grumbling, as well as the warnings of the parapsychologist.

They were shooting a television show here, for crying out loud. Andy had been a good man, a great special effects man, and he did great work. These things were just glitches, and they happened all the time. The only ghosts inside that house were the ones *they* put there. They were the Gowan brothers. They made vampires and monsters, they made werewolves and demons, and they made the goddamn ghosts inside the goddamn house!

"All right," he said, "let's see if we can get through the night without getting anyone killed."

Twenty

"It's a pretty deep cut," Forrest said, after rolling up Jody's pant leg and taking a closer look at the wound.

"Will it need stitches?"

"Probably, but first we have to worry about getting that piece of glass out of your leg."

Jody wasn't looking forward to that.

Forrest looked over his shoulder at the other two women. "Any of you ever take any premed courses?"

Tamisha laughed. "I've been done with school for a while now."

"I went out with a med student once," said Melanie. "For all his study of the human body, he didn't know his way around mine very well."

"Come on, I'm serious," Forrest said. "She's hurt and if you could do anything to help, I'd appreciate it."

Melanie reluctantly got to her feet. "I think they said there's a first-aid kit in the bathroom."

"Can you get it please?"

Melanie headed for the bathroom.

Forrest looked at Jody. "It won't stop bleeding until I pull out the glass."

"Then do it!"

"It's going to hurt . . . a lot."

"It already hurts like hell."

Without another word, Forrest grabbed a firm hold of

Jody's leg with his left hand. "Help me hold her leg steady."

Tamisha came over and put her hands around Jody's knee.

"Okay, I'm going to do it on three."

Jody nodded.

"One . . . two . . ."

Forrest yanked the glass from her leg.

Jody threw her head back and screamed. She could feel the skin on her leg folding back unnaturally, and an intense heat shooting up her leg, as if the whole appendage were on fire.

"There. It's over."

"You said on three," Jody said through clenched teeth.

He smiled. "But you would have been tense then, and it might have hurt even more."

"I don't think that would have been possible." She took a deep breath and let it out slowly.

Melanie returned with the medical kit and handed it to Forrest.

Forrest opened it up. It seemed to be pretty well stocked with bandages and disinfectants, even a small container of extra-strength Tylenol. He took out one of the thick bandages and tied it tightly around Jody's thigh to try and stanch the flow of blood. The wound wasn't bleeding as badly now, but he needed to slow down the flow so he could do a better job of patching it up. He took out a couple of bandages and poured some iodine onto them. "This should help keep it from getting infected, right?"

Jody grit her teeth, pressed her lips together as tight as she could, and nodded.

"It's going to hurt."

"I know."

Forrest took a breath, then dabbed the iodine onto

the cut. Jody did her best not to scream, but ended up letting out a sharp shriek of pain.

And then she felt herself go faint.

"Done," announced Forrest.

She was breathing hard now, and feeling rather light-headed.

"I'm going to wrap it up as best I can," Forrest said, "and it should get you through the night. But as soon as we're done in the morning, you've got to get it checked out by a doctor."

"It sounds so easy when you say it like that, especially for you guys."

"What sounds easy?"

"Making it through the night."

Forrest looked at her strangely. "What do you mean?"

Jody hesitated a moment, wondering if she should say anything at all. She decided she really had nothing to lose. "Well, I'm going to be at a disadvantage with my leg like this. I know people might think I'm soft for saying so, but when I signed on I never agreed to give blood."

"Oh," wailed Tamisha. "It's all different now, isn't it?"

Jody wasn't sure what Tamisha was talking about.

"I get hit on the head with a big ole book and nobody gives a rat's ass about it. But now . . . now the white girl's got a scratch on her leg and we're all supposed to pitch in and help her get through the night."

"It's not a scratch," Forrest corrected her. "It's actually a pretty deep cut."

"So am I supposed to feel sorry for her? What if that thing had hit me, would you all be as worried about me?"

Forrest nodded. "Yes, we would."

"Bullshit! You'd be counting me out and moving on, just like I'm doing with her. If she's hurt as bad as you say, then the door's over there. I'm sure the minute she steps outside, someone will be more than willing to take her to a hospital."

Jody looked at Tamisha in wonderment. The woman had an incredible sense of self-preservation, but apparently didn't have a clue as to how the rest of the world might perceive it. She wouldn't be winning any popularity contests any time soon and was destined to die a bitter old woman who'd never realized that she'd been her own worst enemy. It was as if she were falling down some great spiral and the more time that went by, the less likely it would be that anyone would reach down to try and lend a hand.

"You could always stay here and gather your strength while the rest of us check out the house."

Jody wasn't sure if what Melanie had just said had been said as a friend or foe. Melanie was real competition, Jody realized. She was a hot latino woman with dark hair, dark smoldering eyes, and a self-assured way about her that was difficult not to admire. She was playing the game on a couple of different levels—on looks, on personality, on toughness, and on compassion—and could very well win it all just by winking into the camera at the right moment. Jody couldn't possibly let Melanie get the upper hand, even if it killed her to go on as if there were nothing wrong with her leg.

"No, that's okay," Jody said. "I can tough it out. Besides, the three of you might need my help upstairs."

Tamisha laughed under her breath.

Melanie gave no reaction at all.

Forrest poked gently at the bandage with his finger. "I think it's stopped bleeding. Or at least it's not bleeding as badly as before."

"It's fine," Jody said, getting to her feet.

Her right leg nearly buckled from the pain and Jody could feel the cut stretching and tearing under the gauze. She could also feel fresh wetness pressing against her skin. The cut was going to bleed all night, and it would keep bleeding until she could rest the leg properly and keep it still.

That would be sometime tomorrow, after they were through with the house.

"Good as new," she said, putting weight on the leg and smiling to hide her pain. "So now there's no excuse for you guys holding me back."

"As if," said Tamisha.

"Dream on, girl," said Melanie.

Forrest just smiled at her, as if he approved of her determination.

Hopefully the viewing audience would feel the same way.

This time Roger Kettyls remembered to bring a flashlight with him. There was plenty of light shining on the outside of the house, but there were still many dark places and shadowy areas that the light just did not reach.

In fact the house was pretty spooky looking and he didn't like getting too close to it. It was an irrational fear, he knew, but it was still a powerful emotion, and he had to hand it to the contestants for having the guts to venture inside. He couldn't put his finger on it, but there was something definitely *wrong* with the house. He wouldn't go as far as to say it was haunted, but it was one of those places—like a bad neighborhood—that were simply best avoided.

But a job was a job, right?

When he'd decided on a career in the movie industry, he had envisioned himself working as an assistant director, or a cameraman, but he'd been a production assistant for three years now and the closest he'd gotten to operating a camera was loading the film for the assistant film loader. He would have been better off living in his parents' home in Sacramento and volunteering at the local public access station. At least there he'd be doing something more substantial, and gaining some real production experience while he was at it. Sure, the money was better working for the Gowan brothers, but it wasn't all that great, and he wasn't learning anything more than how to be a good gofer. If he wasn't bringing Ike Gowan a mocha latte, or the latest copy of *Variety*, he was picking up the man's Lexus from the detailers. How do you even put stuff like that into a résumé?

Roger got down onto all fours and shone his light under the front porch. There was a fair-sized crawl space under there and plenty of room for someone to hide . . . if they had a mind to.

He couldn't imagine why anyone might want to hide under there, but he'd looked just about everywhere else and hadn't seen any sign of Vonda McNair.

There had been that bloodstain on the grass at the side of the house, but that had to be fake blood. No one could lose that much blood and just walk away. If that was Vonda McNair's blood, then she had to be close by—either dying or already dead—and that just hadn't been the case so far.

She was nowhere to be seen.

But how could he go back to the production trailer and tell Ike Gowan that he couldn't find her?

"Did you check in the woods?" he'd ask, or "Did you go all the way down to the highway?"

"No," and "No," he'd say and Ike would send him back out to keep looking, having a little less confidence in his abilities than he'd had before the night began.

No, thanks.

Ike Gowan could get pretty scary himself, scarier even than the house in some ways. Ike Gowan held a large part of Roger's future in his hands. After so many years, he might promote Roger to camera assistant on the next production, or even make him an assistant director on the second or third unit. And even if he ended up being a production assistant again, Ike could put in a good word for him at another company and he might be offered those types of jobs somewhere else.

Either way, he had to keep Ike happy and if Ike wanted him to find Vonda McNair he was going to stay out all night looking for her . . .

Just then the bulb of his flashlight flickered.

. . . or for as long as his flashlight held out.

Roger tapped the flashlight against the heel of his left hand and for a moment the light went out completely.

"Oh, shit!"

And then it came back on, shining strong and bright.

Roger breathed a sigh, but then held his breath as he felt something behind him.

"Vonda? Is that you?"

He wasn't sure *what* was behind him, but there was *something* there. He could hear the grass rustling beneath it as it moved, could feel the cold press of its body against his own as it neared.

"Someone there?" he said, trying to look over his shoulder, but still unable to bring himself to turn all the way around.

Maybe there was a crew there with a camera and soundman, taping him being scared silly. Yeah, that made sense. They could use it on the DVD for a *Behind the Screams* feature or something like that.

That'd be cool.

"Very funny, guys," he said softly, not wanting to ruin the take by being too loud. "But you're not scaring me."

No response.

He decided to turn around quickly, shining his flashlight right into the camera lens. That would make a great end to the shot as everything went white. They could use that to set up just about anything they wanted.

In his mind, Roger counted one . . . two . . . three . . . then turned.

But there was no one there.

"Huh?"

Nothing there but shadows and cool night air.

Roger felt his skin begin to prickle and the hair raise up on the back of his neck.

He couldn't see anything, but he *knew* there was something there close by. He could *feel* it moving all around him.

It was evil.

And it was something to be afraid of.

To be very afraid of.

Roger took a step, carefully lifting his right foot and putting it back down onto the grass. Then his left foot, slowly. Then his right again.

He continued putting one foot in front of the other, in front of the other, in front of the other, until he was walking at a decent clip.

Then, when he'd gotten walking right, he became bold and tried running . . .

Running as fast as he could away from the house and not stopping until he was far, far away.

He'd keep looking for Vonda McNair, all night if he had to. He'd take another look around the trailers, maybe even venture out toward the highway.

But he was done searching as far as anything near the house was concerned.

If Vonda McNair was stupid enough to still be any-where near the place, she was on her own.

Twenty-one

"Who's hungry?" Forrest asked.

"I could use something to drink," said Jody.

"Coffee and a donut would be nice," Tamisha added.

Forrest glanced at his watch. "Maybe we should take a bit of a break. There's food in the kitchen, and the bathroom's here for anyone who needs it. We can hang out on this floor for a while and get rested before we head upstairs."

"Sounds good to me," Melanie said.

"We can even explore this floor a bit. There's the living room, dining room, and a storage room behind the kitchen."

"What's in it?"

Forrest shrugged. "I don't know . . . but I guess that's part of the fun."

Tamisha started down the hall toward the kitchen, using her camera to light the way. "This is nice," she said, entering the large kitchen that had obviously been given a quick face-lift prior to the production.

Jody limped down the hall behind the others. The pain in her leg was still there, only not as sharp as it had been. It was beginning to settle down into a dull ache and if it stayed that way, she might be able to make it through the night without too much of a problem. A couple of Tylenols would sure hit the spot, though.

She decided to make a detour into the bathroom to check out the medicine cabinet.

In addition to storing medicine, the bathroom was also camera-free, so if nothing else, she could at least let down her guard here for a bit and relax. As strong as she'd been so far, Jody felt a little like having a good cry. But while that might alleviate some of the pressure and tension she was feeling, not to mention the fear, she knew that once she left the bathroom, with her eyes all red and wet, the others would notice and use that against her. No, she had to be strong. Suck it up for now and carry on. If she won this thing, there'd be plenty of opportunity to cry later . . . like on her way to the bank.

She stepped into the bathroom and closed the door behind her. There was a light switch by the door, so she tried it. To her surprise the light came on and the bathroom was brightly lit. Apparently the Gowans had kept their promise of making the bathroom off-limits and not part of the show. She was thankful for that, because she could really use some downtime.

Jody pulled open the mirrored door of the medicine cabinet and found that there were several different kinds of pain relievers lined up on the shelves, including Extra-strength Tylenol. But before she took any, she put the seat down on the toilet and relieved herself. She didn't have to go all that badly, but she might as well do it while she was here. Better to do it now than all over her leg in some moment of terror later on.

When she was done, she flushed, and washed up, then opened the medicine cabinet again and took out the container of Tylenol. She was happy to see it was still safety-sealed and didn't mind having to struggle with the plastic and foil to get it open. She shook two tablets into her hand, popped them into her mouth, and washed them down with a paper cup full of water. Just knowing they were entering her system was making her feel better already.

Then she shook out four more tablets, wrapped them in the foil from the top of the container, and slipped the tiny package into a shirt pocket. She probably wouldn't need them, but judging by what had happened so far, it wouldn't hurt to be prepared.

She picked the paper cup off the sink ledge and crushed it in her hand. Jody didn't know why, but it felt good to do that, empowering. She tossed the crushed paper cup into the wastebasket, replaced the Tylenol bottle on the shelf, then closed the door of the medicine cabinet.

In the mirror, a face looked back at her.

A face that was not her own.

Jody let out a scream and backed away from the sink, slamming her back into the wall behind her.

Moments later the door to the bathroom opened up.

Forrest was standing there. "What is it?"

Tamisha and Melanie piled in behind him.

"The mirror," she said, pointing a slightly shaking hand at the medicine cabinet. "There was a face in it looking back at me. A monstrous face. Ugly."

"Easy, girl," Tamisha said. "You ain't that bad looking."

Forrest glared at her.

"No, there was a different face in there. It was bloody and bruised and maybe it was trying to say something to me."

Forrest reached over to the medicine cabinet and popped open the door. The mirror reflected their faces back at them, but as he opened the door the light caught the mirror in such a way as to make something else appear in the mirror.

"What was that?" Melanie asked.

Forrest moved the mirror back and forth, back and forth, until it was clear that there was some sort of holographic image behind the glass that could be seen when the mirror was at an angle, but was invisible when looked at straight on.

"Is that what you saw?" Forrest asked.

Jody nodded. She could hear the other two women snickering behind her. "But they said the bathroom would be off-limits."

"For cameras, maybe, but you're still in the house and the game is still on."

Jody smiled, able to breathe easier now, but only slightly. "Well then, that was a good one," she said, vowing never to let her guard down again.

They could hear people moaning in other parts of the house, even a scream or two coming up from the basement. Those things had become old hat now, even corny, and they had learned to block the sounds from their minds.

Besides, there were plenty of other things to be afraid of inside the house and you could never be sure when one of those might jump up out of the darkness and say, "Boo!"

"Who wants a sandwich?" Tamisha asked.

Jody wondered how anybody could think of eating with all that had gone on recently. "I'm not hungry," she said. "But I'll have a Diet Coke if you see one in there."

"Anyone else?"

"A couple of beers would be nice," said Forrest.

"I'll see what I can do."

She put her hand on the refrigerator's handle and was about to open it when Melanie called out to her. "If there's any carrots or celery in there, I could use something to nibble on."

Tamisha nodded, opened the door . . .

And screamed.

She slammed the refrigerator door shut and creeped backward several steps until she ran into the table and chairs behind her.

Forrest came over and stood between Tamisha and the refrigerator. "What now?"

Tamisha pointed to the fridge and stomped a foot in anger.

Jody came up behind Forrest and watched as he opened the door slowly. The light inside had been painted green, and in along with the other usual food and drinks, there were also a few body parts—a severed hand on the top shelf, a leg in the shelf on the door, and in the back of the fridge, looking very red and very fresh, was a man's severed head.

Forrest laughed and reached into the fridge.

Jody recognized the head from *The Night of the Sorority Vampires*. It was used in a scene where the hero enters the sorority house at midnight and kills one of the vampires by cutting its head off with a chain saw. The head in the refrigerator was the same head the hero ended up putting in the trash on his way out of the house.

Forrest stood up straight, a handful of hair clenched in his right hand. Dangling from the hair was a large male head, battered and bruised with the left eye bulging from an eye socket and the right eye buried behind a purple knot of bruised flesh that had pinched the eye shut. A line of fresh blood was still dripping from one corner of the mouth, and pieces of dead flesh were falling away from the tip of its nose.

Jody looked at the head with amazement. It had looked a little fake on the screen, but somehow seeing it *live* made it look all the more real.

"What's there to be afraid of?" Forrest said, laughing.

And then the bulging eyeball moved to the right, as if glancing over at Jody, and the mouth moved slightly, as if the head were trying to say something.

Forrest gasped and dropped the head onto the floor.

Now it was Tamisha's turn to laugh. "Oh, big man." Her voice was high-pitched and mocking. "What's there to be afraid of?"

"Yeah, Forrest," Melanie said, putting a hand on one of her hips. "I thought every guy wanted a little head."

Jody didn't want to laugh at the joke, but couldn't help herself.

Even Forrest gave a chuckle.

"Man, these guys are good."

Tamisha wasn't convinced. "I suppose, if you like that sort of thing."

After the fridge was emptied of snack food, Jody and the others sat down in the kitchen to have a quick bite to eat. There was no beer, so Forrest made himself a cup of instant coffee and decided to check out more of the living room.

Jody popped the top on a can of Diet Coke and glanced at her watch. They had passed less than half the night in the house and still had plenty of hours to go until morning. Jody figured she'd done pretty well so far, showing herself to be tough yet compassionate, feminine yet strong. Of course, that was just *her* impression of how she'd done so far and didn't have any bearing on how the actual voting would go once the show aired. And even then, who was to say the Gowan brothers wouldn't edit the tape to make sure the contestant they wanted to star in their film wound up the winner?

She took a sip from the can and looked around the kitchen. Tamisha appeared as if she'd had enough fun for one night, but Melanie still looked fresh, even taking the time to cut herself a few carrot sticks.

Just then a shout came from the living room, followed by a laugh. The laugh belonged to Forrest, but the shout . . . it could have been anybody's.

Jody and the other women didn't leave the kitchen.

Forrest entered a moment later, a hint of a smile on his face. "There's a pad under the rug in the living room. Every time you step on it, a scream goes off somewhere in the house."

He left the kitchen and a short time later screams and moans could be heard coming from different parts of the house.

A woman's cry from an upstairs room.

A man's shriek of pain in the basement.

Children calling for their mother.

Dogs yelping on the other side of a door.

They all sounded so real, so intense. Jody knew they were fake, but she couldn't help being frightened by them. They were just too creepy for her liking.

And between each scream, Forrest could be heard laughing, jumping off of the pad, and then onto it again, causing another scream to grate against Jody's nerves.

"We get the idea," Jody said at last.

"Yeah, that's enough," Tamisha urged.

There was silence for a moment, as if Forrest was considering their wishes, and then he stepped onto the pad again, this time setting off a long, agonized wail from someone who was clearly on death's threshold.

Melanie grabbed a knife off the rack hanging over the counter and held it loosely in her hand. "I'm going to kill him when he gets back in here."

And at that moment, the rest of the knives fell from the rack, slamming point-first into the wooden countertop as if they had been shot from a gun—

Pock!

Pock!

Pock!

Melanie cried out in pain.

Jody rushed over to the counter in time to see several of the long knives still quivering, their points buried into the wood almost an inch deep. Two of the knives, a steak knife and a cleaver, had narrowly missed Melanie's fingers, somehow finding the small patch of wood between the digits and pinning her hand to the countertop. A third knife however, had caught the little finger and blood was oozing out from it onto the counter.

Forrest came in from the living room in a rush. "What the hell happened?"

Jody tried to pull the steak knife free, but it was pressed too firmly into the wood to remove with just one hand. She put her other hand on the knife and it came free after a couple of tugs. The cleaver came away more easily since the thicker blade hadn't gone too far into the wood.

Which left the third knife.

"Get it out," Melanie said. "It hurts."

Jody didn't doubt it.

She tried the handle, but there was no way she could pull it out without making the cut on Melanie's finger even deeper. She just wasn't strong enough. She moved out of the way and Forrest took her place, grabbing the knife and giving it a hard pull to move it away from Melanie's finger.

After that, one final jerk on the knife had it free.

"Bastards!" Melanie said. "What kind of special effect was that?"

Forrest ignored the comment. "Let's see your hand."

She shook it once to ease the pain—

Jody felt a drop of blood spatter against her cheek.

—and then presented the hand to Forrest.

He ran it under some warm water and the blood that had been running all over her hand and arm washed cleanly away, leaving a tiny scratch between the first and second knuckle of the pinky of her right hand.

"Just a scratch," said Forrest, straining to show a smile. "Nothing to worry about."

Melanie laughed under her breath and shook her head. "You know as well as I do that I could have lost my finger there, maybe even my whole hand."

She had a point, Jody thought.

"But you didn't." Forrest said the words, but there was no conviction in his voice. "You're okay."

"I swear," Melanie said, "if I don't make it out of here alive, I'm going to kill those bastard brothers."

There was a few moments of dead silence.

And then all four of them broke into laughter over what Melanie had said.

"That looked fantastic, Erwin," Ike said, after the knives had fallen out of the rack and into the countertop.

"Yeah, it sure did," Erwin said, his voice flat and un-emotional.

"It scared the crap out of Melanie, too, and she came away with hardly a scratch."

Erwin just nodded.

"This is good stuff. Never mind *Scream Queen*, we'll be giving *Survivor* a run for its money."

Erwin said nothing.

Ike laughed again, only now realizing that his brother wasn't sharing his enthusiasm.

"Come on, Erwin." Ike gave his brother a slap on the shoulder. "What's wrong? This stuff is great!"

Erwin didn't look up. "Only one knife was supposed to fall."

"Huh?"

"Only one knife . . . We only rigged one knife to fall, not three. And it was just lucky for us we didn't cut off her hand."

Ike pressed his lips together, realizing how serious the

situation was. If her hand had really been cut, they would have had to blur it out for television broadcast, or even worse, not be able to use the shot at all.

If her hand had been cut.

"But she's okay. It worked out great, and we're still rolling. This is going to be one hot show, Erwin. We're going to have *Scream Queen Two* in preproduction before we're done with the feature. We are going to be on such a roll . . ."

Erwin looked up at his brother. "Think we could make *Ghosts of the South?*"

The smile vanished from Ike's face. *Ghosts of the South* was Erwin's pet project about the ghost of a black man that haunts the Confederate forces during the American Civil War. It was a stupid idea, expensive as all hell, and there was no place in it for tits or teen sex. Worst of all was that Erwin would never let it go, bringing it up every time Ike started talking about hitting the big time. But as much as Ike hated to talk about *Ghosts of the South* he didn't mind dangling it in front of Erwin like a carrot whenever his brother needed some motivation.

"You bet, Erwin," Ike said, struggling to put a look of sincerity on his face. "It'll move to the top of our list of things to do."

Erwin's face brightened. He sat up in his chair and snapped his fingers. "Give him the signal," he said. "We've got enough stuff on this floor. It's time to send the contestants upstairs."

Everyone in the trailer seemed to come alive with anticipation.

Anticipation . . . or dread.

Twenty-two

The light in the kitchen suddenly got brighter.

It burned white hot for a few seconds, then began to flicker, as if some kid had driven into a telephone pole out on the highway and they were about to lose electricity for the night.

And then the light went out.

"Everyone done in here?" Forrest asked.

Tamisha and Melanie both nodded. Jody emptied her soda can with one last gulp, then placed it on the counter. "I'm ready."

"The envelopes are waiting for us on the dining room table."

"Do we get to choose?" Melanie asked.

Forrest shook his head. "Our names are on them. One envelope for each contestant."

Jody wasn't happy with the news. She'd hoped that the room assignments would be given out by chance, but obviously the brothers weren't about to give up control over any aspect of the production.

Forrest led them into the dining room.

As they gathered around the large hardwood table in the middle of the room, Forrest lit the six candles on the candelabra with a cigarette lighter. Laid out in a circle around the candelabra were six square white envelopes, each labeled with one of the contestant's names in bold black letters.

"How should we do this?" Melanie asked.

Tamisha took a seat at the table. "Our names are on them so it doesn't matter what order we go in."

Jody picked up her envelope, broke the bloodred wax seal on it, and took out the card that was tucked inside.

"What's it say?" asked Forrest.

Jody smiled. "It's a poem."

"Well," prodded Tamisha, "go ahead and read it."

She cleared her throat.

> *Hello . . . hello . . .*
> *While you wait for the sun,*
> *There's someone on the line for you*
> *Down in bedroom number one.*

It just had to involve a phone, didn't it? Jody thought. That psychiatrist, Dr. Katz, he'd done a half-assed job interviewing her, but he'd talked to her just long enough to give the Gowan brothers exactly what they needed.

Perfect.

Obviously she was going to be playing out the now clichéd horror movie scene where the killer calls his victims inside the house. The scenario was made popular by the *Scream* series of films, but was actually done first and best in a couple of films from the 1970s, *Silent Night, Bloody Night* and *Black Christmas.*

She looked around the room at the others and did her best to smile. "Sounds like fun," she said, not looking forward to the audition at all.

Next, Tamisha reached out and picked up her envelope, a nervous smile of anticipation breaking across her face as she fumbled with the seal.

Finally, she was able to open the envelope and read the card.

> *They're coming to get you, Barbara.*
> *Whatever will you do,*
> *When you're their final victim*
> *Alone in bedroom number two?*

She looked up from the card. "My name's not Barbara!"

Jody just shook her head.

Melanie laughed under her breath.

"That's a line from *Night of the Living Dead,*" Forrest said.

"But my name's not Barbara."

Although "Barbara" wasn't exactly the final victim in the original *Night of the Living Dead,* she did play the part in the remake. But final victims could be found in just about every horror movie, from Jamie Lee Curtis in *Halloween* to Heather Langenkamp in *Nightmare on Elm Street,* and maybe even in the next Gowan Brothers epic.

Tamisha didn't have a clue about the part she'd be playing, and that made her just about perfect for the role.

"I'll go next," Melanie said, drawing her envelope across the table toward herself, as if it were her final card in a high-stakes poker game.

She opened the envelope, pulled out the card, and held it close to her chest for several moments.

And then she read it.

> *You're a wild child*
> *Who will never be free.*
> *The devil is within you*
> *On the bed in bedroom number three.*

Melanie smiled. "Hey, I can play that."

Jody didn't doubt it.

While she was a little old to be playing the Linda Blair demon-possessed child from *The Exorcist,* there were plenty of other possessed characters from horror films to base her audition on, especially older women, erotically charged by incubi or vampiric elements.

Melanie was a natural for that sort of thing.

And judging by the look on the woman's face, she was looking forward to giving the audition everything she had . . . and then some.

Jody looked over at Forrest, who seemed to be hesitant about drawing his envelope. "Aren't you going to read your card?"

"Yeah, right," he said.

He picked up his envelope, used his little finger like a letter opener to tear it open, then pulled out the card.

> *The reports are coming in*
> *Through all the radio static.*
> *The monster is waiting for you*
> *Way upstairs, in the attic.*

Forrest smiled. "And here I am without a shotgun, or a chain saw."

Jody laughed.

Obviously Forrest would be auditioning for the role of the hero who defeats the monster in the end. There'd been plenty of those sorts of characters in horror films over the years, from Van Helsing in the original *Dracula* to Donald Pleasance's Dr. Sam Loomis in the *Halloween* series of films. But since Forrest was a bit younger, and would be after some nondescript "monster," he'd most likely be playing the part of somebody like Bruce Campbell in the *Evil Dead* movies. But whatever Forrest did in the audition, it would only be icing on the cake since he'd already done a great job leading the contestants around the house, sort of like the Duane Jones character in the original *Night of the Living Dead*.

"I'm sure you'll do great," Jody said.

"Of course he will," said Tamisha. "Ain't got no competition since Radko's out. And the way he's been pushing us around here and there, it's obvious he's with us to make sure we do what we're supposed to." She looked him straight in the eye. "You've already got a part in the movie, right?"

Forrest said nothing.

Jody decided somebody had to step up for Forrest, and it might as well be she. "I don't understand your problem. If he is in on it, then he's not competing with you."

"No, but he's been helping *you.* Making you look good, and the rest of us look bad."

Jody was going to argue the point, but it turned out she didn't have to.

"You haven't needed any help to do that, girl," said Melanie.

Tamisha just sneered.

"Uh, ladies," Forrest said, breaking the silence, "upstairs is this way." He pointed over his left shoulder.

Tamisha left the dining room without a word, followed by Jody and Melanie. Forrest brought up the rear.

The four of them pooled around the bottom of the stairs and looked up. It was a long wooden staircase that rose about twenty steps from the landing, to a railed hallway at the top that stretched left and right from the stairs and filled the width of the house. The hallway was open to the foyer, and most of it was shrouded in shadow. Even though she couldn't make them out from where she stood, Jody knew from looking at drawings of the house's layout that there was a bedroom at the far left, two rooms facing the staircase, and a fourth bedroom at the end of the hall at the far right. Between the third and fourth bedroom doors, a smaller half-size door led upstairs into the attic.

Jody stared up into the darkness and felt her heart begin to race. She wasn't sure why she felt so frightened, but she was trembling and her knees had suddenly gotten weak. Reason told her there was nothing up there to be afraid of—literally nothing, since it was all blackness and shadow—although she knew that not knowing what was up there was the thing that was supposed to make it all the more frightening. But bedroom number one wouldn't be a total unknown for Jody. She knew she'd be getting a phone call in the room, a phone call that was sure to bring back memories of a phone call she'd received years ago in the bedroom of her parents' home.

The Gowan brothers knew what she was afraid of, and they were going to make her live it all over again.

The silence stretched out into a minute or more.

Finally Forrest cleared his throat and said, "Well, who wants to go first?"

Twenty-three

No one said anything for the longest time, each of them content just to stand at the bottom of the stairs looking up into the darkness.

"Well," Forrest said at last, "somebody's got to go first."

Again, not a word.

"You know, this isn't exactly riveting television," Jody said after another very long moment of silence.

Forrest cleared his throat. "Hell," he said, "I guess I could go first."

Melanie smiled. "That's a good idea, hero man. You charge right on up there and show us girls how it's done."

Tamisha laughed out loud.

Jody gave a little laugh at that, too. Melanie's comment had been meant to be sarcastic, but like the best sarcasm her words had had a ring of truth to them. Forrest had been leading them around the house as if someone had elected him to be in charge. And now that things were getting scary, he'd been a little slow in volunteering to lead them up to the second floor.

"Right," said Forrest, again hesitating for some unexplained reason.

"We haven't got all night," Melanie said.

Forrest shot her a smile. "Well, actually we do."

"Just get up there!"

Forrest turned to look up the stairs, tiny beads of sweat beginning to form on his forehead and at his temples.

Then he took a deep breath, switched on his camera light, and headed up to the second floor.

He took five or six steps when the step beneath him broke under his weight and he stumbled.

Jody jumped at the sound.

The others let out sharp screams.

Forrest turned around, a nervous sort of smile on his face. "Don't worry, I'm okay. The stair gave way under my foot. But just a little bit." He faced the darkness again and continued up the stairs.

Moments later he was on the second floor. He turned left and right, then headed for the door to the attic when his camera light went out.

"What the—"

Jody could no longer see Forrest in the shadows and was straining to catch a glimpse of him. She began to fumble with her own camera, searching for the light switch.

It seemed impossible to find it in the darkness.

There was movement at the top of the stairs . . . a struggle of some sort.

Then the house was filled with the sound of breaking bones, of tearing flesh . . .

And a scream.

Sounding a lot like Forrest in great pain.

And then nothing.

Nothing but a faint dripping sound, like the kind a leaky bathroom faucet might make in the middle of the night.

"Oh, shit," Tamisha said.

"Forrest?" Melanie called out.

At last Jody found the switch on her camera and turned it on. As she moved the camera around to focus the light on the top of the stairs, the shadows thrown up by the railings swayed left and right against the walls, like a row of ominous beings lording over them from high above.

But as the light finally came to rest on the second-floor hallway, it became obvious that Forrest was nowhere in sight.

"Where is he?"

"He's gone."

"What's that?" Tamisha said, pointing to a spot along the rail.

Jody swung her camera around and swept it along the line made by Tamisha's extended arm and finger.

The circle of light from her camera wound up shining on . . .

Blood.

Blood had pooled between two of the balusters and was dripping down onto the foyer floor.

That accounted for the drip.

But where had Forrest gone?

Bump!

Something had struck one of the top steps.

Bump!

Jody swung the light around again . . .

And caught something round rolling from left to right on the second step from the top.

It fell to the third step with another *bump!*

And then began falling down the stairs more quickly.

Bump!

   Bump!

    Bump!

Tamisha let out a shriek.

Even Melanie screamed.

Jody fumbled with the camera, but managed to keep the thing mostly inside the light.

It was a head.

Forrest's head.

Bumping its way down the stairs, step by step, until it came to a stop between Tamisha's feet.

She jumped back in horror.

Jody stepped back, too, trying to keep her camera focused on the head.

Melanie pushed it with the toe of her boot as if it were a mound of roadkill. "Is that Forrest?"

It looked a little like him, although it was bloody and pretty battered after its bumpy ride down the stairs. "It sure looks like him," Jody said.

"Son of a bitch," Tamisha said angrily, nearly giving the head a hard kick.

Melanie had turned her camera on now, as well, so Jody bent down and took a closer, direct look at the head . . .

And laughed.

"What's so funny?" Tamisha said.

"It's a fake," Jody said with relief. "A fake head, made out of latex."

"Son of a bitch," Tamisha said again.

Jody picked up the head by one of its ears. Upon closer examination, the head bore only a passing resemblance to Forrest. The shape of the head was wrong—even after its ride down the stairs—and the hair was too thin and too long. And apart from the blood, it was completely dry with not a trace of sweat to be seen anywhere on the skin.

But it had been real enough to scare the hell out of them, and that was probably all that mattered to the Gowan brothers.

The damned Gowan brothers.

Jody held up the head for the others to see.

"So I guess he *was* part of the production, then," Melanie said. "He led us around the house, then left us here to do the rest of the night on our own."

"Put it away," Tamisha said.

"What?"

"The head. Put it away."

Jody lifted it higher. "But it's just a fake."

"I don't care if it's a pineapple, get rid of it."

"Sure, no problem," Jody said, tossing the head into a dark corner so it was out of sight, and out of mind.

Tamisha nodded gratefully. "Thank you."

"Okay," Melanie said, "I guess the next one up the stairs has to be one of us."

"Yeah," Tamisha muttered.

Jody nodded. "I guess so."

But for a long time, none of the women moved.

Twenty-four

"Who's next?" Jody said.

As she expected, no one said a word.

Melanie glanced over at Jody. "Are you telling me *you* feel like going up there?"

"It's not at the top of my to-do list."

"Hey, girls, if either of you wants out, might I remind you that the door is right over there?"

"Nice try," Melanie said with a hint of a sneer. "But if you're so hot for us to leave, why don't *you* head on up the stairs first?"

"Why should I have to go first?"

Melanie stepped in front of her. "Because you've got the biggest mouth."

They were a couple of seconds away from exchanging blows.

"Hey, hey, c'mon," Jody said, stepping between them. "We all have to go upstairs tonight. What we need to do is figure out a fair way to see who goes up first."

"Alphabetically," said Tamisha. "Jody, Melanie, and Tamisha."

Melanie shook her head. "No, if you do it alphabetically it should go by last name. Menendez, Robinson, Watts."

"Says you."

"That's right, I do."

"We don't have straws to draw," Jody said. "But how about rock, paper, scissors?"

"Fine."

"Sure."

"We'll go first," Jody said to Melanie.

Jody showed rock. Melanie had scissors.

Then Jody turned to Tamisha.

Jody showed paper. Tamisha had rock.

"I'll go last," Jody said.

Melanie squared off against Tamisha.

Melanie showed scissors again. Tamisha had paper.

"Yes!" Melanie said with some relief.

"It's not fair," Tamisha cried.

Jody couldn't believe she was still putting up a fight.

Melanie said, "Yeah, that's what the viewers will think when they see that little contest from four different angles."

Tamisha had no reply to that.

"Break a leg," Jody said.

"Yeah." Melanie smiled. "Both of them."

Without a word, Tamisha put a hand on the rail and lifted herself onto the first step. She took the second step a little more quickly, and in short order she was headed up the stairs. She paused halfway up to look back, then continued on to the second floor.

She lingered at the top of the stairs for a few moments, then went to the second door from the left, opened it . . . and after another moment's hesitation, stepped inside.

The door closed shut behind her.

"See?" Jody said. "Nothing to it."

"Yeah, right."

"Come on, let's get this over with," Jody said. "The sooner we're done up there, the sooner we can come back down and wait for the sun to come up."

Melanie nodded, then said, "Here goes nothing."

She started up the stairs toward the third bedroom.

Jody followed, headed for bedroom one.

The room was dark, darker than the rest of the house had been, and Tamisha could barely see the floor in front of her well enough to walk. She ran her hand over her camera searching for the light switch, and found it.

She turned on the light . . .

And screamed as a pair of dead, dark eyes looked back at her.

After she was over the initial shock, Tamisha slowly brought the light around onto the body again.

I would have to find a body in here, she thought.

Tamisha didn't exactly have a fear of dead bodies, but she'd hoped to get through her lifetime without ever having to chance upon one again. The first and only body she'd ever discovered belonged to her grandmother, whom she'd found dead in a heap at the bottom of the stairs of her home when she was six years old. Her grandmother didn't have a phone so Tamisha had to wait with the body for two hours until her mother picked her up after work.

Two hours with a dead body seemed like two years.

And here was body number two.

Or was it really a body?

She shined the light on the body's face. It was upside down, the body hanging by its feet from the thick overhead timbers that spanned the room. But even with the facial features so disoriented, she recognized the face of Radko Arruda, the guy who disappeared after he'd gone down into the basement.

For a moment, Tamisha breathed easier.

This was all part of the game.

This had to be a dummy or a mannequin made to look like Radko. There was no way he could hang upside down like that all night, and if it really was him, how did he get out of the basement and all the way upstairs without anyone seeing him? And why was the body set back into one corner of the room? Probably so it wouldn't be picked up by the two room cameras and so the first anyone would see of the body would be a close-up from Tamisha's own Digital Handycam.

Obviously, the body was just here to scare Tamisha, because the Gowan brothers knew the story about her grandmother and were using that fear just to freak her out.

Well, that just wasn't going to happen.

She wasn't going to let that happen to her again.

Tamisha could play it cool . . . cooler than anyone.

She stepped up to the body, and cringed slightly at the smell of it. They really went all out, she thought, admiring the realistic coloration of the bruises on his head and neck, and the way the wounds in the chest and abdomen were made to look fairly deep.

Tamisha reached out and poked the body with a finger.

It sure felt real. Not hard and stiff as if it were made of latex, but a little mushy like flesh and bones.

She poked at the body again, this time pushing it harder than before.

The body swung back and forth, like laundry drying in the breeze. There was a slight squeak as the ropes around his ankles rubbed hard against the wooden rafters.

She shined her light up at the rafters . . .

And gasped.

The rope had cut into his ankles, almost to the bone in some places, and a couple of rats were gnawing on the exposed flesh.

It was all too real. The technicians would have had to bring the rats up here and put some sort of food into the wounds around the body's ankles to make the rats so interested.

Either that or it was a . . .

A real body.

She poked at it again, only this time her index finger found a wound in the abdomen and went all the way into the flesh to the third knuckle.

It felt cold and wet.

She pulled her finger away and it came back covered in blood.

Tamisha sniffed at her finger.

It stank like real blood.

Just then there was a sound in one of the room's closets.

Tamisha remembered then that she was playing the part of the final victim, which meant there would be a killer after her. And the sound in the closet wasn't a sound effect . . . it was the killer.

Or somebody playing the part of the killer.

She moved her light onto the closet where the sound was originating and saw that the handle was turning.

There was someone in there, trying to get out.

Maybe it was a zombie from that movie the others had been talking about, *Night of the Living Dead.*

She turned to run.

And slammed, face-first, into the body hanging from the rafters.

The force of the collision knocked her backward onto the floor.

The body was swinging now, the rope straining against the rafters.

And then there was a sound of rope snapping, breaking . . .

The body came loose.

Falling to the floor in front of her.

The head was caught by the light from her camera, Radko Arruda's dead eyes open wide and staring back at her as if he were asking, "Why?"

She pushed aside the body and got up off the floor.

She started for the door, but slipped on the pool of blood that had formed beneath the hanging body.

A door opened somewhere in the room, away from the closet with the moving handle.

Tamisha tried to get up off the floor again but lost a couple of seconds when her right foot slipped on the blood.

Then she was on her feet.

The door to the hallway was just a few feet away.

She took one, two steps toward the door, both arms flailing wildly with the effort. . . .

A dark figure was momentarily caught in the flickering flashes of her camera light as its beam traveled crazily about the room.

The thing came up behind her.

And as she reached for the door handle . . .

It put a shovel blade deep into the middle of her back.

Tamisha fell to the floor.

Dead.

Twenty-five

The inside of the trailer was silent, except for the continuous hum of the monitors.

Everyone stared openmouthed at the wall of screens, utterly stunned and unable to speak.

"Holy shit!" Ike said at last. He slapped a hand against his forehead and rubbed his palm hard against his skull. "Did what I think happened, just happen?"

"That wasn't supposed to happen," said Erwin in disbelief.

"But *did it* happen?" Ike said, his voice gaining some strength. "Did she really get *killed* . . . or was that another goof, or maybe an effect? Tell me it was an effect!"

Erwin shook his head slowly. "It was no effect. She wasn't in on the show. She was a contestant."

Ike looked down the length of the trailer, searching for someone to provide him with a different explanation. "It had to be a goof. We've been pulling stunts like that all night. That's just another one of our stunts, right?"

Erwin just kept shaking his head. "It was real, Ike."

"No, Andy did that one. He must have," Ike continued, desperately trying to find some logical, plausible explanation why one of the show's contestants was lying still on the floor, blood flowing out of her body and a shovel blade embedded deep between her shoulder blades. "He set it up . . . and, and he didn't tell us about it before he died."

"No, Ike," Erwin said.

Ike finally gave in to reality, letting out a long sigh, as if half of his life were escaping from his body along with his breath. He stepped back and half sat, half fell into the seat behind him. "Why do these things always happen to me?" he muttered under his breath.

"It's the spirits," said the parapsychologist.

"Oh, for Christ's sake," Ike moaned, burying his head in his hands.

"I tried to warn you, but you wouldn't listen."

Feroze Mohammed had gotten up from his seat and was walking down the narrow aisle behind the desks on the right side of the trailer.

"Your work on the house awakened the spirits who reside here. Then blood was spilled on the grounds, arousing them further. These are the ghosts of people who were beaten, tortured, abused, and who died agonizingly painful deaths. They've had a taste of blood inside now, too . . . more than a taste, a feast of blood, and they've got only one thing on their mind now. And that's revenge."

"Shut him up!"

"Revenge against any human they find, no matter how innocent. And the more blood that's shed, the more powerful they will become—"

"I said shut him up!"

Several people moved toward the parapsychologist, but no one seemed too eager to lay a hand on him.

"There has to be another reason for it," Ike insisted. "There just has to be."

Feroze threw up his arms in surrender. "I don't know why you wanted a consultant on this project," he muttered. "Your money would have been better spent on another lawyer. . . . I think you're going to need one."

Erwin grabbed his brother by the shoulders. "We've got to do something, Ike. Before—"

"Before what?"

"Before someone else gets killed inside the house."

Ike looked at his brother through a sort of daze. "What do you want me to do about it?"

Erwin's eyes narrowed in anger and he shook his brother several times. "We could stop production and get them out of there for a start."

That seemed to make sense to Ike. "Yeah, right," he said softly. Then more forcefully, "Right!"

Erwin turned around. "Okay, cut it!" he said.

Ike got up from his seat, able to think a bit more clearly now. "Shut it all down, at least until we figure out what the hell is happening here."

"I already told you—" Feroze offered.

Ike cut the parapsychologist off in midsentence with nothing more than a glance.

And then he got down to business.

"We've got speakers in the house, right?"

Erwin nodded.

"Tell them we're stopping. Tell them to get out of the house. They won't be penalized for leaving."

A technician three seats over flipped a switch and pulled the stem mike in front of him closer to his mouth.

"We're shutting down the production. Please get out of the house. . . ." He stopped a moment, looked at the console in front of him, and flipped the switch again. "Test, test."

"What's wrong?" Ike asked.

The technician shook his head. "I don't know, it just doesn't seem to be working."

"Turn the lights on in the house," Erwin said. "All of them."

Another technician began moving slides all across the board in front of them.

The rest watched the screens to see if the lights were coming on inside.

Nothing was happening.

It was still dark as night inside.

"What the hell is going on here?"

The first technician said, "It looks like we can't turn anything on or off." He lifted his hands from the switches at his station. "It's like the whole thing is stuck, just . . . running."

"We've got to get into the house," Erwin said.

Ike nodded. "Okay, let's go." He headed for the door of the trailer, then stopped, turned, and pointed to one of the assistant directors and several of the technicians. "You guys stay here and keep taping no matter what happens inside."

"You sure you want all this stuff on tape?" someone asked.

"You bet I do," Ike answered. "It will either save our asses, or put us away for life."

Twenty-six

Mike Grech, a sound engineer who first met the Gowan brothers in college and had worked with them on their first student films, listened to the girl scream in bedroom two. It was a great scream that he knew he'd be able to sample and insert into the trailers. But after the scream, there'd been the sound of footsteps—hers probably—and then something like a piece of metal striking something soft. And then silence.

Maybe she'd hit her head on something and had been knocked out cold. Or maybe she was crouching in some corner, trembling in fear while she hid from the bogey man.

Mike smiled at the thought.

Or maybe the microphones in that room had been knocked out of commission, or hell, maybe there was an even simpler explanation than that.

Mike checked his headset for a loose wire.

It wouldn't be the first time the brothers' second-rate equipment broke down in the middle of a shoot. Once, two years ago, they had been taping an introduction to an industrial video the brothers made for a soap company and thought they hadn't got a proper recording of the company CEO. The sound track was nowhere on the tape and they had to go with the sound picked up by the camera mike, which was lousy and sounded as if they'd been shooting the segment in a closet. The day before they were to deliver the tape, they discovered that the audio track was fine, it was their editing machine that was broken.

The shit he'd had to endure during that week had been incredible. And the brief apology from Erwin, "Gee, sorry, man," and the "Wow, that was weird" he got from Ike, hardly covered it. He'd been ready to look for work somewhere else, when they made him supervising sound editor for their next feature, which turned out to be *Mad Dogs and Motorcycles*. The sound recordings had been great, with the throaty roar of the cycles being one of the best parts of the movie. Unfortunately, many thought that the sound of the motorcycles was the *only* good thing about the movie and it died in theaters, had a brief life on video, and then was released by a two-bit DVD-releasing company that didn't even digitize the sound into Dolby stereo.

Still, he'd stayed with the brothers. Although they had never treated him like a brother, they'd never been mean or unfair to him either. He did his job, delivered what they asked for, and they basically left him alone to do his thing.

If only they'd invest in better equipment.

Sure, they had gotten some quality stuff this time around, but that was only because the network was paying the bills. Even so, they'd still skimped on a few things like quality microphones. They'd wanted the entire house miked, which was an expensive proposition, especially when so much of what would be happening inside would be at low decibel levels and well below normal conversational tones.

But instead of getting an array of top-of-the-line dynamic cardioid and omnidirectional microphones that could pick up a rat farting a dozen paces away, they decided to cut costs and settle for a bunch of all-purpose mikes that might or might not catch all the subtleties . . . which would probably leave him with the extra headache of looping sound effects and maybe even some dialogue in postproduction.

Mike heard something then, and realized that there was nothing wrong with the wires of his headset.

He could hear the other two women heading up the stairs to the second floor. There was no sound coming in through the microphones in the second bedroom because there was no sound being made in there.

Mike concentrated on the two women moving up the stairs. He'd lowered the levels slightly after the guy had run up the stairs and triggered the broken step since it had sounded like a big crunch and not like breaking wood at all. Now he wanted to catch the creak and squeak of the wood as the two women slowly crept up the stairs.

He raised the sound levels on the two microphones set up between the balusters one-third and two-thirds the way up the stairs. He'd gone from a three to an eight on the board, but there was no difference in the sound he was hearing. The levels seemed to be stuck at three.

He moved the slide on the second mike back and forth, trying to hear some sort of rise and fall in the sound quality, but couldn't discern any change.

It was as if the mixing board was frozen.

"Well, that's just great!" Mike said, talking off his headphones and throwing them onto the board. "And the review will say, 'The show's terrific, but it sounds like it was recorded by a kid with a portable cassette deck and a few blank tapes from Wal-Mart.'"

Mike slid off his chair and went for a little stroll. He'd purposely set up his sound station outside on the north side of the house because it was away from the trailers and the front door of the house. It was quiet and peaceful here and with the stand of trees a few yards away, had plenty of atmosphere.

Trouble was, he didn't have a soundboard that worked.

Mike fished inside his pocket for his pack of Lucky Strikes. He'd tried not to smoke too much while he was working. Over the years he'd learned how to hold a cigarette between the index and middle fingers of his right hand without losing any dexterity, but he'd put a few too many cigarette burns into soundboards over the years and the brothers had gone to deducting payments for such damage from his salary. It was fair, Mike supposed, but at the very least it was better for him to quit smoking altogether, both financially and healthwise.

But with the board frozen, he could step back and have a smoke before trying to find out what was wrong with the equipment.

Mike lit up and sucked in a deep lungful of smoke. He held his breath a moment, then slowly let the smoke escape his lips.

He flicked his ashes of his cigarette at the side of the house and tucked the cigarette between his lips. Then he unzipped his fly and began relieving himself against the side of the house.

That's when he heard something move in the grass behind him.

Must be some technician coming out to check on him, he thought. Maybe everything else was frozen, too.

"My soundboard's all screwed up," he said, his cigarette flapping while he talked, sparks dancing like fireflies around his face.

There was no answer.

He was still relieving himself and it felt like he still had a while to go. *Jesus, I didn't know I had to go that bad.*

"It's still recording," he said. "But I can't seem to change any of the levels."

A giant wet stain—in the shape of the Starfleet insignia—was growing on the side of the house.

Someone was coming up behind him.

He could feel a chill against his back, and the hairs on the back of his neck began to stand up on end.

He glanced over his shoulder . . .

In time to see something sharp and shiny flash down through his field of vision.

His cigarette was cut in two.

Several fingers were separated from his hand.

And the stain on the side of the house became dark . . . with blood.

He opened his mouth to scream, but there was another flash of light as the front half of Mike's face came away from the rest of his head.

His body fell forward, struck the side of the house, and was dragged away, fingerless hand swaying like tendrils in the grass.

Twenty-seven

Jody and Melanie took the last few steps slowly, putting off their arrival on the second floor for as long as they could. Melanie had no trouble with the stairs, but Jody lagged behind because of the cut on her leg. She was still in pain and the blood was now seeping through the pant leg of her jeans.

They were silent when they reached the top of the stairs, studying the forbidding darkness of their surroundings for a long, long time.

Jody was the first to speak. "There's only one problem with that fake head. . . ."

"Only *one* problem?"

"If the head was a fake, then what happened to Forrest?"

Melanie shrugged. "Maybe he's put on a costume and a rubber mask and is hiding in the shadows ready to jump out at us and say, 'Boo!'"

The two women looked at each other a moment, then began shining their lights into the dark corners.

Forrest was nowhere to be seen.

"Maybe he's gone," Melanie suggested. "Like that other guy, Radko."

Jody wasn't convinced. "Maybe."

"Why, what do you think happened to him?"

"Maybe he's hurt . . ." said Jody. "Or worse."

Melanie turned to Jody and threw her hips to one side. "Look, I don't know if you're still trying to freak me out or what, but get it through your head that this is just a freaking television show put on by two sick mothers who think all this shit is fun."

Jody was silent, wondering if she *was* taking this all a bit too seriously. The show was supposed to be entertaining, nothing more. Maybe when she was done, she'd have a good laugh about it all, but right now that moment seemed so very far away.

Still, it might not hurt if she tried to loosen up a bit, or would it? It might not hurt, but it might just get her killed.

"You do it your way," she said at last. "I'll do it mine."

"Suit yourself."

Jody took another look around. "Even if Forrest's head was a fake, then we still have to face his headless body. . . . I mean that would be a logical part of the show, right?"

Melanie put a hand on Jody's shoulder and nodded. "Now you're thinking."

Just then the half-size door on their right opened up, the door that led up to the attic.

Both women instinctively brought their cameras up to shine their lights on the open door.

"Forrest?" Jody said.

The young man stumbled out of the doorway. He looked as if he'd just gone ten rounds with the champ . . . or maybe Jason, or Michael Myers. His clothes were torn and bloody. There were fresh wounds on his arms and chest. His face was bruised, bloodied, and swollen. Part of his right ear was missing, and his nose looked as if someone had tried to move it over to the middle of his cheek. His eyes were open, but just barely.

"Wow!" Melanie said. "What a makeup job."

Jody wasn't so sure. "Forrest, are you all right?"

Forrest's eyes opened wider for a moment and his mouth moved as if he was trying to speak. He motioned with his left arm—from right to left—as if he was telling them to get back, or maybe to get away.

"Is he supposed to be a zombie or something?" Melanie asked.

"I think he's hurt," Jody said.

"Oh, please," Melanie said. "You still don't get it, do you? This is part of the show. It's *all* part of the show. We're supposed to be playing along."

Just then the door Forrest had come out of swung open again. But rather than open all the way, it just opened a foot or two, wide enough to let the darkness through.

"What is that?" Jody asked.

"It's a hell of an effect, whatever it is."

The darkness swirled behind Forrest, rising up in a column until it was roughly the shape of a man. The dark figure's movements slowed as its shape gained definition, and then it grew appendages, things that looked like arms and legs.

"That's going to look great on the show."

The right arm moved, rising up and away from the rest of the dark, dark body. At the end of the arm was something shiny, like metal.

The arm rose up over the figure, the shiny thing glinting in the light of their cameras.

In an instant, Jody realized what was happening.

"Forrest, look out!"

But it was too late.

The shiny end came down in a flash, piercing Forrest's body and coming out the front of his chest, dulled by blood.

Forrest's mouth snapped open and he let out a long, terrible scream.

And then the blade was gone.

Blood started to flow freely from the hole in his chest. The dark figure behind Forrest began to turn, then swirl . . . and in moments it was gone, back through the doorway and up into the attic from where it had come.

"Forrest!" Jody screamed.

He stumbled toward them, clutching at his chest as if he could stop the flow of blood with his fingers.

Melanie grabbed Jody's arm and pulled her back, away from the dying man.

Forrest slipped on his own blood, fell left, and hit the railing.

For a moment it looked as if he might not go over . . . his arms reaching out at the air as if to grab hold of something.

Blood was still spurting from his chest. It spattered in the air, and hit the floor of the foyer below like raindrops.

But his body's momentum finally won the battle, and Forrest finally went over the railing.

There was a moment of silence as he fell—heels over head—followed by a dull thud as his body hit the ground floor.

Then the door to the attic slammed shut.

And there was silence once more.

Jody rushed to the railing and looked down.

"He's gone," she said.

"Of course he is," Melanie said, coming up beside Jody. "That was a great stunt."

Jody found that hard to believe. "But it looked so real."

"That's why they call it movie magic." Melanie turned away from the rail. "There were probably people down there with a net just waiting for him to fall. The man's probably outside getting hosed off right now."

Jody shook her head. She wanted to believe Melanie was right, but she couldn't imagine how what she'd seen could have been anything but the real thing. Forrest had looked too hurt. That blade had passed right *through* him. And the smell, there was no faking that.

The Gowan brothers could be good, but they couldn't be that good.

But if it was real, then Forrest was dead.

Maybe it was better to believe Melanie was right.

At least for now.

"I hope you're right," Jody said. "Because that was just a bit *too* real for me."

Twenty-eight

Several members of the crew reached the front door before Ike and Erwin arrived on the scene.

But none of them had entered the house.

"Go in, for Christ's sake," Ike shouted. "We've got to get them out."

One crew member—a young man in his early twenties Ike remembered hiring because his father was some kind of relation to Ike's and Erwin's parents—was turning the door handle and pushing hard on the door, but to no avail. "It won't open," he said, moving away from the door as if to take a rest.

"What are you talking about?" Ike said. "Open the fucking door!"

"It's not even locked," he said, ignoring Ike's profanity. "It just won't open. It's like it's nailed shut or something."

"Move over!" Ike said, deciding to try the door himself.

He grabbed the handle and found that it turned. Surely the door was just stuck, or caught on something, or maybe just tough to open. He pushed on the handle . . . hard, but the door didn't budge.

"Shit!" Ike said, pounding a fist against the door hoping to loosen it.

He tried pushing it again.

Nothing.

Ike stepped back from the door. "Break it down!" he said.

Everyone started looking around for something they could use to break down the door.

A couple of people began kicking at it, but the old solid wood rebuffed their efforts easily.

"Try the glass!" Ike said.

There was a two-foot by two-foot glass insert in the upper half of the door. It was old, decorative glass with real leaded seams between the panes.

Someone came running onto the porch with a rock the size of a cantaloupe in his hand.

"Get back!" he said, and the two men trying to break the door down moved out of the way.

He threw the rock as hard as he could.

It hit the window almost dead center where a frosted red piece of glass was shaped like a squinting eye.

The rock struck the eye and *bounced* back onto the porch, as if it had come up against a concrete wall.

"What the hell—"

"Do it again!" said Erwin.

Ike hurried over and picked up the rock himself this time. It had to weigh at least six pounds. It would be hard to throw, but there was no way it should bounce off a pane of glass.

Ike put his back into his effort and hurled the rock at the window.

It hit the glass with a dull thud and fell to the porch, where it put a big dent in one of the wooden planks.

"Try that window over there!" Erwin suggested.

There was a large picture window farther down the porch. The glass in it was clear and divided into four smaller panes. Maybe the glass in the front door was stronger somehow because it needed to be a certain thickness to work with the leading.

Someone picked up the rock, cradling it in both hands, then tossed it against the window.

The result was exactly the same.

The rock bounced off the window strangely, as if the glass were not glass at all, but something more.

It seemed like the door and the windowpanes were . . . being protected by some force. *But that's crazy*, thought Ike. There had to be some rational explanation for it. Had to be.

One of the effects men arrived with a fire ax.

"Okay, now that's more like it," Ike said.

The man started on the door, swinging the ax against the glass.

The ax head bounced . . . *bounced* off the glass as if it were made of steel.

He tried again, this time on the wood. The result was the same.

"Let me have that," Ike said, taking the ax from the man.

Ike began swinging the ax against the door handle. The handle broke off on the second swing, and on each subsequent strike smaller pieces of the handle's inner mechanism spilled out of the hole it had occupied in the door. When the handle was completely gone Ike slipped a finger in the hole and tried first to pull on it, then to push. It still wouldn't move.

He moved down the porch and tried the ax on the window.

No luck there, either.

Ike looked at the ax head, lifted his hands slightly to feel its weight, then began swinging the ax wildly at the side of the house. The blade of the ax dug into the wood, but only slightly. The effect was like a nail being dragged across a tabletop. The nail scratched the surface, but it would take years to cut a hole through the entire tabletop.

Nevertheless he kept at it, striking the house over and

over again until his clothes were soaked with sweat and
he could barely lift the ax over his head.

He slumped down onto the porch until he was sitting
with his back against the side of the house.

Erwin and a few others had begun working on the
door, trying to break it down with an assortment of tools.
Someone else had gone looking for a tree branch that
could be used as a battering ram, while a couple of crew
members had gone around the side of the house trying
to break through a window there.

"What the hell is going on here?" Ike said, doing nothing to keep the despair from creeping into his voice.

"The house has come to life."

Ike looked up and saw Feroze Mohammed standing
on the porch, towering over Ike like some ghoul. He offered his hand to Ike and when Ike took it, Feroze pulled
him to his feet.

"What? So now it's not just spirits anymore, now the
whole goddamned house has come alive."

"Will you mock the judge so easily when he raises the
point in court?" Feroze asked him.

Ike said nothing for a while, then moaned, "There has
to be another explanation for this shit."

"There is not," Feroze said. "The spirits were awakened by the first trickle of blood, and once they got a
taste of new blood, they grew stronger, even taking on
more humanlike forms. And now . . . ." He paused a moment, as if thinking. "Well, I suppose the phrase would
be, 'All hell has broken loose!'"

Ike shook his head. "It's just a house," he insisted.

"Which now has either been taken over by the spirits
inside it, or the violent death within its walls has stirred
up the house's own memories . . . and it's feeling all of
its former pain all over again."

"You're crazy?" Ike asked.

Feroze took a look around. "And this," he said,

spreading his hands to make his point, "is sanity?" All around them people were still trying to break into the house with whatever tool was handy. None of them were having any luck.

Feroze smiled then, but there was no joy on his face. "Perhaps I could appeal to you with logic."

"You could try."

"You didn't intend for anyone to die inside the house."

"Of course not."

"And the number of mistakes and gaffs that have occurred so far has been incredibly high, making your outfit look grossly incompetent when, of course, it is not. Am I right so far?"

"Yes."

"Well, then . . . to quote the great detective Sherlock Holmes, when you eliminate the impossible, *whatever remains,* however improbable, must be the truth."

Ike just looked at him, then started shaking his head. "It can't be. There's no . . . no such thing as ghosts and spirits. It's bullshit, and you're just a bullshit artist."

"I'm inclined to respond by saying, 'It takes one to know one,' but I think it would be more educational for me to ask why you hired me on."

"To spin out the bullshit."

Feroze looked hurt. "You, Ike Gowan, deal in bullshit. You pedal fantasy and you try to make it look as real as possible. But this is not a movie, Mr. Gowan. This is a . . . *reality* television show. You can't go in there and say, 'Cut!' and have everyone get up off the floor. People are dead in there, and the blood on the floor is real. . . . It's blood that's on your hands."

Ike had heard enough.

"Get him out of here!" he shouted.

When no one came around he tried again.

"I said get him out of here, now!"

Two men ran onto the porch.

"Get him off the site. Drive him into town if he wants, I just don't want him back here."

The two men nodded and quickly led Feroze off the porch. At the pace they were moving it seemed that the crewmen were eager to get into a car and get the hell away from the house.

"A reality show, Mr. Gowan," Feroze said as he was about to turn the corner on the house. "And the reality here is that the house and the spirits inside it are alive and dangerous, dangerous entities."

"Shut up!" Ike muttered under his breath.

He turned to look at the house again . . .

And noticed that the spot on the wooden siding where he'd struck the house with the ax was bleeding.

Bleeding.

Ike wiped his hand over the blood, smearing it rather than cleaning it off.

He looked at his hand and realized it was stained.

Blood on his hands.

He wiped his hand against a pant leg and hurried to join the others in the fight to get inside.

Twenty-nine

"Maybe we should stick together a little while longer," Jody suggested.

Melanie gave a little laugh. "I don't think so."

"You think everything's going to plan?"

"Of course not. This is a *reality* television show, taped *live*. All kinds of things are bound to go wrong; that's what makes it exciting."

Jody thought a moment about that word, *exciting*. Driving up to the house in the van had been exciting. This . . . this had moved way past exciting deep into the realm of terror.

"I just think we should stay together awhile until we have a better idea about what's going on."

"You're still riding that horse, aren't you?"

"I haven't seen many horror movies, but I've seen enough to know that when someone says, 'Let's split up,' it's usually the worst possible thing they could do."

"Yeah, and what's the best thing we could do?"

"We could join arms and stay close to each other the rest of the night."

"Now I *know* you're talking crazy. I'm not holding your hand all night. And I sure as hell am not leaving this house until I see the sun."

"Just a suggestion, that's all."

Melanie turned to face her. She opened her mouth to speak, then stopped to listen.

There were shouts coming from somewhere in the house, maybe even from outside it. They could hear thumps and bumps coming from all over, too. The sounds didn't seem all that scary now, after they'd seen so much blood and gore.

"You know, whether this house is really haunted or not doesn't interest me," Melanie said after the noises had subsided. "What does interest me is the fifty thousand dollars and the starring role in a movie that's waiting for me in the morning. If you think I'm giving up on that when your leg's bleeding and Tamisha's afraid of her own shadow, then you're about as crazy as the two fucks who dreamt this whole thing up. So, you can just forget about sticking together. From now on, girl, you're on your own."

"Okay, if that's how you feel," Jody said, noticing that while Melanie could sure talk tough, there was still a hint of fear in her eyes.

"See you in the morning," Melanie said. "That is, *if* you make it through the night."

"I'll be there," Jody said.

"Yeah, I bet you will."

It was hard to read Melanie's face in the dim light, but it seemed that Melanie was giving Jody a compliment, and considering her a more worthy opponent than she'd given her credit for previously.

Melanie looked over at the door to her bedroom, but didn't start toward it.

"Break a leg," Jody said.

Melanie smiled at her. "I'd say the same to you, but you might need that other one whole just to get around."

"I appreciate the thought."

"See you in the morning," Melanie said.

"Yeah, see you," Jody replied, wondering if she would.

Thirty

Roger Kettyls wasn't looking forward to stepping back into the production trailer. He'd been out searching the fields between the house and the highway for a couple of hours and there had been no sign of Vonda McNair anywhere. More than likely, the brothers would probably send him back out to keep looking. His only hope was that Vonda McNair had turned up and they'd been waiting for him to get back. If that was the case he'd look like some hardworking loyal employee, instead of someone who had failed at the lone task he'd been given.

He put his hand on the trailer door and opened it.

Instead of the chaotic sound of camera cues and directions coming from the inside of the trailer, Roger heard nothing. The place was silent, as if something major was happening in one of the rooms at the moment, or everyone had decided to go on break together.

Roger pushed the door open slowly, not wanting to disturb anyone's work. But as the door opened farther, Roger realized that Ike and Erwin weren't there, and there were only a handful of other people inside the trailer—a skeleton crew. There were shocked expressions on their faces, as if they'd just been given the news that the sitcom they'd been working on the last five years had been canceled.

"Where have you been?" asked Jerry Nadeau, an

assistant to Erwin who Roger realized, after a quick glance around the trailer, was likely in charge in the brothers' absence.

"Out looking for Vonda McNair, like I was told."

Jerry nodded. "Did you find her?"

Roger shook his head. "Nope."

Jerry put a hand to his head. "Oh, that's just great."

"Hey, I looked all over for her, man," Roger said. "I even went halfway down the highway thinking she might have headed off into town. She's just not around, okay?"

"Yeah, okay."

"I'll keep looking if you want—"

"No," Jerry said, putting up a hand to silence Roger. "I don't think you'll find her."

"Why?" Obviously they knew something Roger didn't. "What's happened?"

Jerry flicked his head at one of the screens. "The shit's hit the fan."

Roger looked at the bank of monitors. He couldn't exactly be sure, but in one of them, it looked as if a contestant, Tamisha Robinson, was lying dead on the floor with a shovel stuck in her back. "What's wrong with her?" he asked.

Jerry turned to look at Roger for the first time. "She's dead."

Roger's stomach began to churn. "How the hell did that happen?"

"The brothers think it's just some sort of major snafu, and the parapsychologist says that not only have the spirits in the house come to life, but the damn house itself has come alive, too."

"Come alive?"

"It won't let anyone in or out, and all our equipment is stuck . . . stuck in the *on* position."

"So—"

"So all we can do is watch, listen, and hope that no-body else gets killed before the sun comes up."

Roger let out a sigh.

"Which reminds me. We haven't heard from Mike in a while. Can you go check on him, see if he's all right?"

Roger wasn't crazy about the idea of heading out to the house again, especially after he'd been told about everything that had been going on. "Can't I stay here for a while?"

"Just go out and see if he's there, then come back."

Roger didn't move. He didn't want to go anywhere anymore, except maybe home.

"Syd," Jerry said to one of the technicians, "you go with him. If Mike's not around, come straight back here."

"Sure," Syd answered, getting up from his seat and hurrying to the door.

Roger hesitated.

"You coming?" Syd asked.

Roger extended his right arm in an exaggerated sweeping gesture. "After you."

They had tried to break into the house through the windows out front and on the west side, but all of them had proved to be impenetrable. Rocks, hammers, steel rods . . . nothing seemed able to break through.

"We need something . . ." Erwin shrugged. "I don't know, *stronger.*"

Ike let out a laugh under his breath. "Something stronger," he said. "To break through a window?"

"Well, we need to do *something.*"

"I've got a chain saw in my truck," someone said behind them.

Ike looked over Erwin's shoulder. "Get it!" he said.

Erwin started to laugh.

"What is it?" asked Ike.

"Now we're going to be ripping off *Massacre* and the *Evil Dead* movies."

"Hey," Ike said. "we're Gowans, we only rip off the best."

Roger and Syd headed off to the northeast corner of the house where Mike had his sound station set up. In the distance they could hear the voices and hammering of the others as they tried to break into the building.

It all seemed so . . . *mad*.

"Mike!" Syd called out.

"Keep it down," Roger said.

"But we have to find him."

"No, we just have to *look* for him," Roger said, keeping his voice down. "You keep shouting like that, then something out here just might *find* us."

"Mike," Syd whispered.

After another minute, Roger said, "Okay, he's not here."

"You want to go back?"

"Yeah."

"What'll we tell Jerry?"

"That we didn't find him."

Syd stopped in his tracks and shone his flashlight on the grass at his feet.

"What is it?"

"Something in the grass." Syd knelt down and reached for the things that were lying there in front of him.

Roger brought his light onto the same spot. "Well?"

"Looks like a finger," he said. "Three of them."

Roger laughed. "Man, these guys have thought of everything."

"What do you mean?"

"It's probably a goof the brothers set up, you know, like a gag reel sort of thing."

"*Behind the Screams,*" said Syd.

"Yeah, that's it."

"What should we do?"

"Let's bring them back and show Jerry. Maybe we'll get on the DVD or something."

"You still think this show's going on the air?"

Roger shrugged. "In Hollywood, man . . . you just never know."

They scooped up the three fingers and headed back to the trailer.

The technician returned with his chain saw. It was a fairly heavy-duty model with an eighteen-inch blade. The name on it read *Stihl*.

"You know how to use it?" Ike asked.

"Sure."

"Then go ahead."

Ike and the others stepped back from the house a few paces, giving the man some room.

The chain saw didn't start on the first pull.

Nor did it start on the second, third, or fourth.

"You use this thing lately?

"Two days ago."

"Maybe it's out of gas," said Erwin.

Just then the chainsaw roared to life, then sputtered and coughed as if it was about to die. But the technician revved its little engine and suddenly the machine seemed to be screaming.

"Try the door first," Ike shouted over the noise.

The man moved onto the porch and leaned in toward the door. Then he touched the whirring chain saw to it . . .

And the blood began to spatter.

Ike felt it spray against his face, thick and hot.

"Jesus Christ!" Erwin cried, his voice so loud it could be heard clearly over the chain saw.

The house seemed to shudder, then let out an inhuman cry of pain.

"Stop it!" Ike said. He put his arm on the technician's shoulder. "Shut it off!"

The chain saw came to a stop.

In the silence, they all looked at the door. There was a deep gash across it, as if it were a throat slashed by a dagger.

"Do you think we hurt it?" Erwin asked.

Ike shook his head. "No, I think we just pissed it off."

Syd opened the door of the trailer and held it open for Roger.

"Well?" Jerry said. "What's Mike's problem?"

"We didn't find him," said Syd.

"What do you mean?"

"He wasn't at the controls," Roger offered.

"Did you look for him?"

Syd and Roger looked at each other a moment; then Roger said, "Of course we looked for him, he just wasn't there."

"Great." Jerry sighed. "We've got people dead inside the house and missing people outside it."

"He might be missing," said Syd, "he might not."

"What are you talking about?"

"We found these near the soundboard," Roger said, holding up the three fingers they'd found in the grass.

"What the hell are those?"

"Mike's fingers, I think."

"It would be just like him to play a gag like that on us." Jerry got up from his chair and moved over toward the two men for a better look. "But he couldn't have picked a worse time for playing games."

Jerry squinted at the fingers a moment, then slipped off his glasses. And then, all at once, his eyes widened and his mouth popped open in a gasp.

"What?" Roger said.

"One of those things isn't a finger."

Thirty-one

Jody was alone in the hallway at the top of the stairs.

There were still sounds coming from various parts of the house, but she'd gotten used to them by now.

What was the old saying?

"Sticks and stones can break my bones, but names will never hurt me."

Well, that was what those noises were to her now . . . names. But inside the house there were things that had sticks and stones, and worse, knives and sharp things that cut even deeper than knives ever could.

Jody thought about an audition she'd gone to once at a motel on Hollywood Boulevard. The producer met her at the door to his room wearing a silk bathrobe and matching boxers. He asked her things like "How important is getting this part to you?" and hinted that "We would be working very closely together, a lot of late nights just the two of us, alone." God, he'd gotten a hard-on just talking to her like that. Well, Jody left without reading a line, since it was obvious that the man was more interested in the casting couch than casting a part. She'd laughed about it later, but at the time she'd been angry that anyone would think she'd sleep with him just to get a part in a movie. But now, here she was risking her life, her *life*, and for what? A part in a movie. And not some great Hollywood epic either, but a crappy movie that was probably going to suck like a Hoover.

But she couldn't just leave the house. Not now. Not after all she'd already been through. What if it was all part of some plan? What if *everything* that had happened, and *everyone* around her, had been part of the production? What if the real audition had been at the Gowan Brothers studio where Ike and Erwin had put her through that terrible, terrible scene? Hadn't one of them said, "You got the part"?

Jody wanted to believe it, but with all that had happened, how could she? The sad truth was she didn't know what to believe anymore. All she knew was that she'd come too far to quit now. She had to go through with it.

All the way.

All or nothing.

And no person, spirit, or thing was going to stop her from getting through till morning.

She grabbed a few of the balusters along the balustrade, tugging on each one until she found one that was loose. When one jiggled slightly at her touch, she took firm hold of it and yanked at it. When it didn't come free, she steadied herself on her wounded leg and kicked at the baluster with the other. It came free, sticking out in the air like a broken bone. She grabbed it with her hand and wrenched it free.

Then she hobbled off to her room, holding the baluster in her right hand like a weapon.

Melanie placed a hand on the handle to the door of bedroom number three. The handle was cold to the touch—ice cold. The feeling startled her and caused her to let go of it and take a step back.

"These boys are good," she said, rubbing her cold, cold hand against her thigh in an attempt to warm it up. "They've got all the angles covered, from fake bodies to real bodies to things that go bump in the night . . . no detail too small. Too bad they don't put as much effort into their movies."

She took a deep breath and reached for the door a second time. This time the handle wasn't as cold. She turned it and pushed the door. It swung open with a long, staccato creak.

"Boys, oh, boys," she said, shaking her head slightly at what she saw. "You really *have* got all the bases covered, haven't you?"

The room was decorated very much like the bedroom in *The Exorcist*. The room was dimly lit, the light seeming to come from the floor, casting long shadows onto the walls. To the left was a four-poster bed, each of the posts wrapped in blankets that were covered with sheets and tied down with rope. There was a door to the left of the bed, presumably a closet, and a couple of nightstands on either side of the headboard.

And on the wall, above the bed, hung a crucifix.

"So, the devil is within me, huh?" Melanie said, running a hand over the sheets of the bed. "I'll give it a try, but I don't think I can make my head spin around. . . ."

Behind her the door to the bedroom closed.

She glanced over her shoulder at the shadow-shrouded door. "I guess that means I should get down to business."

Without another moment's hesitation, Melanie slipped off her shoes, then decided to slip out of her jeans. She wasn't wearing a thong, but she did have on a pair of high-cut panties that she knew looked pretty good on her. She might be playing the part of a wild child possessed by a demon, but she was going to play it as a grown-up woman for an *adult* audience.

She climbed onto the bed, kneeling on it a moment and feeling it with her hands. It was soft and yielding. "This isn't so bad," she said, bouncing up and down on the bed a few times.

She was about to lie down when she noticed the crucifix on the wall above her.

"Oh, wouldn't that push everyone's buttons?" she said.

Melanie got to her feet and, standing shakily on top of the bed, pulled the crucifix from the wall. It felt cool in her hand, but it was just the right size and shape to do the job. A devilish sort of smile appeared on her face as she slowly lowered herself down onto the bed.

"You're a wild child," she said, stretching out her long, slender frame. "Who will never be free . . ."

Melanie knew she looked good in a T-shirt and panties. Many men had told her as much over the years, including her father, who first took an interest in her around her fourteenth birthday. That summer her legs grew long, her hips flared slightly, and her ass seemed to become rounder with just enough tuck where the butt met her legs. And her breasts had grown, too, large and full, yet still firm enough to allow her to go braless when she wanted.

Like now.

Without a bra, Melanie knew her nipples would be hard and erect throughout the night, giving her an advantage over the other women. It seemed like such a small thing, but it was actually a really big thing, teasing men and making them want to see more. Even if she didn't win the lead in the movie, there would be plenty of magazines who would pay large to have her pose nude. It wouldn't be a career in the movies, but it would sure beat the hell out of waiting tables for wetback laborers who figured a dollar tip allowed them to touch her any way and anywhere they pleased.

She ran a hand up and over her belly until her fingers found the buds of her nipples. They were there, hard and firm. She was tempted to run her fingers over them, but that's not why she was here. She was auditioning for a part in a movie, and she was supposed to be possessed by a demon.

If that's what they wanted, then that's what she'd give them.

She picked up the crucifix and brought it up to her chest. Then she used the tip of the cross piece to trace the outline of her nipple. Wouldn't that raise some eyebrows? Better than Linda Blair in *The Exorcist,* that's for sure. The thought brought a smile to her face. She turned her head from side to side, as if she were slowly sliding into the throes of some deep, deep passion.

"The devil is within me," she said, her voice breathy and seductive. "On the bed in bedroom number three."

She closed her eyes, slid the crucifix down between her legs, and ran it slowly up and down the insides of her thighs.

She began to enjoy the moment, knowing millions of people would be watching her.

With any luck, they'd be enjoying the moment right along with her.

"Whoa! She's really getting into this, isn't she?" Jerry said, as he and the others in the trailer watched Melanie on the monitor.

"She doesn't know what's happened, does she?" someone said. "She's still auditioning, still wants to win the damn game."

"Well, she's got my vote," Jerry said.

"Mine, too," someone behind him said.

Suddenly there was movement on the monitor. A black, shadowy shape moving across the screen from right to left.

"What was that?"

Jerry stared at the screen. "What was what?"

"I don't know . . . a shadow or something against the wall."

Jerry shook his head. "There's no one else in the room."

Everyone looked at the monitor in silence.

Finally, someone said, "Oh yeah, then who's that guy?"

On the screen, a dark shape had emerged from the shadows, as if a piece of the darkness had stepped forward, leaving one realm for another. As they watched, the figure began to take a more human shape, morphing slowly into something with a head, and arms, and legs.

"What the hell is that thing?"

"Whatever it is," Jerry said, "it can't be good."

Melanie heard a little moan escape her lips.

Damned if she wasn't getting turned on by all of this. And why not? What was not to like? Sure this whole thing was scary, but that just made it all the more exciting. And although it wasn't live, Melanie knew that it would eventually be broadcast to millions of people across the country . . . maybe even around the world.

Maybe her father might even see it.

The bastard!

The man had insisted on taking her to church every Sunday, but when they got home, he'd watch his daughter get undressed through a crack in the door. She'd told her mother about it once, but she'd laughed in her face. After that letdown, how could she tell her mother about the irritation and soreness between her legs that she'd wake up with two or three times each month? She'd put a lock on her door at age sixteen, but it mysteriously turned up broken just over a week later. Six months after that her father had caught one of her boyfriends in her bedroom and had beaten the boy in a, well, in a fit of jealous rage. . . . There was just no other way to describe it.

Even her mother had thought that it had been strange how he'd been so angry. But she'd done nothing about it.

Days before her seventeenth birthday, Melanie moved out of the house and had never returned since. Not even for her mother's funeral.

But all of that was behind her now.

When she'd left the house she was set free and able to be with any man she chose. Old men with money, young men without a penny to their name. Strong men who were weaklings in bed, small men who were giants between the sheets.

They all loved her.

Loved her body.

Some of them even loved her mind.

And none of them were like her father. . . .

As she ground the crucifix against the junction of her legs, Melanie sensed a presence in the room.

Someone or some-*thing* moving around the bed.

"Who's there?" she said.

She didn't want to open her eyes. If she did, she might see something unnatural, something scary, something that looked like her father. Once that happened, the moment would be over . . . the audition would be over, and it would be a case of "Thanks for playing, next contestant please."

And so she kept her eyes closed, remaining in character and possessed, hoping that whatever was in the room with her was a product of the Gowan brothers' twisted imagination.

Another sound, as if the thing had let out a moan of its own. It was an unnatural sort of sound, something that would seem befitting some sort of hairy beast.

A demon, maybe.

Melanie was frightened now. Really scared. Her body was trembling, no longer in the throes of passion, but clenched inside the grip of fear.

What if Jody was right? What if the stuff that had been happening had nothing to do with the brothers, and everything to do with the haunted house? What then?

Then I'm fucked, she thought.

And that's when she opened her eyes and saw a figure in the shape of a man standing at the foot of the bed. There were parts of it that were whole, looking like flesh and blood, but there were also other parts of it that were missing, filled in by blackness and shadow.

Melanie screamed, a long, shrill, horrified shriek.

The thing at the end of the bed didn't flinch. In fact, something like a smile began to appear on its face.

"Who are you?" she said, but the thing didn't answer.

She tried to move away from it, but there was no room to move on the bed. She backed up on all fours, but was soon up against the wall, with nowhere to run.

"Get away from me," she cried, wondering if this was some man in a suit sent into the room to try and scare her. That would explain it. . . . This was all part of her audition.

But even if it was, it was scaring the hell out of her.

"Leave me alone!" she screamed. "Get out of here!"

But the figure paid no attention to her. Instead, it caught her right ankle in its hand and pulled her back along the bed.

Melanie couldn't believe how strong the thing was. It was as if it were pulling a stuffed toy across the sheets.

"What are you going to do to me?" she asked, kicking her leg to try and break free of its grasp.

This time the thing answered, but not with any words. Its free hand came up from its side.

Clutched in the fingers was a long dagger.

"No, please," Melanie cried. Whether this was all part of

the audition or not, *she* wanted no part of it. She wanted out, *now*. To hell with winning this damn thing. . . .

The thing jerked her body again, pulling her even farther down the bed.

Melanie kept struggling, but it was no use.

The thing was too strong.

And it was too late to try and get away.

It pulled her leg to one side, then shoved the blade deep inside her.

She screamed, louder and sharper than she'd ever screamed in her life.

But the scream eventually died out, once the blade made its way up her abdomen and chest, and cut the vocal cords out of her pretty, pretty throat.

Thirty-two

Even though the lights in bedroom three were dim, and the room was a web of shadows, it was obvious to everyone in the trailer what had happened.

"She's dead," someone declared.

"No shit," Jerry said. "That's usually what happens when your heart and lungs and every other one of your goddamn organs gets exposed to the air!"

No one said a word for a long time.

"Has anybody got any control?" Jerry said. It was a disjointed thing, blurted out as if it were a rhetorical question about a world gone mad.

Not surprisingly, there was no answer.

So he tried the question again. "Are the boards still frozen?"

A few moments passed as slides and dials were pushed, prodded, and turned. Then the responses came back.

"Nothing."

"Still stuck."

"Can't change a thing."

"Frozen solid."

"Why can't they get inside?" Jerry asked, ignoring the reports as if he knew what the news would be even before he'd asked the question. "All they have to do is open the door and get those people out of there. . . ."

"Do you want me to see what's going on?" Roger asked.

Jerry considered going to find out for himself. At least

that way he wouldn't have to watch people dying on the screens in front of him. But he'd been given a job to do and he was going to stick with it, no matter how screwed up it was going to make him by the end of it all.

"Yeah, sure," he said at last. "Go find out what the hell is going on."

Roger headed for the door.

"And while you're there . . ."

"Yes?"

"Tell Ike that another one of his contestants is dead."

Roger's face turned white and he slumped against the wall.

"Syd," Jerry said, "go with him."

"Sure."

Syd put a hand on Roger's shoulder and together they left the trailer, each one helping to keep the other upright and on his feet.

That left just two people in the trailer, Jerry and his assistant, Don.

"How long till the sun comes up?" Jerry said when the others were gone.

"A couple of hours, why?" Don answered.

Jerry shook his head. "Because it might as well be a couple of days."

Thirty-three

When Jody heard Melanie's screams, she stopped in the middle of the hallway and listened. She couldn't be sure whether the screams had been real or part of the woman's audition. If they were part of her audition, then Melanie was an enthusiastic actress who would be pretty tough to beat. If they were for real, then . . .

She tried hard not to think about it.

Eventually the screaming stopped.

And Jody knew it was her turn.

She raised the heavy wooden baluster in front of her like a sword and crossed the last bit of hallway between herself and bedroom number one. She hesitated at the door, knowing that once she entered the room she would have to remain inside until her audition was over . . . however long that might be.

And what was waiting for her behind the door?

Rats? Dead bodies? Mannequins? Monsters? Or perhaps nothing but an empty bedroom and a telephone?

She shivered at the thought, then gathered herself together and opened the door.

It was a decent-sized room, perhaps ten feet by twenty, painted in pale shades of pink, not unlike the room she'd had on the family farm as a child. The bed was a single that sat close to the floor, its pillowy comforter falling over the sides of it like cresting waves. There were a few stuffed animals on the head of the bed near the pillow, and there were pictures on the wall of hot-right-now pop singers and movie stars that would appeal to a sixteen- or seventeen-year-old girl.

There was also a phone.

It was a plain black telephone with a rotary dial. It sat on a small desk that could probably double as a makeup table.

That phone was going to ring, and Jody would be required to act as afraid and as terrified as she knew how. But the thing of it was, she wouldn't have to do all that much acting to be afraid. Just the sight of the telephone was giving her the creeps.

It had been five years ago.

Jody had been seventeen, looking forward to graduating from high school and finding her way in the world. She had plans on going to college. Maybe near home, maybe in California. Theater arts, mass communications, she was even interested in philosophy. She could be anything she wanted to be and no one was going to stop her.

But someone still tried.

His name was Bobby Waldrop. He'd been her boyfriend for three years. His parents had a big spread and when he finished high school they were going to give him a good-sized chunk of it, complete with his own house. Bobby wanted Jody to live in that house with him so they could make a life together. Jody wanted no part of it. She'd seen how hard her mother had worked on their own farm to make things halfway decent for herself and her brothers, and Jody had no intention of falling into that trap, especially so early in life. She wanted to go off and do something on her own, *for herself,* and if it didn't work out, well then, she'd be back, maybe hooking up with Bobby again, maybe not. But whatever she ended up doing in life it was going to be something for her, done on her own terms, decided upon by no one other than herself.

When she explained it all to Bobby, and told him she'd be away at college next year, he couldn't believe it. He'd thought his charmed life was going to keep right on going and hadn't even considered that she might not want the same things out of life that he did.

He cried then, not single tears, but wailing sobs that seemed to shake his entire body. Then he begged her to marry him, pleaded with her not to leave town, all the while saying his life would mean nothing without her.

Jody was flattered, but she felt smothered, and just a little proud of herself for making the right decision, especially in the light of Bobby's strange behavior.

But it hadn't ended there.

Instead, it went on for weeks, getting so bad that Bobby's parents even offered Jody money to stay at home and study at a local college.

That convinced her she *had* to leave.

And then one night the phone rang.

It was Bobby. He'd been drinking, and his voice was hoarse, as if he'd been crying all night.

"I don't want you to leave," he cried.

"Bobby, we've been through this all before."

"I can't live without you."

"Oh, come on, I'll be gone less than a week before you find someone else who'll make you happy."

"Nah," he said, sniffling. "I can't live without you, and I won't."

This was a new wrinkle. "What do you mean you *won't?*"

"I ain't gonna live here without you. You leave, I swear I'm gonna kill myself."

God, what an asshole, she thought. *What a selfish, uncaring asshole. He's trying to heap all of this blame and guilt onto me, just to keep me in town for himself.* Suddenly, Jody had never been more sure of her decision to leave. If she stayed, this sort of cloying behavior would become routine. Of course, it wouldn't be as strong as this, but it would slowly wear her down over time until she was ground into submission by a man who had never heard the word *no* before in his life.

And so she decided to call his bluff.

"Well then, you just go ahead and do that," she said, calmly without a hint of hesitation. "If that's what you've got to do, maybe you should do it!"

And then she hung up the phone.

Damned if the bastard didn't hang himself that very night. Hanged himself from the rafters of the family barn with a nylon cord, but only after he'd written a detailed suicide note telling the world that she'd driven him to it. Told him to go ahead and kill himself in no uncertain terms. And if people had trouble believing it, he thoughtfully left behind a crisp, clear tape recording of their final conversation as proof.

Bobby's parents blamed the death of their son on Jody, calling her everything from a tease to a whore. Half the county blamed her, too, especially after his parents provided the local paper with a transcript of that last call.

Jody got away a few days later, but the damage had already been done. She couldn't go home, and she hated . . . just hated, answering the damned telephone.

And now, here she was, in a room just like the one she grew up in, waiting for the phone to ring . . . and something bad to happen.

She searched the room, looking for a script. They hadn't exactly explained how the audition would work, if there were lines or a specific scene they required the actors to act out, or what.

Just then the phone rang.

It was the same shrill, metallic ring the phone in her room had had when she was growing up.

Jody approached the phone slowly, not wanting to pick it up but knowing that she must.

She put her hand on it.

Lifted the receiver off its cradle.

The ringing stopped.

Slowly, she raised the phone to her ear. Just as she touched the receiver to the side of her head, a voice on the other end of the line said, "I'm going to get you for what you did to me!"

Jody felt her knees goes week.

The blood seemed to drain from her face and she had to grab hold of the desk to stay on her feet.

What was she supposed to say to that? What was the right response? Was there an actor on the other end, a recording, or something else?

"What did I do to you?" she said.

"I'm going to find you," said the voice, filling in the spaces between the words with plenty of heavy breathing. "And when I get you . . . you're going to pay."

"I didn't mean to hurt you," she said, as if she were talking to Bobby. Or maybe Bobby's ghost.

"Cut you up into little pieces." The voice went suddenly high in pitch and finished off with a maniacal laugh.

"I loved you," she said. "And I thought you loved me."

"Feed you to the dog." The voice was low now, demonic.

"Why do you want to hurt me?"

"Kill you slowly." This time like a child's playground chant. "Drink your blood . . . scatter your bones around the neighborhood."

"What?"

It had to be a recording, she thought. The voice on the other end wasn't responding to what she was saying and the effects and rhymes were too elaborate to be done live. This had nothing to do with Bobby's death, just like she didn't have anything to do with it. He'd been a sick individual and his death—his suicide—had been no one's fault but his own.

And this . . . this was just an audition, something the Gowan brothers were using to find out how well she acted, or perhaps *re*-acted, to pressure and fear.

The phone had probably been rigged to ring shortly after she entered the room. The voice track would play out on the other end no matter what she said or did. The trick would be to respond to the voice like a woman frightened for her life, and then somehow turn it around so that she was no longer a victim, but a hero.

"Please don't hurt me," she pleaded, trying to put as much fright and fear into her voice as she knew how.

"Cut you up into little pieces," the voice said again, only this time, instead of trailing off with a maniacal laugh, it ended with a mad giggle.

"Don't do that to me . . . please."

"Food for the dog." Obviously the words that had been said before were being repeated, only with different sounds and effects.

Jody wasn't about to ask the voice why it wanted to hurt her. It was time to stop playing the victim. "You'll have to find me first," she said, punctuating her change in emotion by wiping the tears from her eyes.

"Kill you slowly." The child's chant again, only this time it was in the voice of the demon. "Drink your blood . . . scatter your bones around the neighborhood."

"You just come and get me," she said, confidently. "I'll be waiting for you."

And then she slammed down the phone, holding the wooden baluster high in the air as if fending off some attacker.

There, she thought. *How's that for an audition?*

At that moment, Jody noticed something out of the corner of her eye.

Something dark moved within the darkness.

She turned in that direction . . .

Just in time for her to see a dark shape step out from the shadows and rush toward her.

Thirty-four

Someone had brought a ladder out to the house. If they couldn't get in through a ground-floor door or window, maybe they could break through one of the windows higher up on the house.

It was worth a try.

After all, they couldn't just stand around and do nothing while people inside were in danger.

As the ladder was being propped up against the house, the top of it resting against the sill of an attic window, Ike was entertaining other ideas from the crew about what to do with the house.

"We could cut off the electricity," suggested a grip.

Ike thought about that, but even before he came to his own conclusions, other people voiced their doubts.

"They can use all the light they can get in the house."

"We can try and shut off the generators, even cut the wires leading into the house . . . but that doesn't necessarily mean the power will go off."

Ike looked at the technician who'd said that and realized that as a group, the crew believed something unnatural, maybe even supernatural, was happening to the house. Even Ike was beginning to consider it a possibility, but he wasn't about to admit it.

"Something else," he said.

"We could drive a truck through one of the walls."

Everyone was silent. Ike just looked at the guy, unable to decide if he was crazy, or a genius.

Luckily he didn't have to make a decision on it right now.

"Ladder's ready," someone called out.

"I need a volunteer to climb it," Ike said.

The crew were noticeably silent.

"I'll go," said Erwin.

Ike shook his head. "No, I want you here with me."

Erwin nodded and stepped back.

"Anyone else?" Ike said.

No one was even looking at him. Obviously they needed some enticement. "Whoever goes up gets promoted one position on our next film."

Still no one stepped forward.

"We *will* be making other movies," he assured them.

No takers.

Ike realized he'd have to do it the old-fashioned way. "Okay, two hundred dollars."

Two hands went up.

Ike chose the younger of the two men.

"Give him the ax," he said. "And the rest of you hold the base of the ladder. The last thing I need is something bad to happen *outside* the house, too."

They moved toward the ladder, a half dozen crewmen crowding around the base of the ladder and getting a firm hold of the runners.

"What do you want me to do?"

Ike looked at him strangely. "Climb up there and break the damn window!" he said.

"Then what?"

"Then what!" Ike repeated. "Then go into the house and see if you can open the door from inside."

"You want me to go into the house?"

Ike's head jerked from side to side as if the man had asked a stupid question. "Yes."

"Forget it!" the man said, handing over the ax.

Ike took the ax and looked for the other volunteer. When he found him the man was looking down at the ground trying to avoid Ike's gaze. "Three, no . . . four hundred," he said.

The man finally looked up, and reluctantly nodded.

"All right then, let's go."

Ike handed the second volunteer the ax, then joined the crowd around the base of the ladder.

The volunteer, a grip whose name Ike remembered as being something like Vito or Rico, grabbed the base of the ladder, then hesitated a moment.

"All right, all right, four-fifty," Ike said.

The man nodded, took hold of the ax with his right hand, and began climbing.

As everyone watched the man ascend the ladder, Ike noticed two men coming around the corner of the house.

It was Roger and Sydney.

Whatever they had to say, it couldn't be good.

Ike let go of the ladder and took a few steps away from the house.

Above him, the volunteer had reached the top of the ladder and was about to start swinging the ax.

"What is it?" Ike asked the two men.

"Did you hear that last scream?" Roger asked.

"Sure I heard it. Someone inside got scared by something. What about it?"

"Hit it again!" Erwin said at the base of the ladder.

The man on the ladder swung the ax again, but the attic window was being protected by the same force as the rest of the house.

"Well," Roger said, "that scream was made by Melanie Menendez. . . ."

"Yeah, and?"

"She made it just before she died."

Ike felt the life being drained from his body, as if he

were some victim in a Gowan Brothers vampire movie and the house—this whole project—were sucking him dry.

"How'd she die?" he asked.

"Something . . . inside," Roger said.

"Something?" Ike said, beginning to feel sick to his stomach.

"Or someone," offered Syd with a bit of a shrug. "It looks like a person, or like half a person, half . . . something else."

"It cut her with some kind of a knife."

"Something. Someone. Some kind of a knife. How can you even be sure of what you saw?"

"Might not be sure what did it, but we did see her get killed, and we're sure she's dead." Roger stated, matter-of-factly.

"Blood spurt so far it hit one of the camera lenses in the bedroom."

Ike was definitely sick now.

He turned away from Roger and Syd and stepped up onto the porch.

In the background he could hear the ax striking the attic window over and over again.

Ike walked to the end of the porch, hung the upper half of his body over the railing, and threw up into the bushes.

For a moment, everyone around the ladder stopped and looked over in Ike's direction.

Ike hurled again.

The banging on the window resumed.

And then Ike's cell phone rang.

He spat several times to clear his mouth, letting the phone ring. Then when he was ready, he stood up, fished it out of his jacket pocket, and said, "What?"

"Ike, Ike Gowan."

"Yeah."

"It's Bartolo . . . from the network."

"Hey, how are you doing?"

"Never mind me, I'm calling to see how the shoot's going."

Ike paused to take a breath. "Fine," he said.

"It's going well, then?"

Ike didn't know how to answer. Bartolo certainly didn't need to hear the truth. Not now.

Or maybe he did.

At least a version of the truth.

"Well, I think we're getting footage that . . . no one has ever seen the likes of before."

"That's great, just great. And you'll be happy to know we've decided to give this a big push. Network promotional campaign, billboards, magazine ads, the works."

"Great, thanks," Ike said, "but I really don't think publicity is going to be a problem with this show."

"Why, what do you mean?"

Ike realized he'd probably said too much already. "Sorry," he said, "I gotta go."

He hung up before Bartolo could say good-bye.

Ike pocketed the phone, then leaned over the railing again.

Thirty-five

Jody let out a scream.

The thing was half man, half darkness, and what little there was of its eyes looked evil and angry.

Bent on killing.

Out for revenge.

Jody moved to her left, even though the door was on her right.

She moved between the wall and the bed. There was a window behind her, but beyond the window was a drop of twenty feet and she didn't like her chances, even if she was able to break through the window without tearing open an artery.

The thing moved toward her slowly and deliberately, not as if *slow* was the best it could do, but as though it had all the time in the world and it enjoyed causing the terror she was feeling.

That was fine by Jody. She could use all the extra time she could get.

She waited until the thing was near the end of the bed before she climbed on top of it. The thing followed her, but now it had something bright and sharp in its hand. A knife maybe, or a dagger . . . Whatever it was it could likely kill her in a heartbeat.

Jody leaped off the bed, and as she dropped to the floor, she grabbed the bottom of the bedcover and lifted it into the air, throwing up a thin fabric veil between herself and the figure.

The thing slashed wildly at the cover with its knife, slicing it open and sending the inside stuffing flying through the air like feathers.

On one of the slashes, the tip of its blade caught Jody on the arm near the shoulder, tearing open the flesh and sending blood flowing down over her elbow, wrist, and fingers.

She grabbed her arm, but refused to scream.

She couldn't let the wound stop her.

Not now.

The door was within reach.

The thing was struggling to get free of the cover.

Jody dashed toward the door, yanked it open, and lunged into the hallway.

For the moment, the thing was behind her, and she was alone.

She slammed the door shut, looking for a way to lock it, and realizing it couldn't be done from the outside.

She looked up and down the hallway.

Melanie, she thought. *If we can team up, we'll have a better chance at surviving these . . .* ghosts, *or whatever the hell they are.*

She ran toward bedroom three as well as her wounds allowed.

The cut on her leg was fully open now and the dressing covering it was completely soaked with blood. If she didn't get out of here and have it looked at properly, she might very well bleed to death. *Wouldn't that be funny?* she thought. *After all this, I bleed to death because of an accident that happened in the first couple of hours of the game.*

The door to the third bedroom was unlocked.

Rather than knocking, Jody pushed the door open slowly and slid her body through the narrow opening without a sound.

"Melanie," she whispered, as she closed the door behind her.

No answer.

But there was sound in here.

A wet, slobbering sort of sound, and moans of satisfaction.

Like people having some wild sex, or perhaps someone who was very, very hungry.

Jody switched on her camera light and shone it onto the bed.

It turned out she'd been right on both counts.

One of those things was on top of Melanie, pumping wildly between her legs while it tore large gobbets of bloody flesh from her torso.

Jody's mouth opened, but she was unable to make a sound.

She stared a moment, unable to move . . . unable to do anything.

And then the thing turned, as if only now it noticed her presence and the light she'd been shining on it.

Its face was almost whole.

Almost.

There were still chunks of it that were missing and filled in by shadow and darkness.

It reached out for her, as if wanting her to join it.

Join it and Melanie.

Jody shone the light directly into the darkness of its eyes, momentarily blinding it.

As it cowered slightly, she swung the baluster with all the strength she could muster. It struck the thing on the back of its head.

And something cracked.

She lifted the light again, and could see that she'd hurt the thing. Its skull was open and darkness was rising up out of it like smoke.

She struck it again.

Watched it fall.

Then turned to run.

Run like hell.

Jerry and Don watched Jody strike the thing in bed-room three. There was a loud sound of thudding flesh, maybe even of breaking bone.

Don instinctively tried to zoom in on the action with the camera opposite the bed. To his surprise, the picture changed slightly, the image growing larger as he zoomed in close on the final contestant, Jody Watts.

"Hey, Jerry!" he said.

"What?"

"I think I've got some control back."

"On what? Where?"

"This camera," Don said, still playing with the con-trols. "I can zoom in and out."

On the monitor, Jody ran from the room.

"She's moving," Jerry said.

Don tried a few other controls. "Some of this stuff is working again."

"How much of it?" Jerry began trying a few controls himself.

"Some. I guess it's hit and miss."

"Why now?"

Don glanced at his watch. "It's a half hour to sunrise. Maybe that's why it's coming back."

Jerry looked over at the trailer door. It was open slightly, and the crack around it had lightened some-what. "Any of the effects working?"

"Maybe," Don answered. "I haven't tried them."

"You keep an eye on her," Jerry said, pointing at Jody running across one of the screens. "If there's anything we can do to help her from here, let's do it."

"You got it."

* * *

Jody was back out into the hallway.

She came to a stop at the top of the stairs, slipped on something, and fell backward onto the floor.

Pain shot up the length of her leg. Her arm felt as if it were on fire. She gasped to recapture the breath that had been knocked from her lungs.

She sat up slowly, feeling weak and groggy.

She lifted her hand and saw that it was wet with blood. Her own blood.

She needed to get out, get away, to hell with lasting out the night, and to hell with winning this damn game.

It was obvious now.

There were no winners.

How could you be a winner if you were happy just to make it through the night with your life? She'd had her life when she'd entered the house. This wasn't a game to win a part in a movie, it was a game of survival.

And she was a *survivor*.

Jody laughed at the thought. The contestants on that show had nothing on her. Nobody was trying to kill the people on that show.

A noise sounded from the far end of the hall.

She had to get up, get out of there.

But where?

Maybe if she could get to the attic, she could open a window and call for help. Forrest was supposed to have gone up there, but of course he never did. Maybe the attic was a safe place. At least it was worth a try.

She went to the doorway that led to the attic. It was tucked in between the third and fourth bedrooms, slightly smaller than the bedroom doors.

With the baluster in one hand, and the camera hanging from the other by a strap, Jody opened the door . . .

And was unable to get out of the way in time.

The body's head hit her shoulder, knocking her backward. The body kept on falling past her to the floor, where it hit with a loud, dull thud.

Jody got down on one knee and began bashing the head with the baluster, over and over again until she was sure it was dead, or whatever the term was when these things no longer functioned.

But as much as she beat the thing, it didn't seem to sustain any damage. The head was still intact, and it didn't seem to move right when she struck it.

She touched the thing with her free hand.

It was soft and plush.

Like a stuffed animal, Jody thought. *Not flesh and shadow.*

She grabbed it with both hands and turned it over.

A fake.

Jody smiled.

It looked so . . . *fake,* so *not scary.* It was like a toy, a dummy, a fun-house prop.

But then its hand moved, jerking toward her as if to grab at one of her limbs.

She could hear the electric motors whizzing and whirring inside the thing.

And so she smashed its arm with the baluster, immobilizing it, destroying it.

"That the best you can do, Gowan boys?" she said aloud. "You couldn't scare the shit out of a baby's diaper."

That got her laughing.

The Gowan brothers made all sorts of scary movies, but nothing could compare with this.

The fear for your life.

This—

The mannequin's face suddenly darkened.

Jody looked up.

The dark thing from Melanie's room was standing over her, darkness still wafting up out of the rent at the top of its skull.

Jody jumped back again, sliding through the pool of blood.

The thing's blade came down, striking the wooden floorboards of the hallway and getting stuck in the wood.

It gave Jody the chance she needed to get away.

But where?

The attic was no longer an option.

She'd tried up, now all that was left was down.

She took the steps as quickly as her injured leg would allow.

Halfway down she glanced over her shoulder at the thing at the top of the stairs. It was coming down after her. But rather than taking the steps, it floated down over them, as if it were flying.

She hit the foyer running, heading toward the front door.

It was locked.

She turned around.

The thing was halfway down the stairs now, closing on her quickly.

There was nowhere for her to go.

Nowhere to run.

Nowhere to hide.

She did the only thing she could think of. She set her feet, raised the baluster over her head, and screamed.

The thing approached. . . .

Suddenly, the big chandelier hanging high up over the foyer started to fall.

Jody looked up, then glanced at the thing coming toward her.

They were on a collision—

CRASH!

The chandelier landed squarely on the thing's head, slicing it into pieces, mashing it into the floor.

Tendrils of darkness rose up from the floor, wending through the crystals like snakes.

Jody stopped screaming, and took a few moments to catch her breath.

Somebody up there likes me, she thought.

A smile broke over her face.

Maybe she was going to make it after all.

And maybe, just maybe, she was going to be in the movies.

Thirty-six

"All right," Ike said, "get down from there."

The grip took one last swing at the attic window, then began descending the ladder with slow and careful steps. When he was about five rungs from the bottom, he handed the ax to someone and quickly jumped the rest of the way to the ground.

He turned to face Ike. "Four hundred fifty bucks, right?" he said.

Ike nodded. "That's right."

That should have been it, but the guy wasn't moving.

"What?" asked Ike.

"My money."

"I don't have it on me. You'll get it with your payout."

"If we live that long."

Ike understood the man's fear, but he wasn't about to start paying people on the spot. Then they'd all want their money and it would be Ike and Erwin alone against the house.

"We're all going to live that long," Ike said. "See, this is the part in my career where everyone who's ever worked for me and thinks I'm an A-one Hollywood asshole is going to stand up and cheer, figuring I had it coming to me, that I got what I deserved. You think fate's going to remove me from that humiliation? You think I'm going to die and somehow get away with never having to face the music on this?"

The guy nodded. "Yeah, something like that."

"Well, that would be nice," Ike said, "maybe even appropriate considering what's happened tonight. But, if you haven't noticed, my luck ran out a few hours ago!"

He wanted to continue on, to scream and to cry, but he couldn't. How could he blame anybody for being scared? That's what the Gowan brothers had brought them all here for, and they'd succeeded . . . all too well. In the end, Ike just looked the grip in the eye and said, "Don't worry, you'll get your money."

The man nodded appreciatively.

Ike stood up straight, knowing they had to keep going. "We need to try something else."

"How about the truck?"

Ike glanced over at the house, and considered it. The foundation was solid stone and rose up from the ground about two feet before the exterior changed to old wooden siding. A truck running into the house would smash into the stonework and wouldn't do much damage—with or without something crazy going on with the place.

Ike shook his head. "There's a stone foundation."

Erwin stepped forward. "What if we put a railway tie into the back of a pickup and back it into the house like a battering ram?"

Ike glanced at the house. Putting the tie into the back of a truck might just be enough to have it clear the foundation.

"Okay, do it."

The crew went into motion and about ten minutes later they had a late-model Ford—a truck rented out to the production—rigged with a railroad tie. The tie was set back from the truck's cab with several wooden blocks so that the opposite end extended out about four feet from the back of the truck box. Other ties that were lying around the yard were lifted into the back of the truck, weighing it down to give the makeshift battering ram as much mass and momentum as possible.

"Who's going to drive the truck?" someone asked.

Ike could just imagine them all lining up for an easy four or five hundred dollars. Well, screw that. For that kind of money, Ike could do the job himself.

"I'll do it," said Erwin.

Ike was about to protest when Erwin raised a hand to silence him. "Save it, Ike. I can't stand around and watch anymore, I've got to do something."

Ike sighed and gave his brother a slight nod. His brother was right. When they went to court on this, they'd need to show that they did everything possible to save whoever was left in the house. Having Erwin drive the truck was probably a good idea. Besides, he'd be saving four or five bills this way . . . and they'd be needing every dime they could scrape together for the lawyers.

"Sure," he said at last. "Go ahead."

Erwin sprang into action, hurrying into the cab and making himself comfortable behind the wheel.

"Here," someone said. It was one of the effects people, slipping a large foam cushion behind Erwin's head. "It'll stop your skull from punching a hole through the rear window."

Erwin rubbed the back of his head. "Thanks."

Then someone tied a large towel around his neck. "So your head won't snap your neck too badly."

Ike shook his head, realizing how close he'd just come to getting his little brother killed.

Erwin gave the thumbs-up signal and started up the truck.

A dark figure roamed the outside of the house, something shiny and sharp in its hands. It moved slowly across the grass between the house and the woods like an animal awaiting its prey.

But instead of gliding over the grass, it walked now, its body made up of equal parts of flesh and shadow. It had been a female in another life, perhaps even an attractive one, but now it was hideous. Even the flesh that had been made whole again had been savaged by small gashes and gaping wounds. And through the rents in the mottled skin, shadow wafted like smoke.

As it moved again from the woods toward the house, the figure stopped.

Around the other side of the building, a noise.

A vehicle starting up, roaring like an angry beast.

Many voices on the move.

Too many voices . . . approaching.

The figure began moving again, only now it moved away from the house and across the fields.

Toward the trailers.

There would be shelter from the light of day inside them.

Shelter . . .

And victims.

The crew followed the truck around to the side of the house where the lawn was flat enough for the truck to gain some speed.

When Erwin was in position about twenty yards from the house, he beeped the horn once and revved the engine.

"Everyone back," Ike shouted.

A moment later he gave his brother a signal.

Erwin began backing up the truck, gaining some speed, but not as much as he could have.

At the very least, thought Ike, Erwin was showing a bit of judgment.

The railway tie struck the house about a foot above the stone foundation.

But it didn't break through.

Instead, the railway tie shot forward, crashing through the front of the truck's steel box . . .

And continuing on through the back wall of the cab.

A scream came from inside it.

Ike ran to the truck.

Erwin was still crying out in pain.

Ike looked in through the open window. The railway tie had broken through the back of the cab and pushed forward until it stopped a mere six inches from the dashboard.

Erwin's right arm had been in the way of it and was now broken in what looked like two places, judging by the way it was bent at unnatural angles.

Erwin looked at Ike, managing to overcome the pain for a moment. "Did I break through?"

Ike looked at the house. There was hardly a scratch on it.

He looked at his brother and shook his head. "Sorry, Erwin."

"Shit, Ike, what are we gonna do now?"

Ike shrugged and looked at the ground. "I don't know."

"You're the producer, Ike," Erwin said. "You can't say, 'I don't know.' You have to know."

Ike was all out of ideas. But as he raised his head, he noticed that the sky was a shade brighter than it had been a few minutes before. He shrugged. "Maybe we'll just wait."

Thirty-seven

Jody was hard at work trying to open the front door when she heard the crash. It had come from another part of the house, maybe even from outside.

She tried to think what it could have been. . . .

Something angry and trying very hard to get into the house, or maybe it was something trapped inside the house wanting to get out and get at her.

Either way, it wasn't a good idea to hang around to find out exactly what it was.

She tried the front door again.

It wasn't locked, but it wasn't about to open up either.

She pounded on the glass with her fists, but the glass was stronger than she remembered. Unyielding. Impenetrable.

It was no use. She'd have to stick it out until morning. Whenever that was.

And since she'd tried the attic, and that last horrible noise had come from somewhere on the first floor, she decided she'd have to go down.

Into the basement.

That made the most sense.

After all, even in the original *Night of the Living Dead*, they'd argued about upstairs and downstairs through most of the movie, only to learn in the end that their first choice—upstairs—had been wrong.

She'd go downstairs, and wait.

The door under the stairs was still open. She stepped through it and shone her light down into the basement. When she was satisfied that there was nothing waiting for her at the bottom of the steps, she closed the door behind her and began looking for things she could use to block the door.

Luckily there was a piece of two-by-four lying against the wall. It had been cut to the right length, probably by the previous owners of the house, and it wedged in tightly between the door and the opposite wall.

When the brace was firmly in place, Jody sat down on the top step and peered down into the basement. It was as empty as it had been before, even emptier now that she was the only contestant left.

She'd been down here with the others only a few hours ago, but it seemed more like days, even weeks.

Jody's mind began to rewind and recall all she'd been through, what had been an effect and what had been real and all the things in between that she couldn't be sure what the hell they'd been.

Had it been worth it?

Worth it, even if she was going to be in a movie at the end of it all?

Hell no!

Plenty of actors star in a movie or two, never to be seen again. What if that happened to her? She'd have gone through this night, something that was surely going to haunt her for the rest of her life . . .

And for what?

Her fifteen minutes of fame.

"You bastards!" she said aloud. "All of this shit for a part in one of your stupid, lame-ass cheese-ball movies."

She shook her head in dismay.

Tears began to leak from the corners of her eyes.

"You make some of the worst movies I've ever seen,

and getting a part in one of them is supposed to be the prize for all of *this?*"

She laughed through her tears.

"No part in one of your movies, or anyone else's movie for that matter, is worth all of this shit."

She was right, and Jerry didn't blame her for being pissed off.

The last contestant, Jody Watts, had been through hell and was letting off a little steam.

Well, you go girl, thought Jerry.

They'd done their best to help her. The chandelier dropping onto that *thing* had been great, but it was way too little, way too late.

This shoot had been, without a doubt, the worst he'd ever seen in his twenty-three years in the business. He'd heard of cursed productions before, like *The Exorcist* in the early 1970s and *The Crow* in the 1980s, but this . . . this production was the mother of all snafus. A crew member hospitalized and another dead while preparing the site, and now four, maybe even five, cast members dead during the course of one night.

And for what?

The chance to star in a Gowan Brothers B-movie that would probably end up going straight to video.

That girl, Jody, she had a right to be pissed off. I mean, when you sign up for a television show, at the very least you expect to be alive when taping wraps.

"You sons of bitches are going to pay for this!" she vowed, every word picked up clearly by the basement mikes.

Yeah, I bet they are, thought Jerry. This was likely the end of the road for the Gowan brothers. They'd be lucky to be making pornos in five years . . . if they were still in business.

Just then, Jerry heard a tapping against the outside of the trailer.

"Did you hear that?" he said aloud.

"Maybe Roger's back from the house," suggested Jerry's assistant, Don, the other crew member in the trailer.

There was another sound now, like a piece of steel being dragged against the aluminum skin of the trailer. It was a grating sort of sound, almost as bad as finger-nails on a chalkboard.

"What the hell is he doing?" Jerry asked.

"Maybe it's some sort of game," said Don.

Jerry looked at Don. "What do you mean?"

"Maybe there's a camera inside the trailer, on us."

Jerry shook his head. Even though he wouldn't put it past the Gowan brothers to still be collecting footage, he couldn't believe they would be so callous and unfeeling. "The show's over, my friend," he said. "It's been over for a long, long time now."

The show was over, but tape was still rolling.

A hard knock on the outside of the trailer, as if some-thing solid had struck it.

"Go out and see what the hell's going on out there, will ya?" Jerry said.

Don didn't move.

"All right, I'll go myself."

Jerry took off his headphones and mike and got up from his seat.

He'd taken two steps toward the door when it opened.

Jerry stumbled backward, falling into his seat.

A grotesque figure stood in doorway, half human, half shadow. . . .

The door slammed shut behind it.

And then for several moments, the trailer was filled with the sounds of two men . . .

Screaming.

Thirty-eight

Jody opened her eyes.

For a moment she didn't know where she was. She was tired, and sore, and bleeding. But she was alive.

She took a look around her. She was in the basement of the house at—she glanced at her watch—damn near close to sunrise.

Which meant . . . she'd made it.

She'd made it through the night. So even if she didn't win the fan vote, she'd still get some money for lasting out the night. Then she'd be on the show for four weeks and maybe, just maybe, she'd be able to parlay that into something else, something more.

She stopped herself a moment.

How could she be thinking such things when the others, Melanie for one, probably Forrest as well, were dead? There'd be nothing to win if the others were dead. Sure, Gowan Brothers, or the network, would honor its contractual obligations in terms money and everything else, but how could she move on from this?

Every audition would be—

"And your name is . . ."

"Jody Watts."

"Jody Watts. Jody Watts. Hey, aren't you the girl who lived?"

No, thanks.

Maybe she could change her name, or take the prize money and get something done to her face. Maybe even a boob job. Nobody would recognize her from this show then.

The smile on Jody's face didn't last. She'd made it through the night, and the show hadn't even aired yet, and here she was already thinking about cosmetic surgery. God, Hollywood had a way of creeping up on you. *How about instead I take the money, go back home, and spend some time with the family?*

That sounded good.

But before she could do that, she'd have to get out of here.

Easier said than done. She could get out of the basement without any trouble, but what might be waiting for her on the other side of the door?

She decided she'd be ready for it, whatever *it* was.

Down in the basement she found a couple of pieces of long, narrow wood and fashioned them into a cross. Tying a length of string to the cross, she hung it from her neck, just in case the thing might have some power to protect her. She also found a utility knife—box cutters, they sometimes called them—that she could hold in her free hand.

She pulled the Digital Handycam from her wrist and set it on the workbench. *To hell with the show,* she thought. *I'll need that hand to protect myself.*

And so, with the baluster in her right hand, the utility knife in her left, and a cross around her neck, she turned for the stairs.

Then she hesitated.

She turned back around, knelt down, and looked into the camera. "Well, I'm heading out now. Ike and Erwin Gowan, you're a couple of B-grade assholes. . . . Mom and Dad, I love you."

Satisfied, she nodded once, and turned for the stairs.

At the top, she removed the brace and opened the

door slowly, watchful for anything waiting for her on the other side.

There was nothing there.

The inside of the house was silent and dark.

But it wasn't completely dark. Light from the outside windows was beginning to shine through. It wasn't direct sunlight, but it was pretty darn close to it.

Almost morning.

Jody moved through the foyer. What was left of the shadow thing was still smoking under the chandelier but it was quite faded now, as if it was disappearing with the coming morning light.

She could hear sounds of people outside the house. They were trying to get in the front door.

Jody went to the door and tried it.

It wouldn't open.

Not yet anyway.

She took a long look around. The house seemed different in the light, less menacing, maybe even a bit homey. She would have liked to see it during the day-time, it might have made her feel as if there was less to be afraid of . . . if such a thing were possible.

From where she stood, Jody could see across the foyer and all the way into the kitchen. There was a door there, too, not as grand as the front door, but just as effective for getting in and out of the house.

Even better, that end of the house faced the morning sun.

She headed to the kitchen, and as she entered it, she realized that she could see the sun . . . *the sun,* shining through one of the kitchen windows.

She ran to the door.

The handle turned.

The door opened.

And a moment later she was outside.

Outside.

Out of the house.

A winner.

"I did it!" she said. "I made it."

No answer.

"Hello. Is anyone here?"

There was no one in the yard. Over to her left, a pickup truck was parked on the grass, its cab twisted somehow, as if something had tunneled right through the middle of it.

Over on her right was the soundman's station. She walked over to it, but there was no one there. The equipment was still on, still working.

"Hello," she said into one of the microphones. "Can anyone hear me?"

No response.

She gasped.

There was blood on some of the controls, even more of it on the ground.

In the distance she could see the production trailer.

The bastards were inside it, probably still taping her, maybe even laughing at the fear on her face.

"Assholes," she muttered under her breath.

Well, she had a few things she wanted to tell them.

And they were going to listen.

She ran across the field to the production trailer.

The door to it was ajar.

She dropped her knife and baluster onto the ground and pulled the door open wide, ready to give the Gowan brothers a piece of her mind.

POSTPRODUCTION

Thirty-nine

The first thing that struck her was the smell of it. The inside of the trailer smelled of rot and decay, maybe even blood. . . . Well, what did you expect from a bunch of men holed up in a tiny trailer all night long?

She stepped inside the trailer.

"Who the hell do you guys think you are?" she said, not trying to hide the anger in her voice. She'd nearly been killed playing these boys' game and she was going to let them know how she felt about it.

"This damn movie I'm going to be in better be a good one—and I mean *Exorcist* good, not some cheesy *Night of the Sorority Vampires* crap—"

She stopped herself in midsentence.

There were only two people in the trailer, and both of them were dead.

Jerry, the assistant director, was sitting in his seat, half of his head missing and his arms lying in pieces across the control panel.

There was another man, maybe Jerry's assistant, two chairs over, his head hanging backward from his neck by a flap of skin. Blood was still dribbling out of the stump, which was quite a feat considering how much blood had washed over the panel in front of him.

She could hear sounds.

It was the Gowan brothers.

She turned to face the monitors, watching the one hooked up to the main camera in the foyer.

They had managed to open the front door of the house.

It swung fully open, revealing Ike and Erwin standing in the doorway. They looked as if they'd been through hell, too.

What the hell had happened? Jody wondered.

Just then there was movement inside the trailer.

A shadow crossed in front of the trailer doorway.

And then the door slammed shut.

The inside of the trailer was returned to darkness.

All except for the glow of the monitors.

Jody saw the shadow figure approaching.

She opened her mouth to scream.

And then everything faded to black.

Forty

The front door opened.

"It's about time," Ike said.

The brothers rushed into the house.

"Hello," Ike shouted.

Erwin cupped his hands to his mouth. "Anybody here?"

The rest of the crew filed into the house, some brandishing makeshift weapons, some just moving cautiously about the foyer.

"What the hell happened there?" Ike said, standing over the fallen chandelier and the smoldering mess beneath it.

"Don't know," Erwin said, kneeling down for a closer look. "Might be somebody under there, might not."

Ike turned to take a good look around. With the sunlight streaming in through all the windows now, the house looked absolutely . . . well, harmless. They were going to have a hell of a time proving that they'd been powerless to stop anything that had happened inside.

"Ike," someone called out. "Erwin."

"What is it?" Ike answered.

"A dead body. I think it's Forrest."

The brothers headed into the dining room.

There lying between the dining table and the wall was Forrest, one of the contestants who'd been in on the show, guiding the others around the house and setting up a few of the gags.

And here he was dead, his body bent and broken, his flesh ripped apart as if he'd walked into a meat grinder.

Erwin looked at his brother. "This is bad, Ike."

Ike nodded.

"We're in some really deep shit, aren't we?"

Ike rubbed his eyes with the heels of his hands, then ran his open palms down over the length of his face. "Not only that," he said, "we probably won't be making movies anymore, either."

WRAP

ABOUT THE AUTHOR

Edo van Belkom was the very first horror movie host on SCREAM, Canada's all-horror television channel. As a writer, he is the author of more than two hundred stories of horror, science fiction, fantasy, and mystery, which have appeared in a wide variety of publications including *Storyteller, Truck News, Hot Blood 11, Year's Best Horror Stories,* and *Best American Erotica.* In addition to winning the 1997 Stoker Award from the Horror Writers Association for the short story "Rat Food" (cowritten with David Nickle), he also won the Aurora Award (Canada's top prize for speculative writing) in 1999 for the short story "Hockey's Night in Canada." Edo is the author and editor of more than twenty books, including the novels *Teeth, Martyrs* and *Blood Road,* the story collections *Death Drives a Semi* and *Six-Inch Spikes,* and the nonfiction books *Northern Dreamers* (a book of interviews with writers) and *Writing Horror* (a how-to). He lives in Brampton, Ontario, with his wife and son, but his Web site is located at www.vanbelkom.com.

Scare Up One of These Pinnacle Horrors

__**Haunted**
  by Tamara Thorne   0-7860-1090-8 $5.99US/$7.99CAN

__**Thirst**
  by Michael Cecilione 0-7860-1091-6 $5.99US/$7.99CAN

__**The Haunting**
  by Ruby Jean Jensen 0-7860-1095-9 $5.99US/$7.99CAN

__**The Summoning**
  by Bentley Little   0-7860-1480-6 $6.99US/$8.99CAN

Call toll free **1-888-345-BOOK** to order by phone or use this coupon to order by mail.

Name_____

Address_____

City_____ State_____ Zip_____

Please send me the books that I checked above.

I am enclosing	$_____
Plus postage and handling*	$_____
Sales tax (in NY, TN, and DC)	$_____
Total amount enclosed	$_____

*Add $2.50 for the first book and $.50 for each additional book.
Send check or money order (no cash or CODs) to: **Kensington Publishing Corp., Dept. C.O., 850 Third Avenue, 16th Floor, New York, NY 10022**
Prices and numbers subject to change without notice.
All orders subject to availability.
Visit our website at **www.kensingtonbooks.com**.